Sob Story

Carol Anne Davis

snowbooks

Proudly Published by Snowbooks in 2008

Snowbooks Ltd.
120 Pentonville Road
London
N1 9JN
Tel: 0207 837 6482
Fax: 0207 837 6348
email: info@snowbooks.com

www.snowbooks.com

British Library Cataloguing in Publication Data
A catalogue record for this book is available from the British Library.

ISBN 13 978-1-905005-63-5

Printed and bound in Great Britain

Sob Story

Carol Anne Davis

CHAPTER ONE

He watched as she descended the stair, small breasts outlined by thin white cotton. Her heels tapped against the steel stairway, her mind clearly on other things.

Belatedly he glanced at his fellow prisoners. Ironside was looking at her hips whilst Paul was surreptitiously checking out her legs, and the con who'd just joined them from the Induction Wing clearly had a breast fetish. He, Jeff, was the only man staring at her throat.

Giving a quick nod, the woman passed them and disappeared into the Education Block.

'She's the new education officer,' Ironside said.

Jeff managed a lewd smile. 'Yeah? In that case, it's time I got myself some adult education.'

Everyone laughed loudly. Twat jokes always went down well in here.

Later, as he played basketball in the gym, the new con - Kevin - came up to him and asked for a game. Jeff passed him the ball and they shot hoops for the next twenty minutes. It wasn't a sport he played on the outside, but there was nothing to do around here. Nothing that wouldn't double your sentence, that is...

'So, what are you in for, mate?' Kevin asked. Jeff hesitated - cons didn't usually ask that particular question. But the guy was just trying to make small talk, probably desperate to fit in.

'Let's just say my girlfriend got a bit too mouthy.'

'Yeah?' The newer prisoner licked his lips. 'My girl's alright.' He passed the ball from one hand to the other then added, 'You still with your girl, then?'

With Faith? Only in her nightmares. There was a restriction order, her parents and the local police force keeping them apart. He shook his head. 'She's history.'

She almost *had* been history. At first he'd been charged with attempted murder but they'd ultimately bargained it down to malicious wounding. The courts had gone easy as they thought it was a first offence.

'So, has your girl got a sister going spare?' he joked.

To his surprise, Kevin looked alarmed. 'No, she's only got three brothers.'

Jeff half expected him to add *and they're big guys*, but he wasn't so crass.

'Only having you on,' he said. 'I'll be out soon and able to get my own pussy.'

He might even have the pussy contact him whilst he was still in here. His mother - networking like mad at her computer course - was working on it.

CHAPTER TWO

'We are now approaching Dundee,' the tannoy said. Heart speeding slightly, Amy stood up and reached into the overhead luggage rack. The movement caused her midriff-skimming top to ride up and a youth further up the carriageway shouted 'Show us the rest' and made both his friends laugh and clap.

Damn, she was going red as usual. Dipping her head so that her hair hid her face, she promised herself that this was the last time she'd blush. The new Amy was going to be chatty, self-assured and sophisticated. No one here knew her so she could be anything she wanted to be.

She wanted to be at her new flat. She wanted black tea. She wanted to unpack her case before her clothes became totally crumpled. One of the drawbacks of moving from Aberdeen by train was that she hadn't had space to pack an iron. She'd only brought all her clothes and shoes, a university reading list and enough money to get her through the next four weeks.

Now she'd spend some of that money hiring her first ever cab. New moisture spreading under her arms, the nineteen year old left the train and followed signs to the taxi queue. It was made up of kissing couples and forlorn families. She was the only person on her own.

Forget about them. Think about what you'll say to your new flatmate. It was an odd situation as she'd never met the other girl. All that she knew was that they were both going into first year at Dundee

University and that neither wanted to stay in student halls. Amy's aunt knew someone in the agency that leased the flat and they could see from the map that it was a mere five minutes walk from the university.

Now, as she waited in the mid-morning sunshine, Amy went through the various possibilities in her head. She could say *Hi, I'm Amy*. But did that sound conceited? Why should the other girl care? Maybe, *'Hi, what's your name?'* would be better. After all, the shy person's book said to concentrate on the other person and forget about yourself.

'You want a taxi or not?'

The voice belatedly cut through her thoughts and she jumped and stared at the taxi driver.

'Sorry. Yes.'

Getting in, she scraped her hip then bashed her case into the adjacent passenger door. She gave the driver her new address and he frowned. 'Say that again?'

She did, adding 'It's just off the Perth Road.'

Within minutes they were speeding along the Nethergate, past the university where she'd had her introductory tour only weeks before. Then on past the houses and shops of the Perth Road until the driver turned into a sidestreet and said 'There you go.'

Her new home for the next four years - and maybe more. Amy looked proudly at the row of little houses with their blue, green and yellow painted doors. She squinted through the cab's window, trying to make out the numbers, and the taxi driver said 'That'll be four pounds,' in a bloody-students-shouldn't-be-able-to-afford-taxis tone.

Seconds later she disembarked and walked shakily towards the third house. She'd feel better when she was safely installed in her new room. And she'd surely feel much more confident when she got to meet her new flatmate, had someone to pal around with. She'd never had a best friend before because of mum and dad...

She pressed the bell, waited for an age then pressed it again - but there clearly wasn't going to be a welcoming committee. The agency had sent her a key and after her third attempt she managed to turn it in the very stiff lock. Walking into the hall, she could hear loud music. Cautiously she followed the sound to an open door.

A girl holding a mobile phone was sitting at the kitchen table. Her long honey-brown hair fell in waves to her waist so that she looked like a girl in a shampoo ad, her small nose and long lashes adding to the supermodel effect.

Amy had blow dried her own midlength blonde bob that day but suddenly she felt plain and somehow unworthy. At that very moment the girl looked up and gave a little scream.

'Sorry, I... will I go away while you make your phone call?' Amy said.

'How did you get in here?' the girl gasped, jumping to her feet.

'My key.' Amy held up her key chain.

'Christ, you must be the new girl.' She sat down again with her hand over her heart 'You could have killed me.' Then she looked up and frowned. 'Isn't it five weeks till your course?'

Five weeks in which to make friends and influence people - not give them a heart attack. Amy nodded. 'Till my English course. But my aunt's got me signed up for a computer course first - you know, part of that free adult learning scheme - and it starts this week plus I finished work early as I was due some holiday leave and Aunt Gretchen said I should come through now and get to know Dundee and...' She realised she was in danger of hyperventilating and took a deep breath.

'Right.' The pre-Raphaelite beauty was staring at her strangely.

'I'm Amy Bartlett,' Amy said belatedly.

'I'm Dana. You know, as in the *X-Files*.'

Was that a porn film? No, this girl had too much breeding. It was Amy's turn to mumble 'Oh right.'

There was a brief silence then Dana said 'Shall I give you the guided tour? There's just the two rooms.'

Picking up her arm-numbing case, Amy followed her the few steps from the kitchen to an incredibly long but narrow and dimly-lit room.

'I've taken the bed nearest the door,' Dana said, 'Means I can come home late without having to tiptoe past you.'

'That's great.' Unsure what else to do, Amy walked towards her new bed and put her suitcase there. The agency had described this as a two roomed flat and she'd automatically assumed that meant two student bedrooms: now it seemed that one of the rooms was the kitchen-come-living area and she'd have to share her sleeping space.

'I've left you space in the wardrobe and you can have the third and fourth drawers of the dressing table,' Dana added.

'Great,' Amy said again. The conversation felt really flat and not at all as she'd imagined. Her mind went into overdrive, desperately searching for something interesting to say. 'Do you...' she started and just then Dana's mobile trilled a little tune.

'That'll be Mummy,' she said. 'I was just about to phone her. She's in Dundee for a conference so we're going to do the shops.'

Mummy. Amy forced back a smile. She studied the room as Dana spoke to her mother, noticing that the window had wooden shutters which could be closed and locked to keep out the draught. The rest of the bedroom held no surprises - but she was relieved to see two study desks and wooden chairs. Dana's desk housed a little rubber alien, a bottle of Absinthe and a filofax. There were no books on the shelf above the desk.

Dana ended her phone call. 'Right, I'll get out of your way.'

'Oh. Okay.' Was the girl fleeing the house in order to escape from her? 'When will you be back?' she added then realised she sounded like an anxious mum.

Her new flatmate shrugged and glanced at her watch. 'Mummy has to be back for the afternoon conference at two thirty so I'll see you then if I come back in the car with her. But I may decide to shop till I drop.'

Suddenly Amy didn't want to be left alone so soon in this strange new house and town. 'So what's the conference about?'

'Mm?' Dana walked up to the mirrored wardrobe and finger-combed her shampoo-advert hair. 'Oh, something about the male pill.'

'So is she a chemist or...?' People were supposed to love talking about themselves but Dana seemed the exception.

'A medical lecturer. She and daddy both.'

'And is that what you want to be too?'

The English girl nodded slightly. 'At least until I can think of something else.'

'Well, at least I'll be in good hands if I get something terminal!'

Dana looked faintly alarmed. 'I don't start my course till next month.'

'I know. Me too. I...' They were supposed to be fellow academics, so she turned the subject around to books. 'I'll be reading Austen at night and you'll be immersed in Gray's Anatomy.'

Her new flatmate gave a little laugh. 'I hope to get the information by osmosis,' she said.

She left. Amy sat on the bed for a while and replayed the conversation in her head then wished she could erase it. It was just after midday but the room was already so dim that she switched on the overhead light.

Why wasn't the sunlight filtering through? The window was set high in the wall and she had to stand on the wooden chair to reach it. Now she could see that this part of the house was actually below street level. By glancing up she could see through the railings to the pavement and watch people's feet hurrying past.

She had nowhere to hurry to now. It was Monday and her computer course didn't start until Wednesday. Not that she was exactly counting the hours. She'd never had any interest in technology but Aunt Gretchen wanted her to do the course so that she 'had something to fall back on.' Amy had explained that her English degree would be something to fall back on but Aunt Gretchen had been adamant. And the older woman had had the final word - after all, she was paying Amy's university fees and living expenses for the next four years, was being incredibly generous.

Maybe she could phone mum and dad, let them know she had arrived? Mum had been really anti all of this but surely she'd come round now that it was a fait accompli? She walked into the kitchen and glanced at every work surface but the flat didn't have a phone.

Unless... she opened a door in the kitchen and found that it led to a shower room with a wash hand basin. So where was the toilet? After a ten second search she located it in a tiny room off the narrow hall.

Maybe she'd feel she belonged here if she unpacked. Returning to the bedroom, Amy divided her various pairs of jeans, tops and her long black coat on the three empty wire hangers remaining in the wardrobe. Dana, she noticed, had used all the other hangers for her designer label everything and had also taken up the entire footwear compartment with her boots, sandals and shoes. Not wanting to get off on - no pun intended - the wrong foot, Amy put her own pair of trainers and her ankle boots under the bed then withdrew her hand quickly as it brushed against a carpet of fluff.

Now all that remained in her suitcase was a box of teabags, a large banana and a small banana. Ninety calories versus as much as a hundred and twenty calories. It had been five hours since she'd eaten - but she'd been given a lift to Aberdeen station by a neighbour and couldn't have burnt up much energy sitting on the train. Decision made, Amy took the small banana into the kitchen and made herself a mug of black tea.

Fruitarian lunch over, she decided to venture out and do her first ever grocery shop for the flat. Not that shopping for herself was a new experience. She'd been doing it since she was eleven and the school had... but she had to forget about all that.

New Amy. New life. But the very same foods, the relatively safe foods. After a very short walk she found a supermarket and bought salad, fruit, vegetables, frozen low fat yoghurt, thin cut wholemeal bread, reduced sugar baked beans and rice cakes.

'Nice shop,' she said to the checkout girl. The girl stared then returned her attention to the cash register. *Keep thinking positive.* She'd feel better when Dana got back.

But Dana didn't come back. Amy sat in the flat for the afternoon and throughout the evening, nibbling on apples until finally succumbing to a toasted salad sandwich. She read the second half of *Mansfield Park* and was glad that everyone lived happily ever after. Women had such few opportunities in Jane Austen's day whereas now...She could do anything, go anywhere. She was single and nineteen and new to town, a free spirit. She could... she did a hundred sit-ups then made herself another cup of tea.

CHAPTER THREE

He was to lose the only thing he had, his single cell. Hardly able to believe the words before him, Jeff read the notice again and again. The roof had been damaged during the recent summer storms and the entire wing also required refurbishment. So all of the cons in this wing were being moved to another block where they'd be three prisoners to a cell.

He wouldn't be able to sleep when he wanted or eat a meal in private or... well, do any of the things that a man had to do. It was fucking criminal. How could the system rob him of the only private space he'd known for the past four years? If only they'd waited till January when he'd be out on parole.

Somehow he had to keep his temper, not louse up that long-awaited opportunity. Jeff forced his clenched hands to relax, finger by finger. It was lucky that he'd taken that relaxation course when they first banged him up in here, though the creamy neck of the bitch who'd run the classes had made him feel increasingly tense. She'd had this way of tossing her head back and playing with her long gold earrings, knowing that every man in the room wanted to fuck her hard.

He'd wanted to fuck her too, of course, but he'd wanted to do so with his hands wrapped around her throat whilst riding her into oblivion. He'd wanted... wanted all the things that he'd soon get again on the outside.

CHAPTER FOUR

Amy woke at 6am and immediately looked over at Dana's bed. God, she still wasn't there. Had something happened? She hurried to the kitchen but it was clear that her flatmate hadn't been home. She'd pictured them talking about books and going on walks and to the cinema. She'd had such hopes, such plans.

What did you do in a strange place when you didn't know anyone and were too shy to introduce yourself to strangers? The hours crept past in a lonely mixture of walks and reading followed by an early night.

On Wednesday Amy again awoke early and found that Dana still wasn't back - but at least she had the induction session of her computer course to go to. Now, for the first time, she was actually looking forward to it, or at least to speaking to people there. Back home she'd spent most of her evenings in her bedroom but she'd had some human contact when Mum shouted through offering her various snacks.

Three hours later, part scalded by the flat's temperamental shower, she walked into town and followed her map until she came to the business centre. Aunt Gretchen had signed her up for Basic Word Processing which was going to be a challenge as she couldn't even type.

Entering the foyer, she found a sign which said to go to level three. A middle aged woman in a smart blue wool skirt suit was talking to a plump girl of around twenty. After a moment the girl backed away smiling and made for the stairs. 'Oh well, if you change your mind...' the well-groomed woman called. She turned to Amy. 'Here. I'll get the lift for us.' A moment later it opened and they hurried in.

'I'm going to the third floor,' the woman said in a soft Scottish lilt.

'Same here.' Amy realised that her own voice sounded slightly croaky, probably because she hadn't used it for the last two days. 'Are you doing the Induction Word Processing course?' she added hopefully.

The brunette shook her head. 'The internet course, but I did the Induction course months ago. It won't phase you. They give you a reference number and a folder, get you signed up for at least four hours a week.'

Amy nodded, amazed that such an organised and together woman even wanted to talk to her. This student had poise and confidence though it was clear from the language she used that she'd originally been working class. Maybe she, Amy, could be like this if she could just get over her self consciousness and nerves.

'Are there exams?' she asked as the lift stopped on the second floor and an elderly couple got in. She'd always passed her exams, felt hollow at the thought of her first ever failure.

'There are, but they're not compulsory. I mean, you can just learn the subject for your own satisfaction. That's why I'm here.' They reached the third floor and stepped out onto a carpeted landing. 'Look, we're slightly early. Why don't we have a hot chocolate from the machine? I don't know about you, but I need to wake up.'

'Same here,' Amy said, aware that the building's high temperature was already making her feel tired, 'But do they do anything other than hot chocolate?'

'They do everything.' She followed the tall, blue suited figure to a small seating area with two refreshments machines. 'Water costs five pence and hot drinks twenty so I always bring coins with me,' the woman added. She held up her hand as Amy got her purse out. 'My treat.'

When they were seated with their Styrofoam cups the woman asked Amy why she'd chosen to do the computer course.

She laughed. 'It was sort of chosen for me. My aunt loves value for money and as it's free...'

Her new friend smiled back at her. 'Do you live with your aunt?'

'No, but she's paying my way through university.'

'So what are you studying?' The woman seemed genuinely interested.

'English Lit, but it doesn't start until the 7th of October. I'm really looking forward to it - but I'm not looking forward to this.'

'I was a wreck at first,' the brunette admitted, 'But my son Jeff's been on a computer course and he says it's useful for all sorts of things.' She said hello to two students in their twenties and they smiled and hurried on towards the furthest door. 'I work from home and he said it would help with my accounts.'

'Can I ask what business you're in?' Amy wished that everyone was as easy to speak to as this woman.

'Speciality cakes.'

The teenager's stomach rumbled slightly at the thought of even not-so-special cakes. She picked up her black coffee and gulped it, trying to fill her stomach. It was time for a rapid subject change.

'Did your son do his computer course here?'

The woman hesitated. 'No, he's in Maidstone now.'

'And what does he do?'

'He... was a research assistant at a big lab in Wales. He'll hopefully go back to it eventually.'

She'd read about such things. 'He's having a career break?'

'Something like that,' the woman said vaguely. She gulped her hot chocolate. 'Listen, you'll love your university course. Jeff's got a BSc from Cardiff. He said those years were the best of his life.'

'Well, I've been a lifeguard for the past year so it's got to be better than that,' Amy admitted, remembering the endless treks around the pool.

'At the Leisure Centre?'

'No, at home - I mean, back in Aberdeen.'

There was a loud click and they both looked over at the clock on the wall.

'I'd better go to the internet suite,' the woman said, 'The computers nearest the Tutor's Help Station get booked up fast.' She pointed to a door at the far end of the room, 'You go through there and give them your name at reception. The induction only takes about an hour.'

'Thanks,' Amy said. She was beginning to wish that this woman was her flatmate. 'I'll buy you a drink next time.' She turned to go.

'I'm Barbara, by the way.'

'Amy.' They smiled shyly at each other.

'If only my son could meet a nice girl like you,' Barbara said.

CHAPTER FIVE

He'd have to kill his new cellmates - *kill someone* - soon. He simply couldn't go on like this, sharing his nights with two men in a space the size of a large bathroom. Something had to give - either his patience or his sanity.

Jeff lay in his bunk at 3am listening to Dermott have yet another enraged conversation. At first he thought the poor bastard had repeated nightmares, but now he'd watched and heard him have similar one-sided conversations during the day.

'You fucking with me? I didn't mean it, dad,' Dermott said. 'You want more of what you got yesterday? No, not that. I'll do better, honest. Honest I will.'

In an honest system, Dermott would have been nutted off to Rampton years ago. But he wasn't a danger to the screws or to other prisoners which was all that the medics cared about.

Pulling his duvet over his ears, Jeff wished that he was a man who could count sheep. As it was, Dermott's screams and pleas simply reminded him of his own early experiences. No one listened until...

Thank Christ, the nutter had stopped. Jeff turned on his side then stiffened anew as he heard a different type of racket. What the hell was that? Jesus, it was Tim crying again. He'd been on suicide watch until recently but was supposedly cured by his new sustained-release meds.

One mad con, one sad con - he guessed that he must be the bad con.

But he didn't feel bad, at least not all the time. He'd felt the same as everyone else when he was out on the hills with his neighbour's retriever. He and the dog would walk and run for miles, just enjoying the exercise.

But the moment he returned to a more populated area, the judging began. Another dog walker might look critically at the sweat stains spreading beneath his arms or a teenager would glance disparagingly at his supermarket trainers. And when he went to the Job Club they'd question him closely about his qualifications, about how much he'd actually achieved. His mother and girlfriends had also promoted 'be all you can be' rather than letting him be what he wanted. No one seemed to accept the real him.

Small wonder that he'd eventually snapped, that he'd gone for the jugular. Small wonder that he'd turned on Faith and committed the act which had landed him here. In an ideal world, what went on between a man and his girlfriend would remain private, just wouldn't be a matter for the courts.

All that he could do now was make sure that his next victim didn't take him to court or even take him to task about anything. That someone had to be especially young or fearful of getting old or somehow inadequate. She might have a physical disability - as long as she had her invalidity allowance he didn't care. He simply had to find someone lonely and gullible, a warm-blooded female who would dance to his increasingly demanding tune.

CHAPTER SIX

You could make a frozen yoghurt last an hour by skimming the tiniest amount onto your spoon and licking it off. Amy was halfway through doing just that when Dana suddenly appeared in the doorway, the first time she'd seen her since the day they met.

'Oh, you made me jump!' Heart palpitations aside, she felt genuinely glad to see the other girl, to see anyone. 'Are you getting your own back?' she quipped.

'I'm just in for a change of clothing,' Dana said in her slightly breathless cultured voice. 'I'll be staying at Ken's.'

'Your boyfriend?'

'Uh huh.' She looked around the room, 'Any mail?'

'Mm, it's on your desk,' Amy said. She felt her spirits sink as Dana began to back out of the room. She wanted to ask where her flatmate had been but that sounded disapproving. 'Did you have a nice time?' she asked.

'Super.' Dana's eyes were still sweeping the kitchen, 'Mummy finished her research paper early so I went back to Oxford with her and met up with all my friends.'

'Oh, that's nice. I doubt if I'll be home till the Christmas holidays,' Amy said.

She waited for Dana to ask where home was but Dana didn't. Instead she disappeared and Amy heard a couple of drawers being opened and closed then the front door slammed. Oh well, she'd have to spend another night with Jane happily-ever-after Austen. Wearily she finished her melted yoghurt then picked up *Pride And Prejudice*. At least she had her computer course tomorrow and might get to see Barbara again.

But there was no sign of her in the foyer or in the lift or in the little coffee area. Amy sat there on her own until 9am sipping water but no one else joined her and, feeling self conscious, she moved on to the beginner's computer section and began to follow the exercise book that she'd been given.

'Take a break everyone,' the tutor said at the end of the first hour. Amy again headed to the water machine: water helped burn fat and it filled your stomach. She stiffened slightly as a familiar voice said 'You'd get on famously with my son.'

Taking her cup from the machine, she looked up and saw Barbara facing a long-haired girl wearing a floor length dirndl skirt. The girl was apologetically backing away. 'I must go to Reception and book my next few sessions,' she said, half tripping over her hem.

Barbara nodded. 'I'm booked to the end of my course already.' She turned in Amy's direction and smiled. 'Oh hello. How are you coping so far?'

Amy smiled back. 'Slowly! Most of the others in my group are pensioners but they're much faster than me.'

'Oh, their grandkids teach them,' Barbara explained. She looked wistful for a moment then got herself a white coffee from the machine.

'So are you doing four hours a week or six?' Amy asked as they sat down.

'Oh six. I figured I'm such a Luddite that I'd better do something intensive.'

'Same here,' said Amy, 'I'll be doing two hours each Monday, Wednesday and Friday from now on.'

'And you can fit that around your university course?'

'Well, I may cut back to four hours when uni starts. That's the beauty of being here early - I can do twenty four hours of computer training before my real studies even begin.'

'And keep your aunt happy,' Barbara added cheerfully.

Gosh, the woman had remembered their entire conversation. This was brilliant. 'Well, keep her paying my university fees,' Amy said.

She realised that Barbara was studying her intently. 'So don't your parents...?'

'They couldn't. Neither of them earns enough.'

'They must be very pleased with your aunt for funding you, then.'

'Mm,' Amy lied.

'Everything was so much simpler when Jeff was at university,' the older woman said. 'The state paid his fees and his stepfather and I just had to make a parental contribution. And we got off lightly because our eldest son Damien didn't want to go on to further education at all.'

'Really? What does he do?'

'Part-owns a second hand car dealership.'

'So if I ever learn to drive I know where to come!'

'Well, you'd have to travel a long way. He's in Basingstoke,' Barbara said with a smile.

'And your other son's in Maidstone. Don't you miss them?' To her surprise, she was already missing her parents. She'd phoned them from a kiosk but neither had much to say.

'Oh, my husband drives me to see them when he can - and we hope that Jeff will move to Dundee when he gets out.' She hesitated, gazing directly into Amy's eyes. 'Jeff's a clever young man but he got in with a very manipulative girl. She almost ruined him. In the end they had a fight that got out of control and... well, he ended up in jail.'

In jail. It was Amy's turn to hesitate. She'd always thought of prisoners - if she thought of them at all - as being rough youths from run down housing estates. But Jeff's mother was well dressed and ran her own business. Amy's own background was a lot more spartan than Barbara's was.

'How... how long did he get?'

'Seven years.'

'And how long has he left to serve?'

Barbara looked vague again. 'We're not quite sure. I mean, there are appeals and tribunals that take time off but they can put time on if you're assertive with one of the prison officers or if you're found to have more than ten pounds worth of postage stamps in your cell or... you wouldn't believe the number of rules.'

She would. There had been lots of stupid rules at the swimming baths and she'd already found a couple more on this computer course. Even the rental agency for the flat had rules about not hanging paintings (as if most students brought their favourite Van Gogh with them) and you had to wash the net curtains once a month or else.

There was an awkward silence. 'He's lucky to have you,' Amy said.

'Well, what we'd - his stepfather and I - would really like is for him to find a nice girlfriend. It would cheer him up and take his mind off that woman who... oh you probably don't want to hear about it.'

She certainly did. It was a lot more exciting than learning to type.

'What exactly did she do to him?' Amy asked.

Barbara swallowed visibly. 'Well, she was a lot older than him for a start. And very clipped - she'd been a Sunday School teacher, you know, when she was younger? The whole family was religious. Her parents even christened her Faith. Anyway, she was always nagging him to get married and he really wasn't ready. That's why they were living together, to make sure that they were a good match.' She took a sip of her coffee. 'He used to make her breakfast and drive her to school - she taught eight year olds - before he went on to his own work which was miles in the other direction. She was supposed to get home first at night and cook the evening meal but she'd stay on to mark jotters, knowing that he'd come home starving, knowing that he was coming home to an empty house.'

It was horrible being on your own in the house when you'd anticipated company. Amy began to form an image of Faith and she looked remarkably like a wrinkled version of Dana. 'Why didn't he just leave her?' she asked.

Barbara looked thoughtful. 'Well, he's never been one to run away from things is Jeff. And they'd adopted two little kittens from the shelter. I think he was afraid that if he left they'd be neglected. So he stayed and the stress built up and one night she threw a glass jug at him in the kitchen and they got into a physical fight.'

'And he got seven years for that?' The Home Secretary wasn't kidding when he said he was tough on crime.

Barbara nodded. 'There'd been a lot about domestic violence in the media so we think the judge was cracking down. I mean, it was Jeff's first offence - and his last - and his next door neighbour even took the stand to speak up for him.'

Amy had seen far worse assaults by parents on their children in the swimming pool. 'It doesn't sound like he'd hurt anyone else.'

'Exactly. We think it was a feminist misinterpretation, seeing the man as the aggressor whereas she started it.'

'So do you ever bump into her?' Amy asked, wondering if Faith still saw herself as a potential daughter-in-law.

Barbara shook her head. 'Faith and Jeff were living in Wales at the time and my husband and I lived in Edinburgh. We only moved to Dundee after the trial. We hoped that they'd send him to a Scottish prison but they put him in Maidstone so we can't usually visit during the week.'

They both watched as various smokers walked back to their computers, signalling the end of the break.

Amy blushed slightly as Barbara touched her arm. 'I wonder if you could write to him some time? His stepfather and I write as often as we can but he's only twenty eight so he'd find letters from you much more interesting.'

What on earth would she write about? 'But... well, he doesn't know me.'

'All he knows in there is loneliness,' Barbara said. Amy nodded. She knew all about being on your own and it was hard to say no to this helpful, friendly woman, but she couldn't quite imagine writing to a stranger. Talking to Dana in person was bad enough. 'Tell you what, I'll give you his address just in case,' Barbara continued, pulling a typed card from her leather bag.

Uncertainly, Amy slipped it into her pocket.

'You're so slim,' Barbara added admiringly, 'He loves slim girls.'

'Was Faith slim?'

By now the tutors were giving them dirty looks.

'To be honest, Amy, she'd let herself go and Jeff himself is so trim that they looked odd together.'

'Sounds like he's well rid,' Amy said then realised she'd used her mother's favourite phrase. 'Well, back to the grindstone,' she added, gearing herself up for another boring fifty minutes at the keyboard.

'I'll look out for you on Monday,' Barbara called as she walked away.

CHAPTER SEVEN

At last she'd found him someone. Jeff reread the latest letter from his mother. I met a nice girl, Amy, at my computer course. She's just moved through here from Aberdeen, is starting Basic Word Processing to please her aunt. The aunt is also funding her through university - she starts next month, doing English Lit.

I think you'd like her, Jeff. She's slim and pretty and she obviously keeps fit - she's been a lifeguard for the past year since leaving school. I told her about how you-know-who had treated you and she was obviously on your side. I've given her your details and urged her to write to you, so fingers crossed.

So the girl would be - what? - nineteen at most and on her own in a new city. This sounded promising. And if she was a teenage fitness fanatic she'd probably be the youngest at most sports clubs: leastways the teenage boys who came in here were allergic to the gym. The place was either deserted or used by the old lags who'd been working out for decades: at twenty eight he was often the youngest man there. She'd be lonely and feel different and would hopefully start to think of poor Jeff, also alone and different. Before long the Post Office would be working overtime.

He read on. Dad sends his love. Damien does too. Dad phoned him last night and he's doing well. We asked if he'd come home for Christmas but his girlfriend (another new one!) has already signed them up for some Spanish tour.

As if Damien ever did the happy families bit.

I had an order for a christening cake this week (twins) and one for a fiftieth anniversary. Imagine, fifty years. Do you think dad and I will make it? Only if you continue to avoid talking about anything real in favour of watching the TV, Jeff thought.

Well, son, write and tell me your news. Oh gee, right mum. I've run a marathon since I saw you last and joined the ramblers association and taken my friends to that new Thai restaurant... What kind of news did she expect him to have when he was banged up in here?

The letter ended with *love mum* and her usual two neat kisses. Then there was a PS. *I did what you told me, said we didn't know when you'd get out.*

Ah, so the old dear was firing on all cylinders at last. He'd tried to drum that into her as he got closer to his release. Because the truth was, the kind of girls who befriended prisoners often didn't want a man on the outside. No, they liked him safely locked up where they could write him loving letters and dream romantic dreams and never have to worry about taking a cock up the cunt or up the arse.

With a prisoner for a boyfriend, they could visit if they wanted to or just murmur sweet nothing-of-any-consequence down the phone. A prisoner could spend hours writing them letters - hell, some of the Lotharios in here even wrote or plagiarised poetry - but would never make the lounge untidy, or smoke in the bedroom or come home drunk. It was the equivalent of adopting a monkey at the zoo and having your nameplate on its cage, only this particular monkey was about to run free.

He hadn't realised how important freedom was to him until it had gone. Now there was a thousand little things he missed - making himself a bacon sandwich, walking to work in the sunshine, going to the cinema, renting a DVD or browsing through the shops.

You lost control of so much in here, couldn't even change into a fresh shirt when you wanted one. Instead, you put all your dirty laundry into a string bag and the prisoners in charge of the laundry washed the bag with your clothes in it. Nothing came back clean.

He missed sleeping in late, having a scotch on the rocks, taking next door's dog for a walk or having afternoon sex with a stranger. Here it was all yes sir, no sir and keeping your head down till you'd done your time. It was a noisy, dirty and sometimes brutal place, this world of men.

Ironically, what he missed most in here was having a woman. Oh, not a nagging, frigid bitch like Faith, but his particular kind of woman. The kind who believed that the man's needs were more important than her own. Once upon a time the world had been filled with that sort of female but the rise of the ball breaker had put paid to all that. Now men like him had to pay for what they wanted, pay often and pay dear.

Two hundred pounds a session was what most whores charged for specialist sex. It was no wonder that in the end he'd taken Sonia and... he spent some time reliving that particular memory. But on other occasions he'd kept himself more in check. Even using self control, though, it was a challenge to take himself to peak excitement without taking the prostitute over the edge.

First, he'd order her - it was usually Tanu who had more needle marks than a pin cushion - to strip. She'd take her time unbuttoning her blouse and unzipping her jeans, watching him nervously as she removed both garments. He liked her nervousness more than her nakedness, knew damn well that she only catered for him when she was desperate. Even now he could remember each detail as if it was actually taking place...

'Lie on your back. Put your hands by your sides.'

She lay down on her narrow bed, watching, waiting. The room smelt of stale semen and sweat. It was a typical junkie's flat - dirty, unloved and almost threadbare, yet it was the place where he'd experienced the most intense orgasms of his life.

He walked towards her, noting how her fingers were already flexing as if trying to ward off what he was about to do.

'Two hundred,' he reminded her softly.

With a clear effort of will she kept the backs of her hands flat on the soiled quilt.

'Mummy won't save you now.' It was what... but he had to forget about that. He concentrated on unzipping himself and entering her. As usual, she'd used a lubricant and gave no sign that she'd noticed his cock going in.

But she noticed his hands moving up. He felt her body tense, saw her lick her lips like a bad movie actress. He wrapped his fingers around her throat and began to tighten them with each measured thrust.

Tighter and tighter. She made a little gagging sound and her hands came up off the quilt and moved towards his hands. Tighter and tighter. Her fingers began to claw at his but he continued to thrust and squeeze. Heroin and crack had failed to kill Tanu so a little constriction of the throat was unlikely to do so. Hell, the bitch was damn near indestructible.

Crush and thrust. His cock felt huge with desire, his heart beating so fast that he was sure she could feel it. Crush and thrust, knowing that he had the power to extend her life or bring about her death. Her pulse in his hands, her eyes panicked and wild, her body under his bucking like a wild animal. She pushed up against him with particular ferocity and he cried out and came.

He slumped over her, only half aware that she was wheezing and spluttering and clutching her neck. What did she expect for two hundred quid - a few caresses? No, the bitch knew what she was getting into: she'd accommodated him at least twenty times before. And when she was doing time he found one of her street mates to satisfy him, though some only let him semi-strangle them the once.

Jeff sat back on his bed remembering the others. One had said that he was weird - but you got a lot weirder than him out there. Hell, some people liked to shit on each other or piss in each other's mouths. Others liked to don rubber masks and hang upside down in oversized barrels. He hadn't believed some of the stuff that went on until his enemy had showed him the magazines. He'd been - what? - ten at the time and still at the stage where he thought babies were brought by the stork. Then that bastard had wrapped his hands around Jeff's throat and stared into his eyes and squeezed.

It had been a year or two later that the strangling fantasies had started.

At first he hadn't known that they were sexual, just knew that he'd have these half waking dreams about wrapping his hands around a girl's throat. They'd plead and beg these girls, the girls he went to school with, and he'd get this strange but pleasant tingling between his thighs.

Then one day he'd woken up with his first erection. He'd turned over in the bed and his cock had rubbed against the sheet. Half scared but intrigued, he'd taken over the rubbing, pretending that he was choking that mocking, spoilt Debbie from primary seven, and his first orgasm had wracked dryly through his limbs. That night he'd orgasmed again and the next day and the next. Sometimes he only had to look at a girl's pale, defenceless throat and he got hard.

He was hard now. He stared at his cell door for a moment, then broke one of the prison's billion rules by wedging it shut. After all - he grinned sourly at the pun - if he left it open, any Tom or Harry could walk in and find him playing with his Dick. If Dermott and Tearful Tim came by and saw that the door was closed, they'd also get the message and bugger off.

His privacy assured, Jeff lay down under the blanket and touched himself, reliving another session with Tanu. He remembered her increasingly breathless little whimpers, the livid red marks he'd left around her throat. She'd have worn his marks for many days, a living collar. And the pain would have reminded her that he, and only he, was in charge.

Afterwards he sat up in bed and his mother's letter fluttered to the floor, go-get-her words about the thin and needy Amy. He hoped she had a sensuous, slender neck.

CHAPTER EIGHT

She'd had vegetable soup with reduced calorie toast (160 calories) and an apple (50 calories) for her lunch. Now the afternoon stretched ahead of her. Amy sat in the kitchen and studied Donne's poetry but couldn't quite identify with the man's endless lust. She simply didn't feel that level of desire for anyone. Mum had once joked that maybe she played for the other team, but it wasn't that.

Amy set down the book. She'd already covered half of the textbooks on the reading list - and she knew that Dana hadn't even bought a single medical book yet. She was out again, probably with Ken who phoned her mobile every day.

She, Amy, was never going to have someone to phone. Barbara hadn't been at the computer college this morning or for the two previous sessions. Maybe her course had ended or she'd just grown tired of it?

How could she get through the afternoon, far less the night? In Aberdeen she'd worked from eight to six so was happy to sit in her room reading in the evenings. But she couldn't read for sixteen hours a day. Her eyes already felt tired from the morning session at the computer and she felt increasingly trapped in the airless flat.

She'd go for a walk along the Perth Road, check out the shops. Not that she'd buy anything - Aunt Gretchen had given her enough to live off but nothing to squander. She thought warmly of her favourite relative, wishing that the woman was here with her now in Dundee. They'd spent so much time together back home that they were more like mother and daughter than aunt and niece.

Cheering up at the prospect of an outing, Amy changed out of the denim dress she'd worn for computer college and into her black cords and one of her midriff-baring tops. She'd bought three when she knew she was coming here, one black, one navy and one brown, all slimming colours. The fact that they ended above her stomach would remind her not to overeat. It was easy to balloon out if you were an undergraduate - she'd read that most students put on ten pounds during their first term.

Surely there'd be some healthy eaters on her course? Or on some of the other courses? There again, Dana was a medic and Dana ate butter, full fat milk and blocks of cheese.

Slinging her little rucksack on her back, Amy headed for the shops. She browsed in one of the charity stores noting that they were selling an exercise bike for only ten pounds - but no, she must keep her cash only for essentials. She killed some time in a bookshop, admired the Dundee Rep, then retraced her steps and sat on the wall outside the university's tower block, watching mature students or lecturers enter and leave with stacks of books and bulging carrier bags. Everyone gave off a strong sense of purpose and of belonging to the town. Was that man in the parked car looking at her strangely? Maybe he thought she'd been stood up or that she was a prostitute. She'd better go.

Amy resumed her walk along the Perth Road but slowed down as she neared home, knowing that she didn't want to go back to the empty flat yet. She looked at the office windows, wondering if she'd ever need the services of this accountancy firm or that insurance agency.

Suddenly a large sign in one of the windows caught her attention. Youth Crisis Clinic. Trust us - you don't have to be in the middle of a crisis to talk to our friendly staff. We can help with many everyday problems - a worry shared is a worry halved. Appointments not always necessary. This free service is available to everyone under age 21. There followed a charity registration number and a picture of two talking heads.

Amy hesitated. Were her troubles too fleeting and too trivial? She walked up the stairs to the door and scanned the information posters to find out which problems the clinic specialised in.

'Hello. I'm Jean. Can I help?'

Amy turned to see a small, grey-haired woman with a kindly face. She was holding a carrier bag so had presumably just nipped out to the local shops.

'I just... I wasn't sure if I should go in.'

'Course you should. We're quiet just now because the students are away.'

'I'm a student,' Amy said. This woman looked so calm, so understanding, that she was feeling better just looking at her. 'I came through to Dundee early but now I'm at a bit of a loose end.'

'Loose ends are our speciality,' the older woman said, smiling and touching Amy lightly on the arm. She opened the door and ushered the nineteen year old in. She found herself in a small hall with various doors leading off. 'Do you mind giving your name for our appointments diary? It's entirely optional,' Jean said pointing to a large open book complete with pen. Moments later she added 'That's a nice name, Amy.'

'My mum got it from a film she liked,' Amy said.

Jean knocked then popped her head around one of the doors.

'Shelley, are you free to see Amy here? Oh good. I'll go and do the honours.' She turned to the teenager. 'Would you like a tea or a coffee?'

'A black coffee, no sugar, would be brilliant,' Amy said.

Jean introduced her to Shelley then hurried off. Amy smiled weakly at the pretty brunette thirty-something as they sat down facing each other.

'An Aberdonian, right?' Shelley asked.

Amy felt surprised. 'Most people don't think I have much of an accent.'

'My grandfather was from Aberdeen,' Shelley said. She leaned back in her chair and Amy marvelled at how relaxed, how *right*, she looked. 'So, how long have you been living here?'

Amy smiled wanly. 'Three weeks - but it feels longer.'

Shelley nodded. 'Why do you think that is?'

'Well, my arts degree doesn't start till next month but I came through early to do a computer course. Unfortunately it only takes up six hours a week so I've still got lots of time to kill.'

'I can imagine.' The counsellor paused. 'You couldn't befriend some of the people on this computer course?'

Amy nodded. 'I did get chatting to a nice woman but she seems to have left.' Barbara had hinted that she'd like her as a daughter in law. Maybe she should have sounded more interested in her prisoner son?

'Aren't there other nice women?' Shelley asked.

How did other people manage to make friends so easily? Amy felt inadequate for about the zillionth time.

'Well, it's difficult to talk because you sit facing your computer and most of the students are pensioners - you know, husband and wife teams? - and hardly anyone takes a coffee break so...'

'So what did you do back in Aberdeen?'

Hid away in my room. 'I was a lifeguard who patrolled the indoor pool all day so I was happy to curl up with a book in the evening. And I was living at home then so technically my parents were there if I wanted a chat.'

'Technically?' Shelley echoed lightly, her already large eyes widening.

The last thing she wanted was to talk about her old life - she was different now. 'Oh, you know, they have their own routines and don't like to be interrupted,' Amy said, feeling disloyal. She changed the subject. 'I'd hoped to get to know Dundee with my flatmate but she's out with her fiancé all the time.'

'So could you get a third girl in to share or...?'

Amy shook her head. 'We already share a bedroom. It's just a two roomed flat.' She realised that she'd been grumping away non-stop since she came here and searched for something positive. 'But it has shutters to keep the draughts out and it's incredibly close to the university.'

There was a lull in the conversation and Amy stared awkwardly at the floor. She shouldn't have come here. Just what, exactly, had she wanted the counsellor to do?

'I should go,' she said standing up.

'No, please stay,' Shelley said, looking as if she meant it. 'I'm just thinking. Do you still like swimming? The university has its own pool.'

'I'd be allowed to go there now?'

Shelley hesitated. 'You might have to show your acceptance letter and pay the visitor's rate. I could phone for you.'

'Oh no.' Amy shook her head more violently than she meant to and they both smiled as something in her neck clicked. She didn't want to make a fuss.

'Don't worry - we'll never do anything that you don't want us to,' Shelley added. She smiled. 'There's also the swimming pool in the city centre. It's open to everyone.'

'I'll go there then,' Amy said quickly, glad that Shelley wasn't going to represent her to the university as some special sad case.

'It's just that exercise helps alleviate depression,' Shelley added. 'I should know - I walk home every night and it takes well over an hour.'

'Same here.' Amy felt glad that someone else still walked. Dana was always getting lifts from Ken or taking taxis. 'I bought a map and walked all the way to Invergowrie last week.'

There was a knock on the door and Shelley shouted 'Come in.'

Jean appeared holding a tray. 'Coffee and something to go with it,' she said happily setting it down on the little table to Amy's right. Amy stared at the large vanilla slice, cream oyster, triangle of gateau and éclair. 'It's my sixtieth,' Jean added, 'I'm afraid Zoe and I have already bagged the meringues.'

'I'll have the éclair if that's alright with you, Amy,' the counsellor said.

Amy nodded. Jean handed Shelley her cake on a napkin and put her coffee on the little section built into each chair. Then she turned to Amy. 'Help yourself.'

Amy stared at the juicy-looking cherries on the black forest gateau. The whipped cream in the centre and on top looked equally tempting. Her stomach rumbled. She looked at Shelley who was happily nibbling her éclair.

'I wish we had two birthdays - you know, like horses?' Shelley said, reaching for her drink.

Or none, Amy thought. She looked at the plate of cakes again then reached for the gateau, hoping that she'd feel less anxious if she could lift her blood sugar. She'd just have a little of the dark sponge and the cherries from the top.

'So what are you going to be studying?' Shelley asked.

They spoke about Amy's course for a while as she ate a little of the sponge then a little more. All too soon it was gone.

Shelley grinned at her. 'Would you mind if I had the vanilla slice as well? There's something about cream.'

Whipping cream - a hundred and five calories an ounce. Double cream, a hundred and twenty five. Clotted cream - a hundred and sixty five. She picked up the plate and took it over to Shelley.

'Help yourself to the other one,' the counsellor said.

'I'm fine thanks.' Amy returned to her seat and set the plate down but her eyes kept returning to it. Resolutely she picked up her coffee but her stomach, mind, taste buds still screamed out for cake.

'Could you have any of your friends from Aberdeen come to visit you?' Shelley asked between nibbles of her vanilla slice.

She hadn't had any friends at school after mum... 'No, they've all moved away,' she lied and felt herself blushing.

'I know how difficult it can be moving to a new town on your own,' Shelley said.

'I suppose I thought Dana and I would... have you heard of the *X-Files* by the way?'

'Yes, it was a cult TV programme.' Shelley looked surprised.

'Oh, I hardly ever watch TV.'

'Maybe that's something else worth considering,' the counsellor said.

Amy thought of all the nights when her parents had turned on the TV and...

'I think I prefer keeping fit.'

'Well, there are walking clubs in Dundee, ramblers associations, dance classes.'

'Won't there be clubs run by the Students Association when I get to university?

Shelley nodded. 'Oh yes, they've got everything. But I thought you were bored now?'

'I am, it's just - it hardly seems worth joining those things when it's only seventeen days till my course.'

The counsellor finished her éclair. Amy's willpower ran out and she reached for the remaining cream cake. She listened to the older woman as she ate the floury sweetness, saving the cream - the best bit - for last.

'I can appreciate that you're sort of stuck in the middle,' the counsellor said. 'On the one hand, seventeen days spent entirely alone is too much for any mortal but on the other hand you don't want to make expensive long term commitments when you'll have a whole new social life by October 7th.'

'So what would you do?' Amy asked, using the question to delay taking the next bite of cake.

'I'd keep my exercise up, as you're doing. Maybe go swimming at the Leisure Centre - see if they have water aerobic classes or something similar where you can chat. If you'd had a longer time to fill I'd also have suggested some voluntary work.' She reached for a file by her feet and rifled through it. 'I'll give you these leaflets from other helpful organisations. You're very welcome to come back here if you need more advice but obviously we're just open office hours whereas some of these services offer twenty four hour help - and you can just phone them for a chat.'

But I don't have a phone, Amy thought. She decided not to say so. Just talking to Shelley had helped and she didn't want to keep sounding negative.

'Thanks for everything.' She stood up to go.

'The university has its own counselling service,' Shelley said. 'But you're equally welcome here. I just wanted to make you aware of the option.'

Amy nodded. 'I knew about that from the prospectus - but as I haven't matriculated yet...'

'You'll love it,' Shelley said. 'All those books, all the facilities, complete freedom. If I could afford it I'd go back to uni too!'

'I'm really looking forward to it,' Amy admitted, envisaging the endless hours discussing books and authors with other students.

'Well, feel free to drop in and let us know how you get on.'

She'd have to make sure that it wasn't anyone's birthday. As she walked out into the late afternoon sunshine, Amy calculated how many calories she'd just consumed. God, she allowed herself a thousand calories a day and she must have eaten seven hundred of them in the past half hour. Plus the cakes were virtually all fat which was harder to burn off than calories from fish and fruit.

They'd tasted brilliant at the time but now they seemed to lie, undigested, in the pit of her stomach, and if she was just sitting in the flat all night she'd never burn them off.

Breaking into a run, she broke the speed record returning to the charity shop. Thank goodness they were still open. More importantly, the exercise bike was still there.

'You look like you need a seat rather than a bike,' the elderly volunteer behind the counter said sympathetically.

'I was scared that you'd have sold it,' Amy gasped, swaying as she picked up the bike and blushing as she reached the desk.

'Are you parked outside?' the woman asked.

'No.' *That was the understatement of the year.* It hadn't occurred to her till now that the bike might be difficult to transport. She prayed that the woman wouldn't start to make a fuss. 'I don't have far to go.'

'You could probably park outside for a moment or we could bring it to you for a small additional charge.'

She'd eaten cake now. She needed to exercise now. Amy smiled bravely. 'Really, it's no problem. I'm stronger than I look.'

She huffed and puffed and reddened and perspired as half of Dundee watched her stagger with the stationary bike along the Perth Road, but at last she got it home, had one of the flat's famous scalding-hot-to-freezing-cold showers, put on her lifeguard's shorts and T-shirt and pedalled until the lactose flooded her thighs.

CHAPTER NINE

The bitch wasn't going to write. It had been almost a month since Amy had been given his address and he hadn't had as much as a post-it note. By now she'd be starting university, making friends. She clearly didn't give a fuck about him being stuck in here with Tearful Tim and Demented Dermott, neither of whom were big on two-way conversations. Christ, they couldn't even read or write.

Other cons had the habits of a pig. One man regularly let his nasal secretions drip into his food whilst another hadn't learned how to use a toilet roll and smelt like a skunk. Luckily Dermott and Tim liked to eat in the canteen, so he'd put his lunch on a tray and taken it to his cell, enjoying a welcome lunchtime hour to himself.

Not that an hour of privacy was nearly enough. Sometimes he wanted to start swinging a chair, killing both of them. At other times he found himself pacing the exercise yard, idly wondering how he could make his escape. It would be madness to do a runner now when he was due out on parole in January - but he needed to imagine taking control of his life again in order to relax. How could a man spend a day doing menial work in the prison sweatshop, only to return to a cell shared with two weeping, shrieking men?

He needed a woman beneath him, squirming as he tightened his grip, silently beseeching. He needed to know and see and feel that he was in charge.

For the past couple of weeks - with no letter from Amy or from anyone else to fuel his fantasies - his thoughts had turned again and again to the pretty young officer in the education block. He knew which part of her he'd like to block, thrusting hard.

Weekday mornings were no good as she had classes then, usually comprising five to six cons who were desperate for a glimpse of cleavage. They all sucked up to her so much that she seemed to have forgotten she could be at risk. Not that her situation was unusual - female staff were regularly left alone with groups of prisoners in unlocked rooms.

Now he mentally reviewed her schedule for the hundredth time, determined to be right about every detail. She disappeared most days after lunch but put in an appearance every Friday afternoon to teach big boastful Barney who needed remedial help. Jeff personally thought that Barney needed a whole new brain but Lisa, the education officer, had a more naïve viewpoint and believed he'd be a changed man if he could only learn his vowels.

Barney, then, with his retarded IQ and his constant tales of who he'd killed was going to be the patsy. And he, Jeff, was going to have the strangulation session of his life. It was surprising, he mused, the number of cons who only became murderers in prison, though in his case - unbeknown to the world - he'd murdered before.

It was 1.50pm now. She'd be there on the hour and would sit marking books till 2.30pm when Barney skipped proudly in with his My First Story Book. Except Barney would find a dead Lisa rather than a live Lisa and would hopefully take the blame. So far the idiot had claimed responsibility for everything from the wing cleaner falling down the stairs to the budgie in the next cell dying. Why should this strangulation be any different?

It was time to get his ass to the education block. Jeff's fingers tingled as he left his cell. His growing erection made the walk down the stairs increasingly difficult so he forced himself to think mundane thoughts until it deflated against his thigh. He used peripheral vision as he walked, making sure that no one he knew saw where he was going. After all, he could hardly say that he wanted to talk to Lisa about joining the Open

University when he was due for release within months.

Getting there. His heartbeat speeded as he approached the classroom she always sat in. *Almost, almost.* He looked through the glass partition and could see her behind the desk, frowning in concentration at a book. He opened the door, closed it quickly and walked towards her. Any second now...

He was about to clasp his hands around her throat and pull her to the floor when the door burst open again and three cons came racing in.

'Baz wants to enter the poetry competition!' the youngest said. They looked at each other and fell about laughing. Jeff stood there in shock, his long-cherished fantasy breaking into a million shards.

'Then he'll have to wait his turn. Sorry, can I help you?'

He realised belatedly that the woman was talking to him.

'Need a dictionary,' he mumbled.

'No problem.' Her face cleared. 'You'll find them in the library.'

He knew what he wanted to find - and it wouldn't be in the fucking library. He felt like a ravenous animal that pounces and narrowly misses its prey.

Only after he left the room did he realise that there were clammy pools under his arms, that his shirt was also sticking to his back. Fuck it, he'd have a shower and... No, he wouldn't. He'd do what he'd come here to do, albeit no longer with a bitch.

Pulse racing again, he strolled with pretend-casualness to the shower block and loitered a respectable distance from the entrance, knowing that the shadows concealed him. He'd considered this strategy before but discarded it as altogether less appealing and too risky. But now he had to do something to take the heavy edge of depression and almost constant irritation away. Tonight, when Tim sobbed and Dermott yelled, he'd retreat inside his latest killing memory. Tonight, and many other nights, would be enriched by the act he was about to carry out.

The first man to go in was tall and heavily built. Jeff watched till he eventually left. The second was smaller but looked strong and soon swaggered out. The third man to enter was five foot four and thin as a pencil. *Gotcha.* He struck fast.

Jeff raced over before the teenager even had time to untie his laces, tackling him to the floor. Then keeping both hands tightly around his throat, he pulled him into one of the adjacent toilet cubicles and shut the half-door. Now they had privacy, for anyone seeing or hearing two men would assume that they were doing a drug deal or cottaging.

Not that he had any intention of fucking this guy. He'd never... well, he'd had a few thoughts as a twelve year old. But in those days it had all been about getting even whereas now it was about making himself feel good.

Clasp hands here comes Jeffrey. He tightened his grip on the boy's neck. The teenager cried out and his hands clawed at Jeff's fingers. Jeff shifted position until he was kneeling on the youth's arms, forcing them hard against the floor. The boy's feet scuffed against the concrete but Jeff's muscular weight ensured that he couldn't throw him off.

Now he could take his time with the next bit. Not as much time as he'd taken with Sonia, of course, for then he'd had the entire flat to himself, he'd been in clover. But he could still make this into a reasonably slow session given that they were behind closed doors.

He increased the pressure slightly, stared into the youth's eyes.

'Say thank you.'

'Th... thank you,' the boy stammered, obviously finding it painful to speak. He stared up at Jeff, probably wondering what he'd done wrong. There were lots like him in here, little pretty boys willing to confuse the fuck out of a straight man for the price of a Mars Bar or a bit of protection in the showers.

He'd have to make sure not to shower the little bastard with his come. Jeff moved his groin away slightly and the boy seized the moment and tried to buck him off. Jeff increased the pressure.

'Don't fuck with me, sonny,' he muttered. Now where had he heard that before?

'Oh please. What do you want?'

Total control. He'd show rather than tell. He squeezed tighter and tighter. The youth started to gasp but because his throat was so constricted the sound came out like a child's first attempt at whistling and his face soon went an unbecoming red, a red which would eventually turn to blue.

Get used to it, kiddo. Jeff kept the pressure constant, knowing that he could keep the boy at this level until his hands started to tire. He liked this moment best, when his prey was still conscious, still moving beneath him, still trying to plead for mercy. After they lost consciousness or died - and one followed the other so quickly that he couldn't tell the exact moment of reckoning - it was all over in the fun stakes. Thereafter, he'd wash and go.

He lessened his grip a little. The boy said something unintelligible but clearly respectful.

'You deserve this,' Jeff muttered, and the words held an echo of the distant past. 'And now you're getting it.' He throttled a little harder, enjoying the boy's squirming. 'You saying something?' he added menacingly as air again whistled through the constricted throat. 'Don't rush me. I like to take my time. You don't want to get on the wrong side of me. You don't want to make me angry again or I'll...'

Fuck it, someone was coming. He crushed the teenager's warm, pulsing neck as if his own life depended on it. No way was this little tramp going to give the game away.

He squeezed, stared, watched the boy's eyes bulge, the mouth go slack, the strange almost mauve-like hue spreading over his features. The very last moments were physically ugly but the feeling of control, of power, was beautiful beyond belief. *I take your life and it's as if I suddenly have two lives. In your very last moments you belong to me.* And then it was over as quickly as it had started. Jeff stayed, immobile, in the cubicle, listening hard, until the other con went away.

Now it was time for a little damage limitation. Working quickly, he got the dead youth into a sitting position then lifted him up so that he was propped on the toilet seat. Fingers aching, he unbuckled and unthreaded his victim's belt, looped it over the horizontal pipe high above the cistern, leaving enough space for the youth's head.

The next bit was going to take all of his strength and then some. Breathing deeply, he stepped onto the toilet seat, his feet on either side of the body, leaned down and put his hands under the boy's wet underarms, pulled the corpse up, up, up. It felt like shifting a ton and his shoulder and arm muscles felt torn by the effort. *Do it quickly*. Now that the thrill of the kill was over he felt increasingly exposed.

With a last lunge upwards, he got the teenager's head through the noose, adjusted the belt around his neck, stepped down and admired his handiwork. Perfect. With luck, the swinger wouldn't be discovered for some time, and even if he was found immediately, chances are the pathologist would find no suspicious circumstances, just another homesick kid who'd committed suicide.

Hoping that Dermott and Tim were vegging out in the Rec Room after lunch, Jeff hurried back to his cell and casually entered it. Thank Christ, it was still vacant. He'd have found it difficult to speak casually to anyone just now. Jeff sat on his bed and picked up his *Life After Parole* handbook and pretended to be immersed in it. If anyone looked in, they'd see a thoughtful, forward thinking man who didn't want to be disturbed. They wouldn't see a man whose skin was wet, whose heart was racing, a man who had just killed for the second time.

Christ, he'd been brilliant, really gone for it. Got in there fast and fixed the kid like a moth on a pin. And he hadn't panicked when someone came into the shower block - no, he'd taken the bastard down, kept control then hung him high. The only hitch was that he really needed a shower - but given the circumstances he'd have to wait. Now he just had to keep his head down for a few more months and he'd be free as a bird.

But not free *with* a bird. He thought again of Amy who didn't have the decency to even write him one small letter. It was a pity that his mother hadn't found out her address or he'd have made her very sorry when he got out.

CHAPTER TEN

God, she was starving. Dana hurried into the student's union and followed the scent of burgers and chips till she found the canteen. Only half of the tables were occupied. Most of the students had matriculated then gone off to join one of the student clubs but she knew from her mother that the clubs would be there all year, that there was plenty of time.

She picked up a tray then caught sight of a familiar figure studying the food. Oh, it was Amy. She'd been out so much with Ken that she hadn't really had a chance to talk to her flatmate yet.

The medical student glanced at the serving girl. 'I'll have a slice of cheese and onion quiche. Mm, and a green salad and a tea. Oh, and a bowl of chips.' She accepted her food then sidled up to Amy. 'Big decision?'

Amy jumped then said 'Oh hi. It's all salads in mayonnaise.'

Dana broke off a piece of shortcrust pastry and popped it into her mouth. 'The quiche is fine.'

To her surprise, Amy shuddered. 'I'm not that hungry. I think I'll just have beans.'

'Beans on toast?' the serving girl asked.

'No, just beans on their own please.'

'A double portion?'

'No, a single. With a black coffee, please.'

Dana pointed out a clean table and they both sat down. She started in on the tangy onion centre then looked up to see Amy self consciously spearing a bean.

'Have a few of my chips if you like.' She pushed the bowl into the centre, 'I'll never eat all those.'

'Er, no thanks - I had a big breakfast.'

'A cigarette's my dead strength in the morning,' Dana admitted. She laughed and held up her hands. 'I know - medics shouldn't smoke. But Ken got me started and now I'm hooked.'

Amy smiled then speared a second bean.

'So, you finding your way around?'

The girl looked uncertain then nodded. 'I joined the vegetarian society today.'

'Oh, I didn't realise you were a veggie.'

'No, I'm not but I wanted to join something and there were lots of men standing around the walking club stall whereas the vegetarian girl was on her own.'

'Ah.' Dana cut off another chunk of quiche and ate it hungrily. The silence stretched.

'I just want to eat healthily,' Amy added softly.

'Oh you can get away with eating what you like until you're twenty five,' Dana explained, remembering various dinner conversations about food. 'Mummy said so. After that your metabolism slows, so you might as well live it up while you can.' She wondered if Amy was waiting for some hardship grant to come through, if these sad-looking beans were all she could afford. 'Listen, help yourself to anything in the fridge. I'm always starting on cheese then going away for days and its green when I come back. Thing is, with Ken being on call at the hospital, I have to stay with him rather than him staying with me.'

'Oh no, really, I'm fine. I hardly ever eat cheese and I've got in lots of salad and beans.'

Another silence. The menu seemed to be beans, beans, beans and beans. Mummy had given her a generous allowance and now Dana wondered if she should offer the girl a loan.

She hesitated then decided to do the right thing. 'I'll be home tonight. I could cook us a meal.'

'Let me,' Amy said - and Dana noticed that she actually smiled. There was another silence then she added 'Would a stir fry with prawns be okay?'

They talked some more about food then Dana saw that it was time to meet one of her friends. 'See you at six?' she asked.

Amy nodded and smiled widely. 'I'll have been to the supermarket by then.'

Dana went into her jeans pocket and found a fiver. 'My contribution. Seafood isn't cheap.' She walked to the door then glanced back and was pleased to see Amy reaching for the virtually-untouched bowl of chips.

That night the two of them ate at the kitchen table. Dana had to admit that the crispy beansprouts, peppers, sweetcorn and prawns tasted great, flavoured as they were with garlic, grated ginger, chopped spring onions and soy sauce. But half an hour after the meal she still felt hungry so made them both buttered toast.

'I shouldn't,' Amy said, staring hungrily at the plate.

'You're thin as a rake.'

'And I want to stay that way.'

'A slice of toast won't kill you.'

The silence stretched, only broken when Amy grabbed and munched.

'You're a good cook. Will you have your parents through for a meal soon?' Dana asked, wishing it wasn't such hard work talking to this girl.

'No, they don't...' Amy spoke through a mist of crumbs then blushed, 'They have commitments. This is very nice toast.'

'Oh, what do they do?'

'Dad owns a sweet shop. Mum works from home, addressing envelopes.'

'I thought they had machines to do that nowadays.'

'Apparently not.' Amy looked glum.

'Still, having access to a sweetshop must be fun.'

Amy shuddered.

'I'll do the dishes.' Dana put the wok in the sink. She took her time scrubbing the plates then said 'Lets open a bottle of wine. Mummy brought through six bottles last month. It's red - very healthy.'

'I don't usually...'

'Think of it as christening this place.'

The one glass stretched to four and the other girl opened up a little, talking about her work as a lifeguard, about her aunt and about the boring-sounding computer course she'd been talked into. But it was still an awkward conversation and Dana was very glad when her mobile rang.

She spoke to Ken for an hour whilst Amy disappeared next door, presumably to do some more course-related reading. She didn't reappear when Dana's phone call ended but popped her head around the door at eleven and said she was going to bed.

'Sweet dreams,' Dana said, reaching for her cigarettes and the wine bottle. She put her walkman on and listened to music until 1am then hit the sack, smiling to herself as she heard Amy snoring in the adjacent divan.

Some time later she awoke and realised that there was an odd, rhythmic clicking in the room. As her eyes adjusted to the darkness, she saw a thin figure sitting on an exercise bike and pedalling furiously. Dana squinted at the glowing figures on her alarm clock. It was 3am.

'Amy, for fuck's sake,' she muttered.

The figure froze. 'Sorry.'

There were further sounds as she disembarked and walked back to bed. Seconds later Dana heard the mattress creak and looked over to see Amy lying on her back on top of the bed. Her slender legs were raised and she was cycling as if her very life depended on it.

CHAPTER ELEVEN

Shelley searched for the words which would pacify Amy. The teenager was much more keyed up than when she'd seen her five weeks ago.

'It's a gamble, moving in with a flatmate you've never met,' she said sympathetically, 'And it may be harder for you given that you grew up as an only child.'

'She made me buttered toast,' Amy muttered.

'Sorry?'

'She keeps offering me things I don't want.'

Again Shelley felt sorry for the girl. She knew that most adults refused to take teenager's problems seriously - but that didn't make the problems any less acute for them. Girls like Amy were trying to make friends, build homes, start their academic lives and possibly establish their first sexual relationships. It was a lot for an inexperienced girl to cope with, and sometimes something had to give.

'So don't take your flatmate's snacks. Just refuse politely.'

'But she leaves opened bottles and packets around. It's just not fair.'

For the first time Shelley wondered if the nineteen year old had an eating disorder. She'd specialised in such disorders for years before moving to the clinic so she usually recognised the symptoms. This girl wasn't shivery enough or hunched enough to be a full blown anorexic - but it looked as if she might be a fledgling one. She thought back, remembering how Amy had taken ages to eat two cream cakes. She'd just thought that the girl was eating daintily in company, but it could equally be a ritualistic approach to food.

The thirty-nine year old sighed. The general public thought that anorexics hardly ate anything. But some did: they just half starved themselves then binged then starved again.

'Would you be happier in student halls?'

Amy looked alarmed then shook her head. 'You can't cook for yourself there and you have to eat at set times and...' She tailed off apologetically.

'And is cooking for yourself so important?'

Amy nodded. 'There's lots of things I can't eat.'

'Can't or won't?' She knew that she sounded harder now, but saw no point in ignoring the girl's issues. Okay, she'd presented here today saying that she wasn't fitting in an university but if the real problem was food...

'I may have a dairy allergy,' Amy muttered.

It was a myth shared by most of the dieting nation. 'So don't eat your flatmate's dairy products.'

'But she keeps offering me snacks.'

At this stage most parents and older friends just laughed and the teenager's problem simply wasn't talked through. 'So why do you think she does that?'

'I suppose eating together gives us something to do.'

'Then maybe you need to suggest something different, like going to the cinema?'

'I would but she's got Ken for that,' Amy said.

Eventually the teenager left and Shelley updated her notes. Amy was a bright - if somewhat needy - girl with an inability to relate to other teenagers. She'd apparently gone swimming twice a week since their first counselling session but hadn't talked to anyone at the Leisure Centre. She'd also joined the vegetarian society but did the four minute mile from the introductory session as it involved cheese and wine.

Shelley smiled wryly to herself. In a way, Amy was old beyond her years which made her easy to counsel. She needed what most adults needed - a sense of belonging to someone, of having a balanced life. She was simpler to understand than more typical teenagers, like those baffling sixteen year old boys who preferred a skateboard to a girlfriend. Shelley was also confused by teenage girls who spent years growing beautiful long hair, only to scrape it back with an ugly elastic band.

'Shelley, do you have time to see...? Oh good, you do.' She smiled weakly as Jean ushered in another female client. 'You've half an hour till *he* arrives,' the older woman added ominously.

He was Dougal who managed this clinic plus the much bigger ones in Perth and Inverness. They'd eventually nicknamed him Dougal With The Digits as, left to his own devices, his fingers went everywhere.

The first time he'd slipped an arm around Shelley's shoulders she'd tensed up and talked nineteen to the dozen. Afterwards she'd been annoyed with herself - hell, she counselled sexual harassment victims on how to stand up for themselves. The second time he did it she'd shot up like a rocket and shrugged him off. After that she'd talked to Jean and they'd come up with the perfect solution - Jean would make sure she always had an arm around Shelley when Dougal was around.

It had worked perfectly so far, given that The Digit only visited every three months and tended to phone ahead. He looked suspiciously at their sudden affection but didn't attempt to make it a ménage a trois.

That night, whilst preparing to lock up, they talked more about how they'd fooled him.

'He'll start on me next,' Jean said in her usual deadpan tone, 'He's probably already bought a granny fanny mag.'

They were crying with laughter as Zoe, the youngest counsellor, joined them in the hall. Zoe had been Dougal's preferred candidate after their male counsellor left - and Dougal had the casting vote.

'Busy day, Zoe?' Shelley asked, choking back her mirth and changing to a safer topic for the PC Queen.

'It had its moments,' Zoe said.

It would, Shelley knew, have had many more odd moments if Zoe had her way. The younger counsellor embraced everything from rebirthing to primal scream.

'See you tomorrow, girls,' Jean called, hurrying over to her husband's car.

'Bye for now,' Zoe said brightly, turning to unlock her rainbow-coloured bike.

Shelley waved to them both then set off on the hour-and-a-quarter trek home. It was something she'd done since accepting the job at the clinic. It gave her exercise and meant that the nights in the house weren't so long. Not that she was bored at home - she was almost finished a year-long paper on teenage eating disorders. And if she did need a chat, she could always pop in to her next door neighbour, Netta, whose husband often worked away from home.

As she prepared paella for her evening meal, she thought again of Amy and of the other anorexics that she'd known. What must it be like, every cell in your body screaming out for nutrition whilst every cell in your mind thought it was virtuous to starve? Glad that she'd never had a problem with food, Shelley snipped spring onions into the olive oil coated rice. That was one of the good things about having your own house and kitchen - you could eat what you liked.

Not that her former husband had been difficult about such things, but living with someone else was always a compromise. He'd often wanted to chat after a day spent in the operating theatre whereas she was talked out from her day's counselling and wanted to sit and stare at the TV.

Which was exactly what she was going to do now - eat, watch and be merry. Living alone, she thought, as she slotted James Spader into the DVD player, was great.

CHAPTER TWELVE

She had to talk to someone today or she'd go mad. Amy left the empty flat and walked to the nearest kiosk to call Aunt Gretchen. But the phone remained unanswered and she eventually left with her head still full of unshed words.

Maybe today she'd make a friend at her seminar group. They were studying T S Eliot's *The Wasteland*. She'd already written the essay although it wasn't due for another week.

Shyly, Amy entered the seminar room and took the seat that was furthest away from the tutor's own. She was first as usual. He looked up from his book and smiled at her in a not-quite-connected way. She smiled back then went slightly red, hoping that he didn't think she fancied him. Just then Shevonne and Emmaline came in and both said 'Hi' to him as if he was a person of no importance. The tutor said 'Hi there. What have you two been up to this fine morn?'

Shevonne grinned as she sat down. 'Sleeping! Let's just say that last night involved Pete's Bar.'

'Enough said. I shall speak quietly and solicitously,' the tutor said, gave a wide smile then returned to his book.

It was now or never. Amy took a deep breath. 'Is Pete a friend of yours?' she asked.

'What?' The other student stared at her blankly for a second. 'No, Pete's Bar is one of the pubs in the students union.'

'Oh, right.' She'd only been to the union once to buy a plate of beans.

'They have some good bands on,' Emmaline added.

'Oh, right,' Amy said again. Her parents had monopolised the TV when she was growing up so she'd never seen any of the music programmes that the other school pupils talked about. She knew as much about the charts as the average pensioner.

The two boys from her seminar group came in and took their seats. The boys talked to each other and the two girls talked to each other and the tutor read his book. Amy felt like the odd one out as usual. Her spirits lightened as the tutor looked at his watch but he just said 'We'll wait another couple of minutes for Chrissie if that's all right with everyone else.'

Amy turned back to Shevonne, knowing that if she didn't speak to her - to anyone - soon, she wouldn't have another chance all day. 'So, what did you think of *The Wasteland*?'

'The what?'

'The T S Eliot poem.'

Shevonne glanced at the tutor then lowered her voice, 'I haven't read it yet.'

'Oh right,' Amy said for the third and final time.

'We've been practically living at *The Liar*,' Emmaline added in a dramatic whisper.

Amy smiled but decided not to ask.

An hour later the session - a self-conscious duet between herself and the tutor - ended and she went for a walk, encompassing everything from Roseangle to the Blackness Road. Thirst eventually drove her home and she sat at the kitchen table sipping a black tea, unable to believe that it was still only 2pm.

Where could she go next? Amy got out the map. She could walk up the Hilltown and look at the shops or find Constitution Road which would lead her to Dudhope Park or... *or she could go home for an overnight stay*. The moment the idea popped into her head, she felt happier. Okay, so she'd promised herself that she wouldn't return to Aberdeen until December, but she hadn't told her parents that. She could tell them about Dana and her medical family, the computer course, her English studies and about joining the vegetarian society. She could describe the flat, the town, the university and the lecturers. She'd stay over in her old room and maybe even call into her old workplace the next day.

The next two hours were action-filled as she packed a bag, went to the kiosk to phone about train times then bought gifts (aftershave for dad and perfume for mum, both with *A Present From Dundee* embossed on them) and a crystal swan to add to Aunt Gretchen's already sizeable collection. Then she walked to the station and was soon on her way back to Aberdeen.

It was cold - a lot colder than it had been in Dundee - when she finally disembarked but she felt happy at seeing all the familiar landmarks. Ignoring the expense, she took a taxi back to her childhood home.

For the first time she climbed the tenement stair as a visitor rather than as an occupier of one of the flats. As she neared her parents' door she fancied she could smell vinegar-drenched fish and chips.

Amy rang the bell. For a moment there was silence but she waited patiently, knowing that they never went out at night. Suddenly she heard the familiar thump, thump, thump of feet, then the door slowly opened and her father filled the doorway looking even larger than he had when she'd last seen him seven weeks before.

'Only me,' she said brightly, trying not to stare.

'Oh, your Mum didn't say...'

'I thought I'd surprise her.'

'Well, *Emmerdale* is about to start,' her dad said.

He seemed to turn in three painful stages, spreading his huge legs obscenely apart as he moved. Amy knew that if he tried to walk normally his thighs rubbed and bled.

An unwilling voyeur, she followed him back down the hall, trying to blank out the huge rolls of shirt-covered fat, the enormous buttocks in the baggy cords, the crushed-to-bits slippers. The stench of perspiration lingered in his wake.

'Surprise,' he gasped as he entered the living room.

'Only me,' Amy said again, popping her head around the door.

'Jim - put another bag of popcorn in the microwave for Amy,' her mother said.

'No need - I had a sandwich on the train.'

'A sandwich won't fill you up.'

'It did.'

'Have a wee taste of *my* popcorn then.' Her mother indicated the large steaming bowl perched on the edge of her chair, 'It's savoury butter.'

Probably not your first bag of the day. Amy stared in disgust at her mother's enormous arms and legs.

'Mum, I came to see you, not to eat.'

Her mother looked at her vacantly. 'You're not pregnant?'

'No, I just thought I could tell you about my course and...'

'Tell me later,' her mum cut in, '*Emmerdale* is about to start.'

It was like walking back in time. Nothing had changed here. Amy took a deep breath and fought back her hurt and anger. 'I'll nip out to the kiosk, see if Aunt Gretchen's home.'

Hurrying from the tenement, she walked to the nearest telephone kiosk only to find that it had been vandalised. The second kiosk only took phone cards. By the time she found a third, she was cold and miserable and felt completely alone in the world. It was a feeling which intensified when her aunt's phone wasn't answered. Damn, she must be out at one of her musical evenings or at her friend's.

Amy returned dispiritedly to the tenement and rang the bell. Again her father answered. Did mum not walk nowadays? She couldn't remember when she'd last seen the woman stand.

'She's out,' Amy admitted as she sat down in the living room.

'She usually is,' her mother said in a disapproving voice. She glanced at Amy. 'Would you like a toffee apple? Your father brought them in.'

'Sell them in the shop,' her father said.

'Oh, that's new. How are sales?'

'Same old,' her father said, 'This man sold me his wife's homemade tablet, vanilla fudge and peanut brittle.' He held out a multi-divided plate and Amy saw that each section was filled with a different sweet.

'I ate on the train,' she lied again.

'Sh, here's *The Bill*,' her mother cut in, then reached for the toffee apple which had now replaced the popcorn on the side of her chair.

The three of them stared as the actors fell in and out of love, shouted at each other a lot, chased a few villains and shouted some more. Amy tried to resume the conversation at each of the adverts.

'You'd like my new flat.'

Her mother sniffed. 'We should do at that price.'

'Well, Aunt Gretchen's paying.' She tried again, 'Mum - it's not that expensive at all, it's just that you're used to subsidised council house rent.'

'Are you saying our house isn't good enough? Jim, can you bring me the cola? It's on your other side. I'm parched.'

'No, I'm just saying that private landlords charge more. It's not a penthouse or anything - in fact, the shower room is off the kitchen and Dana says that's illegal.'

'Dana as in the *X-Files*?' her mother said.

Amy nodded hopefully. 'That's right. What's Dana like? The one that I know is...'

'Time for *Casualty*. It's getting to a really good bit. Would you like a glass of this coke?'

Amy shook her head. 'Aunt Gretchen will be home by now. I'd better go round.' She stood up as the medical soap began.

'Are you coming back?' her father asked.

'Mm, at Christmas.'

There was no point in telling them that she'd planned to stay the night.

'Well, take a snack for the road,' he said and she realised belatedly that he wasn't going to see her out.

'No, honest, I'm not hungry.' *She was always hungry.*

'They've covered that anorexia illness on this very show,' her mother added, not taking her eyes from the screen.

'Mum, how often do I have to tell you I'm not anorexic?' Amy could hear the tears in her voice. She grabbed her bag, planning on a quick exit, and heard a clink. Remembering, she took out their presents.

'Just a small thing from Dundee.'

'Wasn't that *Taggart* set in Dundee?' her father asked.

'No, Jim, that was Glasgow,' her mother said, unwrapping her present then putting it to one side of her chair.

Back on the street, the air seemed even colder than before and Amy pulled her jacket more closely against her bare midriff. Please let Gretchen be in...

She wasn't. For a few minutes she sat on the doorstep but quickly began to lose all feeling in her thighs. Resolutely she got to her feet and walked up the long residential road to the very end, turned and retraced her steps. At least she was burning calories and keeping warm. After half an hour of pacing the block she saw a taxi draw up outside her aunt's small bungalow. Then she was waving and running and Gretchen was squinting into the darkness then waving back and for a few moments everything seemed alright.

'We've been to Edinburgh for the day,' her aunt said as she searched for her keys in her bag, 'Isobel's daughter was doing a lunchtime concert. If I'd known you were coming through...'

'It was a last minute decision.' She glanced at the older woman and saw that she looked worn out. At forty four, Gretchen was only four years older than Amy's parents but she looked closer to fifty, her thin face pale and prematurely lined.

They walked into the house and Gretchen smiled at her then asked hesitantly 'Have you seen your mum and dad?'

'Uh huh. I went there first. They'd made popcorn.'

Gretchen switched on the lounge light then seemed to appraise her. 'I'll make us a coffee,' she said.

A few minutes later she was back with the coffee jug and two rice cakes, each topped with a scraping of hummus and a generous portion of king prawns. Crouching in front of the gas fire, Amy ate and drank gratefully.

'So how was the concert?' she asked.

'Oh forget the concert. How's university? The flat? Tell me all your news.'

Where to start? 'The flat's great - I can even go home between lectures if I've an hour to spare and it's got these wooden window shutters to keep out the cold and...' There was a limit to what you could say about two rooms, a WC and a shower.

'And your flatmate's nice?'

'Dana? She's a medic.'

'Handy if you go down with anything.'

'That's what I said!' Amy laughed. She wished for the zillionth time that Aunt Gretchen was her mother, then felt guilty for having such undaughterly thoughts. 'They were... Dad had brought home loads of sweets again and mum didn't get up at all.'

Her aunt nodded. 'I went round there the other day with some fruit and veg. Your mum told me to put it in the salad rack and I found the veg I'd taken them a fortnight ago. It was completely rotten.'

'Mum ate a toffee apple while I was there,' Amy said defensively then wasn't sure whether to laugh or cry.

'What we need to get them on is toffee cabbages and toffee sprouts.'

They shared a sad smile then Amy went off to have a bath. When she returned to the lounge, the older woman was fast asleep in her chair. Her mind still full of unshed words, Amy fetched a blanket and tucked it around her favourite relative then left the fire on low. Fetching another blanket for herself, she curled up on the settee and lay there for hour after hour, listening to Gretchen's rhythmic snoring. Eventually, as the birds started singing, she fell asleep.

She awoke to the sounds of the toaster catapulting out its contents. Gratefully Amy accepted the slice of wholemeal toast and black coffee that Gretchen brought her on a pretty rose-painted tray.

'I've to leave for work now, love. Will you be here when I get back at six?'

Wishing that she could be, Amy shook her head. 'I've a lecture at two.'

'Well, promise that you'll phone me whenever you can.'

That would be hourly, then. 'I promise. Oh, I got you something.' Amy found the little crystal swan and her aunt said how much she loved it. Then she was gone and the day loomed ahead, peopleless yet again.

Amy walked slowly to the station and took the train home. The flat was empty but there was a carton of double cream, a half finished bowl of fruit salad, four Spanish beer bottles and a red wine carafe sitting on the table. She went into the bedroom and opened the window to let the smell of alcohol out.

What should she do now? She went to her desk and fetched the folder which held her computer course notes, intending to memorise some of the word processing short cut keys. As she leafed through the various papers, an expensively-embossed address card fell out. *Jeff Metcalfe, Weald Wing, HMP Maidstone, Kent.* He was lonely. She was lonely. What harm could it do? Taking out her notepad, Amy began to write.

CHAPTER THIRTEEN

Oh good, the gullible little cow had cracked and written him a letter. Jeff sat in the Rec Room and read it, glad of something to do other than watch TV.

Dear Jeff,

Greetings from a cold and windswept Dundee! I've been doing a computer course here and met your mother. She suggested I write to you.

The computer course is just part time. (I'm a complete Luddite but a relative talked me into it!) I'm also studying English Lit at university. It's part of an arts course which means I have to choose two other subjects for my first two years. I've opted for Psychology and Philosophy. The latter doesn't make any sense to me at all so if you've got any hints...!

Barbara tells me you have a science degree. Can you take additional courses where you are now? How do you spend your days? If you have the time, please write and tell me.

Very Best Wishes,

Amy (Bartlett)

Apart from the fact that she was studying psychology and might psych him out, she sounded just right. Out of her depth at her computer course and at uni. Nineteen but definitely not living the teenage dream.

He liked girls who were a lot younger than himself or a lot older. Faith had been thirty eight when they met and he'd been a boyish twenty three.

She'd had her own flat whereas he'd been in one of Cardiff's cheaper bed and breakfasts. He'd been unemployed since dropping out of university, couldn't figure out exactly what he wanted to do.

One night he'd gone for a drink to a classy hotel looking for a pick-up and met her and her colleagues in the lounge, enjoying a works night out to celebrate the school's headmistress getting married. He'd noticed Faith looking wistfully at the woman's ruby-and-diamond ring.

'Isn't ruby the birthstone for Cancerians?' he'd asked. They usually liked to talk about astrology, did women.

'I don't... my religion doesn't allow me to study astrology,' she'd said.

Well fuck you. He'd bitten back the words - she was plain but her clothes were good and she looked desperate to get a sparkly rock on her finger. He could shoot a few lines about wanting to settle down with the right woman and loosen her up a bit. Christ knows, he couldn't stand living in bed-and-breakfastville much longer and she looked rich enough to have her own pad.

He'd been right, too, but he didn't get to see her place until they'd been dating a month. And he didn't get to see the bedroom for another six months. By then he'd been sick of sweet talking her and was ready to cut his losses and run.

Maybe she'd sensed this, for she'd invited him back that night after they'd seen an unexpectedly erotic film at the cinema. They'd sat on her settee drinking low alcohol wine and he'd started kissing the side of her neck, waiting for her to say 'we shouldn't.' But she hadn't said anything, merely moaned and breathed faster. So he'd kept going, taking his time, knowing that he'd get a decent roof over his head if he could persuade her he was Mr Right.

It was slow going as she was Miss Everything-Is-Wrong. She tensed when he slid his hands inside her very big knickers, tensed when he stroked her pubic hair, almost shot over the top of the settee when he found her clitoris. It took him a moment to realise that the last shudder had been one of pleasure as he touched her bud. Hadn't she ever...? He caressed around the perimeter of her clit slowly and rhythmically. God, had she never done this for herself?

She hadn't. He did. Within seconds of her first orgasm she'd been ready to marry him.

'I love you,' she said, which was Faith-speak for make-a-respectable-woman-of-me-and-give-me-children.

'I love you too.' Well, he loved her cosy terraced house, her Fiat Uno, her salary.

'We... should we make this permanent?' she asked, rebuttoning her blouse and pulling her grey woollen skirt back over her hips and knees.

'Yes, I'd love to move in,' he said beatifically.

'Oh, I didn't mean... The Bible says...'

'It was written a long time ago, Faith.' He stroked her slightly-greying hair back from her face to take the sting from his words. 'I mean, men were ignorant in those days, heard thunder and told themselves it was the voice of an angry deity. Locusts ate their crops and they assumed that the same angry god had sent them as a punishment. They tried to make sense out of a clearly indifferent universe.' He kissed the top of her head. 'Are you really going to spoil what we have because of a book that was written thousands of years ago?'

'Mummy says that when I think like that I'm backtracking.'

He knew what he'd like to do to Mummy's backtrack. 'Faith, it's your life now - you're thirty eight.' He watched her wince. 'Are you really going to live as she's lived?' Mummy was a bigoted relic, a dried up, miserable old prune.

'No, but - I never thought I'd live with anyone.'

'Nor did I,' he said sentimentally, 'We're so lucky to have found each other.'

'And Daddy won't be pleased because you don't have a job.'

'I've been thinking about that.' *Thinking about how long he could avoid joining the rat race.* 'I think it hurts my chances with employers, the fact I'm living in a bed and breakfast. If I could give a proper address like this one I'd look much more stable to them.'

'But what will my friends say?'

He knew she didn't really have friends, only colleagues. 'They'll be pleased that you've found someone to share life with and happy that you can start a family one day.'

'I could never have children outwith wedlock, Jeffrey.'

Thank fuck for that. He'd copied her solemn look. 'I agree with you there, Faith. Children need stability.'

'So why can't we get married now?'

Because I've other fish to fry. 'Because we have to be sure that we're absolutely right for each other - just think of the many marriages which break up nowadays.'

'But we'd work at it.'

'We can work at living together, make absolutely sure.' He'd started to kiss her again, worked his way down till his lips found her still-soaking clitoris. Not even stopping to spit out the occasional pubic hair, he gave her the second orgasm of her life.

Gotcha. He'd waited for her to hand him the keys to her house. Instead she'd said dazedly 'Alright, we can live together - but there's one condition.'

'Name it.' He'd probably have to say grace before every peanut.

'We can sleep together but we can't have full sex until we're wed.'

She'd meant it, too. No matter how often he tried, her thighs became welded together whenever his hard-on approached them. He'd been reduced to bringing her off with his fingers or tongue then bringing himself to orgasm like a kid. He'd tried putting her hand on his shaft but she'd pulled away as if she'd touched a live wire. So she got the orgasms and paid the mortgage, the bills and the upkeep of the car.

It hadn't been a bad deal - except that it didn't accommodate his strangling fantasies. Let's face it, a woman who wouldn't let you have straight sex wasn't going to take kindly to a little jugular squeeze. Which meant that he had to lie about the grocery costs and put aside some money each week until he could afford to treat himself to another junkie whore.

Talking of whores, he'd write back to this one now. Oh, she didn't want money from him - but she would want something. It might be romantic letters to show the other girls at university or the eventual dubious status of bearing his name.

He knew what he wanted her to bear - but that would have to wait for a few more weeks until they let him out of here. For now he must keep her sweet.

Leaving the Rec Room, he returned to his cell, found his notepaper and pen and sat down on his bed.

Dear Amy,

What a beautiful name. Did your parents love the book *Little Women*? My mother called me Jeffrey after a close family friend so I lack your classic pedigree!

You tell me that Dundee is windswept. I remember reading that Mary Shelley hated the town's wintery greyness. Have you read Frankenstein? What does your first year reading list include? The world can look very bleak when you've been given a seven year sentence but I find the day is much brighter if I have recourse to a book.

Talking of Scotland, I'm a fellow Scot. I was born in Edinburgh and still retain my Scottish accent. My parents moved frequently when I was young so I've lived in Perth, Inverness, Ayr (Burns territory!) and Giffnock, a suburb of Glasgow. Then I went to university in Wales!

I used to have a girlfriend there who was studying Philosophy and, like you, she found it difficult. Can you perhaps switch subjects? I know that when I did my BSc we chose various modules but could change them within the first six weeks simply by going to see our student advisor. Let me know how this works out.

I envy your access to a good library, to untold numbers of books. In theory we can take courses here but in practice both funds and staff are very limited and as one of the better educated prisoners I feel it would be wrong of me to use up resources that less literate men really need. As such, I try to help others on my wing with their letters home to loved ones. I can also help them if they are victims of a miscarriage of justice and need recourse to the law.

Please write back when you find the time and let me know how you are, what you're reading etc. I try to stay optimistic but it's hard to have lively conversations with people who don't (sometimes can't) read.

Warmest Thoughts,

Jeff (Jeffrey Metcalfe)

There! That should impress her. He'd used a very similar style of writing to her own and had echoed her interests. With any luck he'd just snared himself a brand new girlfriend.

He'd carefully slotted in the info about serving a long sentence. And it was long - it was just that it was automatically reduced and he'd already served most of it. But it would make her happy, thinking that she could enjoy closeness whilst keeping him at arms length - and at cock's length, of course. For her notes would soon become love letters: he knew that from watching the other guys in here, the ones in penpal clubs. Inadequate women in their fifties soon convinced themselves that they were in love with these thirty year old cons. It suited the men as they were sent everything from duvet covers to tracksuits and even had money credited to their accounts.

These letters from the needy, the stupid, the eternal optimists and the endearingly naïve were like gold in a place like this, so he'd take care to keep his mail hidden. After some thought, he filed the note away in his duvet cover alongside his coins and stamps. Otherwise one of the other cons would nick it and would soon be telling Amy a sob story to steal her away.

You also had to make sure that a nutter like Dermott didn't get hold of the letter and frighten the sender off. One guy had lost interest in his penpal so had written her name and phone number beside the wing telephone alongside the words *soft touch*. The poor bitch had received so many calls asking for money that she'd had to go ex-directory.

But most of the guys held onto their girl's names and wrote to them daily. It gave the men something to do, someone to manipulate and it gave the women a written kiss to build a dream on. So everyone was happy - until reality bit when the con got out.

He was going to be out soon and he'd go straight to Dundee, to his friendless little Amy. And he was damned if she'd play coy like Faith and remain a virgin - to sex or to strangling - for very long.

CHAPTER FOURTEEN

It had been a hell of a day, so busy that she hadn't been able to see Amy or Sheila the thirteen year old mum or Alan who had become college phobic - but they'd all been given alternative counsellors or different dates. Now, as Shelley prepared to leave, Zoe came rushing in. 'Dougal needs to see the accounts.'

Dougal needed a kick up the arse and a change of name. Okay, so his parents had called him after the dog on *The Magic Roundabout* but why hadn't he simply shortened it to Doug?

'They're in the accounts cupboard,' - *like, where else?* - Shelley said impatiently, then remembered that, as the longest-serving counsellor here, she had the keys. Wearily she fetched them from her bag and handed them to Zoe. What was The Digit doing back here so soon? It was weeks till their next financial report was due.

'And if I could have the casenotes for these clients?' the younger woman continued, indicating her section of the appointments book. Shelley looked at the names then located the numbered files for Amy, Sheila and Alan, files which were becoming larger and more angst-ridden every week.

Zoe glanced at them. 'The first girl doesn't stay.' Whenever Zoe was stressed her Scandinavian accent became more pronounced and her English faltered.

'Amy didn't stay?'

'I say she can't see you, to see me - but after a minute she says it doesn't matter, she hurries out. But I talk to this Alan about his first day at primary school and to Sheila about post natal depression and they are very pleased.'

Talking to Alan about his first day at *college* would have been more help, but Shelley knew she couldn't influence the other therapist. The clinic's brief was simply to help young people and Zoe believed she was doing just that. Shelley herself was happy to talk through whatever difficulties the client had carried over from childhood but Zoe was obsessed with the minutiae of their lives from the moment they left the womb.

'I'll be out of here in a minute,' she said now to her colleague. Taking an apple from the fridge, she ate it quickly whilst adding to her own notes. Meanwhile, Jean popped her head around the door and said goodnight.

Shortly afterwards Shelley called her own goodnight to Zoe and Dougal and left the clinic, putting the Closed sign on the door. She walked briskly along the road and it was only when she stopped to buy a copy of the *Big Issue* from a half frozen youth in the Nethergate that she realised her bag no longer contained her keys, including the keys to her house.

Damn, she'd given the bunch to Zoe because it included the accounts cupboard key. She'd only left the clinic ten minutes ago so if she ran all the way back, her colleague might still be there. Remembering why she'd hated sports at school, the thirty nine year old broke into an ungainly run.

When she arrived back, gasping, at her workplace she was relieved to see that the lights were still on. She hurried through the main door, opened Zoe's room and stopped, at first unsure exactly what she was seeing. Dougal was standing behind Zoe, his trousers at his ankles. The twenty eight year old was bent over her desk, her batik dress unbuttoned down the front. Shelley blinked and focused. She realised that Zoe's dress had been lifted high up her back and that Dougal was - or had been - penetrating her. Jesus, had her colleague just been raped?

Suddenly Dougal turned his head and stared at her. 'For Christ's sake, get out,' he muttered.

Zoe scrambled up and turned awkwardly around. 'Shelley, leave now. Please!'

'I... are you alright?'

'What we're doing we have a right to do,' Zoe said, her face flushing.

'Oh right. I didn't...' Shelley stumbled out of the room and out of the clinic. She felt like crying but it was probably mild shock.

Slowly she walked home, reaching her bungalow before realising that she'd once again left her keys in the cupboard at work. Luckily her neighbour was home and she was able to collect her spare set.

'That's not like you,' Netta - part Earth Mother, part shrewd financier who did all her husband's accounts - said cheerfully.

'Trust me,' Shelley muttered, 'It hasn't been a typical day.'

She let herself into the house and saw that the answering machine light was flashing to indicate several calls. Shelley pressed *play* but all of the calls were slightly creepy silent ones. Sighing, she pressed 1471 and was told that the last caller - and, of course, possibly the earlier caller - was from Birmingham. That was strange - she'd had several hang-ups this week from the same number. Determined not to have any more alarms or surprises today, she dialled the number but got an unfamiliar answaphone. No, she definitely didn't know a Veronique who wasn't at home right now. The elderly-sounding woman probably wanted to talk to the previous owner of the house.

Usually she worked on her report for *Psychology In Practice* after dinner, but tonight she felt restless so cleaned out her cupboards and looked out some of her clothes for charity. Then she sat down to watch the late night movie but the image of Dougal's bare bottom intruded again and again.

Christ, she was supposed to be tuned in to people so why hadn't it occurred to her that he'd started something with Zoe? Especially when he'd turned up again today and made straight for her room. More importantly, how was she supposed to act when she saw the other woman tomorrow? She'd never be able to look either of them in the face without imagining their arses again.

Think of something nice, something good. She thought about her report, which was almost finished. She'd written for *Psychology In Practice* for years but this was the most detailed project she'd undertaken for them. It had involved interviewing a hundred anorexic girls and their parents and correlating numerous factors, weaving them through other findings she'd made in clinical practice for herself. The feature had become so large that the journal planned to issue it as a pull-out supplement which practitioners could keep.

Forget about work. Concentrate on the film. For a while she lost herself in *The Sixth Sense*, even jumping a couple of times when the central heating made its usual cracking sounds. It had to be a good film to scare her when she didn't believe in ghosts.

She cried a little at the end and was glad, once again, that she lived alone. There was just so much uncertainty in personal relationships. People could grow in very different directions, want opposing things. When her marriage had broken up, a couple of the women she worked with at Relate had hinted that she'd miss the sex but, to her surprise, she hadn't. It was as if someone had switched off her libido when her husband emigrated to the states. Yet in the early days of their marriage they'd been really good together and had intercourse two or three times a day.

Now her bed was for sleeping in - and it was time to go there before she fell asleep on the settee. Switching onto automatic pilot, she put off the downstairs lights and made her way upstairs to her attic room. It was the cutest part of the house with its small highset windows and sloping roof. And it had its own little WC and washhand basin tucked away behind a wallpaper-covered door.

Yes, the house was worth every penny of the mortgage Shelley thought as she climbed into her divan and stretched out on her sleepy side. It was her sanctuary from work, and from arseholes like Dougal The Digit, on days like this.

It was a sanctuary that she longed for the next morning when she arrived at work to find Zoe outside the clinic, padlocking her bike to the fence.

'Hi there,' Shelley said. Normally she'd have asked 'Did you have a nice night?' but as Zoe had spent part of it with Dougal's cock up her it didn't seem appropriate.

'Hi,' Zoe echoed stiffly then marched up the stairs and started fumbling for her keys to the clinic's door.

Shelley turned as a car drove up and was pleased to see Jean in the passenger seat. The older woman might ease the atmosphere as she didn't know about the after hours sex.

'Well, what have you two been up to?' Jean asked cheerfully.

Zoe glared at Shelley, who in turn felt herself blushing. Damn, she hoped the girl didn't think that she'd phoned Jean and told her about the knee trembler over the desk.

Inside, they each took the day's appointment sheet from the book - which was interleaved with carbon paper so that each entry appeared four times - and disappeared into their respective counselling rooms. Shelley was relieved to see that most of her scheduled clients were ones she'd was already helping with practical problems which simply involved her giving out advisory leaflets or phoning everyone from the council to Citizens Advice.

The next day passed in a similar vein, with her workload remaining straightforward and Zoe largely avoiding her. But on the Friday afternoon Amy came in.

She yawned like a crocodile as she entered the room.

'Have you been watching lots of late night movies too?' Shelley joked.

'Mm? No, we don't have a TV. Sorry, I'm useless just now. I'm not sleeping.' She lowered herself slowly into the client's chair.

'Not at all, or...?' It was Shelley's experience that insomniacs got more sleep than they realised.

Amy pushed her fair hair back behind her ears and Shelley realised that it looked lank and vitamin-starved. 'Not till about 3am then I have to be up at eight.'

'And you've always slept well before?'

Amy nodded.

'Have you changed your diet in any way?'

The girl shook her head so hard that it was in danger of twisting off.

Of course, the teen was probably on a restricted diet. 'You know that having a coffee before bedtime can keep you awake?' Sometimes she felt as if she was simply echoing the basic advice found in women's magazines.

Amy smiled apologetically. 'I mainly drink tea.'

'Okay, are you going swimming very late? Exercising vigorously in the evenings can make you feel more alert.'

'Well, I've been using my exercise bike when Dana's with Ken,' the nineteen year old admitted, looking thoughtful.

'Okay, well try using it earlier in the day. Oh, and a glass of hot milk is supposed to aid restful sleep.'

'I'd rather remain awake forever,' Amy said in a heartfelt voice.

Shelley laughed, sharing the aversion to warm milk. 'I have to agree with you there.' She moved on to other likely source of woe. 'Are you worrying about anything? Stress can keep you awake.' She'd only slept for three hours a night when her marriage was breaking up.

Amy nodded then said 'You must think I complain all the time.'

In truth, the girl wasn't half as negative as many of the teenagers Shelley saw, some of whom presented with vague complaints like failing to become famous. 'Not at all. You have concerns that I'm here to address.'

'Well. it's really an academic problem - I just can't make head or tail of Philosophy. They ask things like "whether man?" I mean, whether man what?'

Whether man what indeed. Shelley smiled gently. 'Have you spoken to your tutor?'

A shake of the head. 'I kept hoping it would all click into place but yesterday I got another of the set texts from the library and it doesn't get any better.'

'Then switch to another subject. You can do so before the sixth week.'

'That's what my friend Jeff says,' Amy added, smiling at last.

Aha. Friends were what this girl desperately needed. 'Is he here in Dundee?'

Yet another headshake. 'Maidstone in Kent.'

Feeling ready to pay the boy's relocation fees, Shelley consulted her notes. 'What about your flatmate? Have things gotten any better there?'

Amy hesitated, and Shelley suspected she was searching for a positive slant. 'No, but now I'm used to her being out.'

'And you're still doing your computer course?'

To her surprise, the teenager tensed further, as if expecting a row. 'To tell the truth, I've given it up. I hated it and I kept sleeping in and they sent me an official warning.'

It sounded like the course from hell. 'So what will your aunt say to that?'

'I'm just going to pretend that I'm still there - and when the time comes I'll tell her I've passed the exam.'

Shelley made her face and voice as sympathetic as possible, sensing that the teenager was close to tears. 'I agree that there's no point in making yourself miserable studying a subject you hate - but if I was you, I'd be honest with your aunt.'

She heard the sudden catch in Amy's voice. 'But she might withdraw my funding for my uni course - and it's all I've got.'

'Then we need to find you something more,' Shelley said firmly. She had a horrible feeling that they'd had this exact same conversation when Amy first arrived at the clinic. 'What about the various university clubs?'

'The Vegetarian Society's all about food and I couldn't find the trampolining club.'

'Ask the janitors - they tend to know where everything is.' But she suspected that the club's location wasn't really the problem, that Amy had simply lost her courage and couldn't face joining anything else. University prospectuses always gave the impression that making friends was easy - but it was bloody hard if you'd never had a friend before.

'I'm sorry to take up so much of your time,' Amy continued, sounding far too polite and world weary for a girl of her age, 'I just thought that everyone would want to talk about books. I thought that being a student would be different. But all the others seem to discuss is texting and dates and clubs.'

'Nothing is ever as we imagine it - but it can be different and still be better,' Shelley said, recognising that it had taken her years to find this out for herself.

Amy glanced at her watch then stood up to go and the counsellor noticed that she was wearing another of those tops which exposed her waist and that her flesh was mottled with the cold.

'My next appointment cancelled,' she said casually, 'We can talk for another twenty minutes if you like.'

Amy sat down again so fast you'd have thought she'd been suctioned to the chair. 'I just... I try to keep busy but sometimes I get really bored. Everyone else goes about in groups and Dana has Ken. And my studying doesn't take up as much time as I thought and Dana brought home chips last night.'

'And are chips so terrible?'

'They're soaked in fat.'

'But chips will fill you up for a few hours and give you vitamin C,' Shelley pointed out. 'You can include a few chips in a healthy diet.'

'I don't want to.' Amy thrust her hands into the pockets of her hooded top and Shelley just knew that she was feeling the reassuring shape of her hipbones jutting out.

'Do you worry about gaining weight?'

'I won't gain any.'

'You know that you're already underweight if anything?'

'That's what mum says,' Amy muttered, looking completely unconvinced.

Shelley took a deep breath. 'I helped run a residential home for people with anorexia for years and I still have contacts. If you wanted to talk to someone in confidence?'

'No.' Amy stood up. 'I'll just switch from Philosophy to History then I'll start sleeping again and I'll be fine.'

She wouldn't be fine if she fretted about the calories in everything. How could she go to any of the clubs, knowing that the other students would offer her pints of beer and peanuts? How could she ever became true friends with her flatmate if she was fretting about the other girl bringing home a cake?

'So what will you do tonight?' Shelley asked as she walked Amy to the door. She hoped that the hungry emptiness of the evening which stretched ahead might make her realise she should have anorexia counselling - or some more formal type of life counselling.

Amy paused then smiled widely for the first time that visit. 'I'm going to write a really long letter to Jeff.'

CHAPTER FIFTEEN

She'd written back by return post yet again, a fish to his hook, a willing captive in his web of lies. Not that she was exactly truthful with her upbeat missives - a genuinely busy girl didn't write six to eight closely-written pages every other day to a man she'd never met. He saw the paragraphs about the books she'd read, the seminars that she'd enjoyed, her trips to the Barrack Museum and the Wellgate Centre. Saw them and read the loneliness between the lines. Occasionally her flatmate, Dana, got a mention but it was clear that they weren't exactly soul mates and that Dana spent most of her time with her beloved Ken. Moreover, Amy hardly wrote of her parents apart from mentioning in passing that they - and the aunt who was funding her - lived in Aberdeen.

It was too obvious to ask outright for a photo, he mused as he started to write back, but he'd send her one in this letter. He had a nice snapshot, taken whilst he was still at university, which he kept for occasions such as this. It made him look boyish yet somehow manly, the academic backdrop adding to the illusion of wealth and casual intellect. It was a shot taken from a distance so that she'd never recognise him now if she passed him in the street. That was useful in case he wanted to observe her for a day or two, knowledge being power, before he rang her doorbell and swept her off her feet.

Jeff smiled at the thought of watching his prey, of learning about her habits. It was time to start making such plans now that it was November.

After all, he was out on parole just after the New Year. Just a few more weeks of bunking down alongside Tim and Dermott, both of whom were thankfully out at their basic literacy course.

He knew what he wanted to teach Amy, wondered what she'd be like in bed. Passive probably, yet wanting to please. She sounded totally inexperienced, would be unlikely to say 'my previous boyfriends didn't do that' when his hands encircled her neck.

He could keep her at the semi-strangling stage for several months, simply aroused by the fact that she was new: Ted Bundy had done so with one of his many girlfriends. It was only after other girls in the neighbourhood had started to disappear that the girlfriend had suggested his name to the police. And even then the police had dismissed the suave young man as a possible serial killer, sure that the culprit was a less educated and less well connected man.

Ted, Jeff knew, had started his killing spree by taking every possible care, tempting his victims into his car then driving them to remote locations. He picked the girls up at night or in areas where he was unknown - and it was only when he snapped the handcuffs on that they realised they were trapped because he'd previously removed the handle from the passenger door. By then he was heading towards the woods or the mountains where no one could hear their screams.

Not that strangling for strangling's sake had been Ted's thing. No, it was just a means to an end for what he really wanted was the girl's dead body. He'd returned to their naked corpses for gratification again and again.

Feeling himself grow hard, Jeff thought about rubbing himself against her letter but realised that he had to keep her words legible so that he could refer back to them. Keeping a databank was important - a fortnight from now he'd casually introduce some of the topics she mentioned today. He'd already done this several times in a continuing bid to make her believe that they were on the same wavelength, that they were meant to be.

He checked that her letter was dated and then wrapped the bright pink envelope around his cock, imagining her choking and writhing defencelessly beneath him. There was one born every minute - and, luckily for him, most of them were women.

CHAPTER SIXTEEN

Quietly Dana let herself into the flat. It was 3am but she felt too wired to sleep and she was starting to feel thirsty. Determined not to wake Amy, she tiptoed down the darkened hall.

To her surprise, there was a light shining under the kitchen door. She edged it open then let it make its usual creaking sound as she saw her flatmate sitting at the kitchen table, writing.

'The lecturers must love you.'

Amy looked up and seemed to take a few seconds to focus. 'Mm?'

'Writing essays all night.'

The fair haired girl smiled. 'Oh, it's just a letter. My essays are all up to date.'

'Is it to your parents?' She hardly ever mentioned her parents.

Amy looked bashful. 'No, to a very good friend.'

Dana hesitated. She'd promised Ken not to tell anyone yet but she was dying to share her news.

'Ken and I just got engaged.' She held out her left hand with its emerald and sapphire cluster ring.

'Oh, Dana!' Amy took her hand and turned it so that the gems caught the light. She looked into her face and smiled with what seemed like genuine warmth. 'Oh, it's perfect. You're so lucky.'

'Well, we won't be able to marry till I've graduated so it's the only ring I'll have for the next six years.'

'Of course, I always forget that medical courses take longer than the arts,' Amy said. Her smile faltered. 'So you'll still be here after I move on.'

Dana hadn't thought that far ahead until now. 'Unless you find work here in Dundee.' Not that finding a replacement for Amy would be a problem: hundreds of students would give anything for a house this close to campus. And by then Ken would have finished his residency and might even move in.

A lengthy silence descended.

'So, when will you be getting married?' Amy asked.

'As I said, not for six years.'

'Will your parents be pleased?'

More like devastated. Dana grinned sheepishly. 'Don't laugh, but we're not going to tell them. Mummy wanted me to wait until I'd started work and Ken's parents want him established in private practice.' She leaned forward, 'So it's really important you don't tell anyone.'

Amy put down her pen again and smiled crookedly. 'Who would I tell?'

'Well, if Mummy pops in to see me...'

Silence descended again.

'Coffee?' Dana asked, already heading towards the cupboard.

'I'll skip it, thanks. I've got a class at nine tomorrow so I'm off to bed as soon as I've finished this last paragraph.' Moments later she said 'I'm really pleased for you both,' walked slowly towards the kitchen door and called a sleepy 'Goodnight.'

It had indeed been a very good night. Dana went to the fridge and emptied a mini-carton of cream into her coffee then sat down at the table to relive her engagement surprise. Smiling, she put her hand out on the ivory coloured table cloth, the better to admire the gems brilliant sparkle. Amy, she saw, had left her notepad and peaking out from under it was a bright pink envelope. Curiously, Dana took a closer look. It was addressed to a Jeff Metcalfe at - or should that be *in*? - Maidstone Prison. So the close friend that Amy had mentioned was in jail.

Ken might have to spend the next few hours administering to his patient - or he could have stabilised her by now and already be back in the resident's flat. Unwilling to risk waking him, Dana sent a text message. A moment later her mobile rang and she eagerly picked it up.

'We have breaking news - Amy's writing to some guy in Maidstone Prison.'

To her surprise, Ken sounded faintly alarmed. 'What exactly did he do?'

Dana picked up the envelope then realised that it was hardly likely to be addressed to The Breaking And Entering Department. 'I don't know - she took the letter to her room.'

She could hear Ken moving about his residency flat, something he tended to do when he was angry or upset. 'Are you sure he isn't a warden?'

Dana studied her flatmate's neat writing. 'No, he has a number next to his name.'

'That's a worry. Dana, you have to find out what he did.'

'And panic if it's not white collar crime?' She stopped smiling as she heard the increasing seriousness in her fiancé's voice.

'Listen, we had a beautiful young girl in here last month who'd been stabbed so often that she lost six pints of blood. And do you know who her attacker was? Her flatmate's ex-boyfriend. He'd gone to his girlfriend's address straight after being let out of prison - only the girlfriend wasn't home so he stabbed her new flatmate instead.'

Suddenly her ring didn't look so sparkly and the shadows in the kitchen looked especially dark. Nervously Dana went to the outer door and made sure that she'd put on the mortice lock.

'Ken, I never thought of that.' She tried to imagine shy, awkward Amy as a gangster's moll and simply couldn't. 'What if he just stole something on impulse?'

'Then he could do it again. Do you want your engagement ring to go missing? Or that locket your mother gave you for your eighteenth?'

'No,' When she'd lived at home all her jewellery had been insured,

'But can't people change?'

She heard her fiancé snort. 'Maybe they can, but do you want to be part of some social experiment? You have to be realistic, Dana - this prisoner is a completely unknown quantity. You don't want him turning up here.'

She certainly didn't. 'Trust me, I'll talk to her,' Dana said. She glanced at her watch. It was three thirty so Amy would be up again in about four hours. She'd just wait here in the kitchen and casually quiz her flatmate when she picked up the telltale envelope.

She dozed in the armchair then was woken the next morning by Amy flushing the loo. A moment later she stumbled into the kitchen and into the adjacent shower room. Dana listened to the water rushing, a short scream followed by a swear word, more water then the sound of Amy saying 'brr' as she presumably towelled herself dry. Moments later she hurried out of the shower room in her dressing gown with a towel wrapped around her head.

'Oh hi. Scalded again! Were you there a moment ago? I didn't see you.'

'I fell asleep in the chair for my sins,' Dana said. She stretched slowly then got up and put the kettle on. 'I definitely need some tea and toast.'

'Just black tea for me,' Amy said, 'And I'll have one of my apple-flavoured rice cakes.'

'I've never felt the urge for hot buttered rice cakes,' Dana admitted as she toasted herself two thick slices of crusty bread.

They ate and drank in silence at the kitchen table then Amy stood up and reached for her book and her envelope.

Dana took a deep breath. 'Amy, I couldn't help noticing the address.' She pointed at the envelope.

She watched as Amy stiffened and blushed slightly.

'Who is he?' She kept her tone light.

'He's a very dear friend.'

'So how did you meet him?' She didn't normally pry like this - but she had to protect herself.

'We... I used to know his mother. She's really nice.'

So Amy was a friend of the man's family. 'And what did he do to end up inside?'

'He got into a stupid fight,' Amy said. She fidgeted with her dressing gown cord. 'He's not normally violent. I mean, he's got a BSc from Cardiff and he's really well read and his parents and his brother just adore him. And he's so keen to rehabilitate himself that he's even helping other prisoners with their appeals.'

'A fight,' Dana said. This was the heaviest conversation she'd ever had with anyone - and probably the longest conversation she'd ever had with her flatmate. 'How many months does one get for a fight?'

'I'm not sure,' Amy mumbled, starting to back towards the door.

'Well, shouldn't you find out? I mean, I don't want anyone violent turning up here when there's only the two of us.'

'He's not violent.'

'But you just told me he'd been sentenced for a violent crime.'

'Anyway, he won't be out for years yet,' Amy said.

This just wasn't adding up, Ken was right to be alarmed. 'You don't serve years for a fight.'

'You do if the judge has been clamping down.'

Dana shook her head. 'Even if that were true, he could get out early on parole or... And Ken told me men can just walk out of these open prisons.'

'But he wouldn't just turn up here unannounced.'

Dana took another deep breath. 'You can't know that for sure, Amy. You're not psychic.

'He's more of a penpal.'

'To you - but what's his take on the subject?' she asked.

Another silence. Amy hung her head and when she looked up there were tears in her eyes. 'I've got to get ready for my lecture,' she said and left the room.

Dana made her flatmate a black tea, but the girl didn't come back.

Soon she heard the front door click closed. Wearily, she texed Ken again, wondering what to do next.

CHAPTER SEVENTEEN

He got a hard-on now every time he walked past the shower blocks. It had been the perfect crime because no one had even remotely suspected him. The little pansy had been cut down and cremated, written off by the authorities as just another suicide.

Jeff lay on his bed and remembered the kill. He'd climaxed hard - but not nearly as hard as when he'd killed Sonia. She'd been his first kill, though snuffing her out hadn't originally been part of the plan.

Rather, she'd started off as yet another pro, desperate to fill her veins with manufactured toxins. She'd given him the come-on in a Cardiff pub and they'd gone back to her basement flat.

'Sweetie, let's unzip your pants,' she'd said, which had irritated the hell out of him. She was as British as he, but must have watched too many American movies. 'Honey, see what I've got for you?' She'd been such a walking cliché that he wanted to kill her there and then. *He'd strangle this one a little harder* he'd decided as he took off his T-shirt, leaving his jeans on just to thwart her. *He'd show her who was in charge*.

But first he had to tell her what he wanted and negotiate the price. With his first few whores he hadn't mentioned the throttling but they'd panicked when he started to compress their throats and clearly thought he was going to kill them. They'd scratched his hands, and one bitch must have had dirt under her nails as the wounds had become inflamed. Over time he'd learned that a strung-out junkie would do anything as long as she knew what was coming so now he said to Sonia 'I'll pretend to strangle you just before I come.'

'Cost you extra,' she said right away. Her brown eyes would have been pretty if they hadn't been so cold. Her hair was cut in a geometric bob that would have looked good on a younger, more toned woman. But this bitch must be pushing thirty and she'd shoved so much shit through her system that she looked fifty under the bare bulb of her bedroom light.

'How much?' He'd deliberately worn a T-shirt and jeans rather than his suit. He looked clean and safe but not wealthy. It was hard enough skimming money from Faith to pay for cut price - far less expensive - whores.

'A hundred.'

That was half the usual cost for his speciality. He tried to feign shock, deciding to see if he could push her lower. 'Eighty's all I've got.' He waited, half expecting her to march him to the nearest cash dispenser, but instead she just smiled. 'Alright, hon. Seeing as I like you.'

And seeing as she'd already stripped off her vest-top and lifted her skirt to show her crack. He knew that next time she'd demand more - and that even then she'd only let him strangle her if she was experiencing serious withdrawal cramps.

'It's all yours.' He took the notes from his wallet and she briefly disappeared into the other room. *Don't even think about doing a runner*. He loitered by the bedroom door to make sure she didn't leave the flat.

Seconds later she was back.

'Lie down on the bed,' he said curtly. Christ, he loved this bit. She clearly didn't, looked like she was about to have open heart surgery. He gazed at her tits but had to admit that they were so small that she could have passed for a boy. Her waist was equally tiny. She'd rucked her skirt up so that he could see the slender tops of her thighs.

'Want me to hand-start you, hon?'

Patronising bitch. He'd be the one doing the hand-starting. He'd start handling her so hard that she'd forget the Americanisms, let out some good old British screams.

Ignoring her, he shucked off the rest of his clothes, folded them neatly on the floor beside the bed. He wasn't hard yet - he didn't get hard until he circled their necks and applied even the slightest pressure. He could see the woman staring glumly at his flaccidity.

He climbed over her, one knee to each side of her waist and put his hands around her throat, just savouring the visual experience. He'd take his time before he started applying the pressure, allow himself to get aroused slowly. He was in no rush.

She was, though. 'Want me to suck it?' she murmured.

Not in this lifetime. He squeezed a little harder.

'He'd like a little lick.'

He squeezed harder still and this time she forgot about sucking and licking and hand-starting him and clawed at his hands instead.

'Easy,' he muttered, letting his palms go limp. She tried to sit up but he pushed her back.

'Hon, I don't like...'

'Well, get used to it.'

But she sat up with more force and resisted harder when he tried to hold her down.

'Ain't gonna cost you nothing,' she mumbled. She'd be right about that if he could find his cash and take it back. But first she was going to get a good throttling. He tightened his fingers around her throat again then cried out as she scratched at the back of his hands. Instinctively he lashed out, hitting her in the face. Her body went limp beneath him and her features slackened. He stared down at her, feeling his pulse speed up. She'd come round in a second and do him more damage unless...

He reached for his jeans and used them to awkwardly bind one of her wrists to the metal post of the bed then he used his T-shirt to bind the other wrist. The lack of symmetry offended his sense of neatness and he went in search of matching - and lasting - bonds.

He found what he was looking for on an armchair in the adjacent room. It was a chair which appeared to hold her entire wardrobe. He rifled through ridiculously short skirts, skinny rib tops and well-shrunk jeans until he found two thin fashion belts and two summer scarves. Hearing a sudden cry from the bedroom he grabbed a pair of tights from the untidy heap: she'd have to be gagged.

She didn't like the gag. She didn't like the wrist restraints. He tied her ankles together to prevent any sudden kicks. It would make entering her difficult but he knew that he could come from the strangulation alone. Hell, he'd always found pussy to be over-rated, especially with a poxy bitch like this.

He straddled her again, looked down and saw the fear in her eyes. She knew what was coming. He'd treat himself to a nice long session, part-strangle her again and again.

'You've been bad,' he said quietly, taking his time, letting his hands close in. 'Very bad.'

He felt her shudder. She tried to say something through the gag but her words were muffled and indistinct.

'I don't want to hear a peep out of you.' His fingers encircled her neck. Her breathing quickened. He squeezed a little and watched her eyelids flicker, her head jerk back.

'You get on my tits.' He heard the words come out of his mouth, knew they were another person's words - but now he felt like a different person. He was no longer Faith's kept man, a man without future plans or a job. 'You shouldn't have scratched me,' he added conversationally, 'You really shouldn't.' He allowed his hands to tighten more, more, more.

She retched and arched. He shifted one of his knees so that it was on top of her rather than just jammed to one side, kept the pressure constant. She tried to arch some more but he held her down, enjoying her struggling, helpless warmth. Watching her eyes half closing, her face stretching as she tried to scream through the makeshift gag.

'Quit that noise.'

But she couldn't or wouldn't. Noticing the first blue tinge appear on her face he took his hands away, observing her closely as she fought for breath. He could do anything. Walk away now and leave her for the next punter to find - or play with her some more.

It was playtime. When her breathing had returned to normal, he smiled down at her and flexed his hands. She moaned into the gag, her bloodshot eyes frantic.

'What a pretty neck,' he murmured, feeling himself grow hard again. He must have climaxed during the first session, realised belatedly that her stomach was smeared with his come. 'Shall we just encircle this neck a little and see what happens? It'll cost me extra I know.'

He pressed. She bucked. He crushed harder. She writhed wildly. He orgasmed again, sat back on his heels for a moment and watched her gasp.

'Now wasn't that fun? Aren't you looking forward to the next session? I'll bet it's taken your mind off your next fix.'

He got some more mumbles in reply. She really hadn't mastered gag-speak. But then she hadn't mastered the Queen's English or the art of seduction or anything else.

Clasp hands, here comes Jeffrey. He wrapped his fingers around her throat again and began to increase the pressure incredibly slowly, staring down at her as he did so. Suddenly he felt a warm deluge spreading across his naked thighs. Christ, the dirty bitch had only gone and pissed herself. Wanting to blot her out, to obliterate everything she stood for, he squeezed and squeezed and squeezed. *People couldn't just do what they'd done to him and continue to get away with it. People had to pay.*

Afterwards he found himself staring at the wall above the bed and he knew that his mind had been elsewhere for the past few minutes. When he looked down, the whites of her eyes had turned completely scarlet and there was a trickle of blood coming from beneath the gag. Hundreds of tiny veins in her face and neck appeared to have broken. She was clearly dead.

A dead woman with his semen on her belly. He had to sort this out - and quickly. It was lucky that he'd studied science at university, was used to looking at a situation logically and objectively. The first thing to do was to get this bitch clean. No, the first thing to do was to make sure that he wasn't disturbed whilst cleaning her. He went to the front door and found that it was only on the latch, slid both bolts along.

Then he ran a deep cold bath, her last bath. Judging by the stench that already permeated the little flat, she hadn't found much time for soap and water this week.

Picking her up took all of the courage he had. She was like something from a refuse tip - ugly, tainted. He felt disgust at himself for ever wanting to have sex with her. Admittedly she'd looked better in the dimly lit pub when he'd had a couple of drinks and was in search of excitement. She'd looked better before... before she made him mad.

Now he carried her to the tub and lowered her in, ran a worn piece of soap over her flesh before washing her hair including her pubis. After letting the water drain away, he hauled her out and took her back to bed.

Junkies often died in bed and weren't discovered for several days. He tucked her awkward limp limbs under the covers, bringing the top sheet up over most of her face. The flat wasn't centrally heated but he found a small electric fire in the corner and turned one of the bars on, made sure that all the windows were tightly closed. The flat would heat up and she'd start to putrefy, hopefully before anyone found her. The putrefaction might obscure the strangulation marks.

He'd done all that he could. It was time to go. He put his clothes back on, checked that nothing had rolled out of his pockets. It didn't matter that he'd touched the doors and the taps as the police didn't have his prints on file.

Gotta love you and leave you. He felt nothing as he exited stage left. It wasn't as if he'd killed a future prime minister. She'd lived like trash and died like trash. He'd saved her from another twenty years of hell.

He walked back to Faith's feeling completely spent. It was only when he tried to insert his key in the lock that he realised his fingers were numb and strengthless. It took him two minutes to open the door. *No one had warned him that killing could hurt so much.* An hour later his hands started to throb so badly that he had to fetch ice cubes from the freezer and wrap them in a handkerchief. He soothed them like this for the rest of the day. As usual, he took next door's retriever out for one of their twice daily walks (which earned him a tenner a week) but couldn't hold the poor creature's leash, had to wind it around his wrist. That night the pain had kept him awake.

But it was more than the pain which had kept him awake. At four that morning he suddenly remembered he'd left his eighty quid in the dead woman's flat. Was there anything to link the twenties to himself or rather to Faith? Say she went to the same cashline every week, would they have a record of which notes they'd given her? He lay there, trying to imagine how he'd feel as the police handcuffed him.

Keep calm. No one will suspect you. He reminded himself that he was a man with a respectable cake-baking mother, a man who almost had a degree, a man who was living with a woman who was practically a nun.

'You alright, mate?'

Jesus. Jeff stared at the other con who'd popped his head around the cell door. 'Great, Phil. Just doing a bit of thinking.' *Just reliving my first ever kill.*

'Okay, well I'll be in the TV room if you want a laugh. Don't wear your brain out,' the man said with a gormless grin.

Jeff forced his thoughts back to the past and away from the mindless tedium of his cell. No one had tied him in to the junkie Sonia's death and as far as he knew it had never become a murder enquiry. If he hadn't attempted to strangle Faith a fortnight later he'd still be free.

No, no one knew that he'd strangled a whore on the outside and a little pansy on the inside - and increasingly no one believed that he'd really wanted to kill Faith, his legendarily dull girlfriend. It was just a domestic, just a lovers tiff that had gone too far. After all, who wanted to think badly of the guy who helped everyone write their letters home, who worked tirelessly on their legal appeals? He was a model prisoner - a model prisoner who would soon be gloriously free.

CHAPTER EIGHTEEN

Faith jerked away as the man touched her arm.

'Sorry, didn't mean to startle you,' he said with obvious surprise, 'Can you take one of those and pass them on?'

Smiling weakly, she accepted the bundle of papers.

'Busy, isn't it?' he asked.

Faith felt her heartbeat quicken and her mouth went dry. She got self consciously to her feet. 'Excuse me. I have to look for my friend.'

She hurried into the lobby of the conference hall, pretended to search for her imaginary mate then spent five minutes sitting fully-dressed in a cubicle in the Ladies. *Get a grip. Relax, relax, relax.* When she re-entered the room she took a seat next to a woman - but thirty seconds later a man came in and took the seat on her other side. Faith scanned the room for an alternative seat but every single chair was taken. Moments later the vocational seminar - which had attracted teachers from throughout Britain - began.

Breathe deeply. His thigh was almost touching hers: she could feel its territorial certainty and unpleasant warmth. *Ignore him.* He took off his jacket and rolled up his sleeves and she could see the hirsute power of his arms.

'They always overheat these places,' he murmured in her ear.

She nodded, not trusting herself to speak. *He's just being civil.* She had to stop imagining that men were trying to chat her up. After all, no one ever had before... before Jeffrey. Before Jeffrey saw how good life could be driving her car, living off her salary and lounging about in her flat.

She'd been a fool, Faith thought for the thousandth time, but she'd paid dearly for her foolishness. Even now, almost five years later, she sometimes woke up remembering the hatred in his eyes as he crushed the life from her throat. His rage-filled eyes had seemed to look through her rather than at her and he'd been oblivious to her early cries and later gasps for breath.

Yet at the beginning he'd been a man like the one seated next to her - a man who was well dressed and well spoken and well educated. A man who was everything but well.

For there was a sickness within Jeff which made him lie even when the truth served him equally, a sickness which made him strike out at innocent targets. She'd given him her love but he'd offered nothing in return except his increasingly distant presence. But he'd taken lots - her cash, her sense of safety, her trust.

Faith pulled her left leg as far away from the stranger as she could, tucked her elbows in and tried to block out his tall, square shouldered presence. Was she always going to relive the part of an attempted-murder victim? Would she never feel safe in male company again?

CHAPTER NINETEEN

Amy sat in the Youth Crisis Clinic's hallway, patiently waiting for Shelley. Not that this (touch wood) was a crisis - but the counsellor had said to let her know how she fared after giving up Philosophy. She'd already told Jeff about it in an earlier letter. They'd only been friends for six weeks but were already writing to each other every day.

She checked her pocket for the third time that morning, making sure that she hadn't lost the stamps she'd bought him, his favourite currency. It was one of the limited number of things that prisoners' families were allowed to send. The rules let you mail a prisoner a shirt, jacket and jeans but not pyjamas. Instead the men had to buy these by mail order or they could be handed in by a visitor. Colours were also restricted, with very dark shades forbidden. As Jeff himself had put it, light brown was the new black.

She smiled, remembering his many jokes. Dana was so wrong to judge him. Her flatmate had a fiancé, friends, visits from Mummy and regular phone calls to her mobile from Daddy. Was it so wrong for her, Amy, just to have Jeff? She now wrote her letters to him at her bedroom desk rather than at the kitchen table, but every few days Dana noticed and gave her an anxious look.

'Amy, come through.'

She looked up to see a smiling Shelley standing in the doorway. With her cute brown bob, brown eyes and crimson shirt with matching jeans, the woman looked both lively and neat. Amy suddenly felt that her own black top and blue cords were unco-ordinated, that her very presence was dull.

They took up their usual chairs in Shelley's office and Amy started the conversation, glad that she wasn't a moaning minnie for once. 'Well I did it - switched from Philosophy to History and it's working out.'

'That's great!' The counsellor looked genuinely pleased. 'So, how's the rest of your course working out?'

'Well, I got seventy five for my first English essay and sixty eight for my Psychology essay. And the tutors say that university marking is harder than school essay marking, that sixty or over is good.'

'It certainly is.' The woman glanced at her folder then asked 'Was your flatmate impressed?'

'Dana?' It would take the Kohinoor diamond to impress Dana. 'I hardly ever see her these days. She's engaged to Ken so she's practically living with him at the hospital and...' She had to tell someone. 'And we had a bit of a row.'

She looked at Shelley and the counsellor widened her eyes in a 'tell me' expression.

Amy had wanted to tell someone - anyone - for ages. 'She doesn't like my friend Jeff.'

'He's being staying at your house?'

'No, he hasn't - and he won't. I've told Dana that. We're just penpals.'

'And her objection is...?'

Her objection is that she thinks he's a psycho. Amy hesitated, wanting to lie but at the same time desperate to talk to someone about the person dearest to her. 'He's in jail.'

'Ah.' Shelley sat back in her chair. 'What did he do?'

Very little. 'He got into a heated argument with this woman and she threw something at him and he defended himself.'

'What the police used to call a domestic,' Shelley commented.

'Exactly,' Amy said, glad that someone understood.

'Until recently most people had an odd take on domestics, saw it as different to street violence,' the counsellor continued, 'But if a stranger punches you in the street or your boyfriend punches you in the house, does the punch hurt any less?'

God, everyone was determined to see Jeff in a really bad light but he wasn't like that. He was the sweetest, most gentle and funny man she'd ever known.

Amy searched for the words to make the counsellor understand.

'He's not normally violent. It was a first offence. In fact he's really caring.'

She watched as Shelley pursed her lips. 'Every wife beater - or husband beater come to that - starts with a first offence.' She was looking increasingly serious. 'In fact, the first assault often happens when the couple are only dating.'

'They were way beyond dating - they were living together,' Amy said, hoping that she'd scored a point, 'They just weren't suitable for each other and she wasn't good to him.'

'And is it okay for you to hit the person you're living with? Would it be alright for you to batter your flatmate?'

Sometimes she'd quite like to batter her flatmate. 'No, but...' She'd thought so often about what Jeff had been through that she understood why he'd lashed out, 'He was much younger than his girlfriend and she manipulated and neglected him.'

'According to the man himself?'

'No,' Amy said, glad that she had external corroboration, 'According to his mum.'

She doubted that Shelley had ever been manipulated or neglected. She suspected that the thirty-something had never felt even a momentary rage.

She noted the counsellor's surprise. 'So you've met his mother?'

Amy nodded, brought out a little lie. 'And his brother Damien. He owns a car dealership. The whole family is very successful - his mother makes made-to-order speciality cakes.'

'And what does this prisoner do?'

'He has a science degree. He'll get a good job when he gets out, but that's not for years yet. That's why Dana's so wrong to get upset.'

She watched Shelley closely, desperate for the woman to be on her side. 'Amy, they don't sentence you for years if you've just slapped your girlfriend,' the counsellor said.

'Okay, so he got carried away, but he's different now. He loves to read and think about life and he tells me all about his day and I tell him about mine and it's perfect. We love the same books, the same kind of food, want the same pets.'

'He sounds too good to be true,' Shelley said in an unconvinced voice.

Amy forced herself to make eye contact with the counsellor. 'I'm very lucky to have him in my life.'

She watched Shelley sigh, hesitate, clearly preparing to fire another verbal shot. 'Amy, if you have him in your life there's less room for a real boyfriend.'

'But I don't want a real boyfriend.' Having a real boyfriend meant going out for midweek pints and Saturday night curries. It meant being given boxes of chocolates and having to drink wine.

She could see that the counsellor was perturbed. 'You've done very well here as I said before, moving to a new city, starting a new course - but I think you'll admit that you're somewhat isolated. This prisoner is only going to add to that isolation. I mean, you'll be writing to him when you could be out meeting other men.'

'I don't want other men.'

'That may change.' Shelley stared at her own hands for a moment. Amy did too and was pleased to see that they were ring free.

'Do *you* have a boyfriend?' she asked bluntly, amazed at her own daring.

Shelley smiled. 'No, but this isn't about me. For the record, I've been divorced for years.' She leaned forward. 'Amy, I'm not one of these desperately conventional women who thinks that everyone needs a man. All I'm saying is that you came here because you wanted more people and outside interests in your life - and spending hours at home alone writing to a convict isn't meeting those needs.'

Jeff was the best thing that had ever happened to her, yet the woman was suggesting she give him up. If she did, she'd have no one in her life that really mattered. Oh, she loved Aunt Gretchen of course, but mum was always saying that her aunt wouldn't be around forever, that she must find a man.

'Maybe my needs have changed,' Amy said, realising that she was close to tears. She felt protective towards Jeff who seemed completely misunderstood by the world.

'Maybe you shouldn't let your needs change? Amy, making friends at university is always going to take courage. Are you sure that you aren't choosing the easy option?' the counsellor asked.

If she had to start one more conversation with an indifferent stranger, she'd go mad. 'You don't know everything.'

'Then tell me everything.'

'I mean, you don't have all the answers.'

Shelley smiled at her. 'Of course I don't. But I know that this supposed relationship isn't ideal for someone in your position - and you've said that it's already causing friction between your flatmate and yourself.'

'But Dana's never been a true friend to me. Jeff has.'

'He may just be a friend while it suits him.'

'Well, it suits both of us so where's the harm?' Amy asked.

She watched Shelley grimace. 'If it was an occasional letter, I wouldn't be concerned but you seem to be putting your real life on hold whilst writing to this stranger.'

She was so wrong. They already knew lots about each other. 'I really know him through his letters. He is real life.'

'If you were to write to him every Monday night, and spend at least three other nights socialising?'

Amy shook her head emphatically. 'He'd be so lonely between letters. He always writes back by return post.'

'You said yourself that he has a mother and a brother.'

'And a stepfather. But it's not the same. They're not avid readers like he and I.'

'So maybe you both need to join separate reading clubs.' Shelley stared at her until she felt so exposed that she looked away. 'Amy, you came here in September looking for friends and by December you've settled for a man you've never met who is locked up hundreds of miles away for an act of violence. He's hardly a soul mate.'

'He is. He really is!' Afraid that she might cry, she got to her feet then added a reluctant 'Thank you for your time.'

Shelley stood up too, looking sad. 'Really, I'm not judging you. You've achieved a lot so far. I'm just worried that this is a backwards step.'

'Whatever.' She hurried from the office then from the clinic and began to walk quickly home, wondering how she could tell Jeff about the incident without mentioning the fact that she was attending the Youth Crisis Clinic. It was one of the few things she hadn't told him about her time here, in case he thought her unbalanced. She also hadn't mentioned her life before the age of twelve.

Hurrying home, she wrote to him at length about the walks she took (including a particularly long one across the Tay Road Bridge and back), the jokes the lecturers had told, the recipes she'd copied out from a board at the local wholefoods store. She wrote to him about how bigoted Dana was towards prisoners, about how another friend (she didn't name Shelley) had suggested that a once-violent man was always a risk. She reassured him again how much she believed in him and knew that he'd been driven to that one enraged act. *I know that some people are just incredibly difficult to live with - my flatmate leaves cheese in the fridge and tells me to help myself. She seems to have no idea that it's sixty percent pure animal fat. She's not health conscious like we are. She takes taxis everywhere and can drink an entire bottle of red wine after she'd been to the student union club.*

She also reminded him that it was almost the end of term and that she'd be going home to Aberdeen for the Christmas holidays. She gave him her parents address again and ended the letter with her usual self conscious kiss.

The kisses were a more recent development. For the first few letters she'd simply drawn a smiley face after her signature and he'd reciprocated. Then, one day, he'd drawn a kiss next to his name and - not wanting to seem unfriendly - she'd done the same with her reply. But when he'd drawn a heart, she hadn't responded in kind. Oh, she loved him all right - but she couldn't quite imagine holding his hand or hugging him, far less going any further. Just writing to him was enough, made her feel warm and happy inside.

The outside world was much harder to embrace. After posting the six page letter, she attended her three lectures for the day then sat at home reading her latest set text, Hogg's *Confessions Of A Justified Sinner.* But her thoughts kept returning to the way that she'd stormed out of the clinic, ignoring Shelley's pleas to come back.

Now what? She didn't want to make another appointment today as that would make her seem really sad and friendless. But there was nothing to stop her accidentally bumping into Shelley as the older woman left the clinic at closing time. That way they could part in good terms and she could go and see the woman again, assuming her circumstances warranted another visit, in January.

Glad of the wintery darkness, she loitered a few doors away from the YCC at five thirty. The motherly counsellor, Jean, left first and got into a car with an Oldest Swinger sticker on the back window. She was followed five minutes later by Shelley and the young Swedish counsellor, both talking at the same time as Shelley locked the clinic door.

The Swedish girl knelt to unchain her bicycle from the railings. Oh good, she'd cycle off in a minute and Amy could approach. But her excitement turned to disappointment as the two women began to walk along the Perth Road, the younger woman pushing the multi-coloured bike.

Amy walked slowly some distance behind, figuring from their body language that they were having a heated discussion. They walked and talked all the way along the Nethergate and into town. She trailed behind them through the city centre until they reached an upwards sloping road that she hadn't previously encountered and started to walk along Victoria Road. When they reached Albert Street, the younger counsellor got on her bicycle and pedalled away.

Shelley kept walking and Amy followed. She was too far from home now to pretend that she'd just bumped into the woman, for what if Shelley asked what she was doing out this way? *Er, stalking you in order to apologise.* But she might as well keep walking, checking out this part of Dundee.

Albert Street was busy, with shoppers hurrying in and out of the many little stores. Amy window shopped whilst still keeping a watering, windswept eye on Shelley. They walked endlessly through a residential area until they came to a street made up of bungalows, each with its own little front lawn. Shelley stopped at a neat whitewashed house with a red door, fished a big bundle of keys from her cavernous shoulder bag and went inside.

So that was where she lived. For a moment, Amy thought of buying an address book, but then she reminded herself that she'd promised to keep her bills down to a minimum. And the only people in her life were her parents, her aunt, and - of course - Jeff, all addresses that she knew off by heart.

She took a last look at the pretty bungalow then began the long walk home. The wind-chill factor was increasing if anything, the pavements becoming icy. The fish and chips shops and chicken bars sent out olfactory signals: *buy, buy, buy.* How she envied the counsellor her perfect home, interesting job, effortlessly good figure and intrinsic *rightness*. If it wasn't for Jeff, she'd be happy to swap lives.

CHAPTER TWENTY

Her talk with Zoe hadn't gone well. Shelley felt uncomfortable in her body as she let herself into the bungalow. Her body was hot from walking for so long, yet her face was numbed by the freezing wind. On a good day she could make the journey home in seventy minutes but with Zoe pushing the bike it had taken an hour and a half. She'd wanted to stay behind and talk to her colleague in the clinic but Zoe had said she had to meet a friend.

Still, at least she was home for the night, there was a good film on at nine and - she scooped up the mail - the latest bumper issue of *Psychology In Practice* had arrived, albeit belatedly. This should be the issue that her extensive report - *Early Onset Anorexia And Relevant Family Dynamics* - was in.

Hurrying to the kitchen, Shelley filled the kettle, put a large potato in the oven to bake then had a quick shower. Nursing a cup of tea, she settled down in the lounge to look at the magazine.

The first disappointment was that they'd spelt her name wrongly on the cover, calling her Shelley Smarr rather than Shelley Smart. The error, she was relieved to see, was not repeated in the actual article. She flicked through the pages, noting that someone had removed the explanatory notes from beneath her diagrams, rendering them useless, and that the subheadings had been printed in such an odd, curly script that they were indecipherable.

Increasingly dismayed, Shelley began to read her report and was surprised to find that the words didn't flow. Surely she hadn't written such jerky sentences? And she'd never have used the clichés which now marred every other page.

She read on, finding that someone had changed the instances where she'd written 'this author' to 'I.' But saying 'I' was considered amateurish in academic circles. Worse, the changes must have been made using the *search and replace* command on the word processor - and the operator hadn't bothered to reread for sense. In several instances Shelley had written 'this author thinks that' and it had become the nonsensical 'I thinks that.' God, they made her look like a remedial student - and one who made sweeping statements devoid of methodology.

Two hours later Shelley glumly rescued her over-baked potato from the oven, grated some Red Leicester over it and ate at the kitchen table. But the way that her work had been bastardised still played on her mind. She'd once worked with another writer who was close to the editor. She'd call her and find out what was wrong.

Five minutes later she put down the phone, glad that she knew the answer. The editor was having treatment for Non-Hodgkin's Disease so a trainee had been left to edit the manuscripts.

'Will she be there long?' Shelley had asked.

'Even if she goes, it's still chaotic.' Maressie hadn't sounded hopeful, 'He's got his wife working in the office and I swear she's dyslexic. I phoned to complain after they fucked up my piece and she replied that they have the right to edit as they see fit.'

'They'll not be editing any more of my work, then,' Shelley had said morosely. Now, as she rinsed her plate and mug, she wondered how she'd fill her evenings and weekends for the next few weeks. It was only mid December yet most people were already gearing up for Christmas. It wasn't the time to pitch to other psychology magazines.

She might as well be good to herself, given that the rest of the world was currently indifferent. Shelley opened a box of chocolate brazil nuts that a client had given her weeks ago and ate two. She'd always eaten exactly what she wanted, when she wanted - working with anorexics for so many years had shown her how dangerous it was to become obsessed with calories. So far it had worked, and she weighed almost the same as she had in her twenties, though that might be about to change for she'd be celebrating her fortieth birthday on Christmas Day. Apparently every seven years or so the metabolism slowed a little further, making minor weight gain a very real possibility.

What the hell - they'd ruined months of work and jeopardised her reputation. Shelley crunched her way through a third brazil nut. This was clearly going to be her night of living dangerously so she went to the kitchen and fetched a bottle of white wine, took it back to the settee.

Robbed of writing her latest report, the night stretched emptily before her, and she couldn't fill it with good memories of the day just passed as she'd spent part of it fighting off Dougal. She'd actually had to knock his hand from her waist when he entered her office unexpectedly and she'd come close to telling him to stick it where the sun don't shine. Instead, she'd tried to remonstrate with Zoe during the long walk home, explaining that work and pleasure should be separate but the girl simply refused to see that there was a conflict of interest in her sleeping with the boss.

Shelley sighed as she looked around her recently-painted bungalow. Years of living-in at the anorexia unit had allowed her to save up the mortgage for this place and when she'd landed the Youth Crisis Clinic post, she'd been doubly euphoric. She had her own home, a great job and an article-writing hobby which brought in extra cash. But now *Psychology In Practice* had left her feeling that months of research simply weren't worth it. And work had become oppressive with the love blind Zoe and octopus-like Dougal around.

For the first time, Shelley wished that the bungalow was close to the city centre so that she could take a walk around the shops which were open for late night Christmas shopping. She could only hope that none of her clients felt as restless and let down as she did tonight.

CHAPTER TWENTY ONE

Now she'd have to go home for the holidays without having apologised to Shelley. And Mum and Dad would offer her snacks all the time and sometimes - just sometimes - she'd weaken and accept. Afterwards she'd usually rush to the local baths and swim length after length, but the baths would be shut on Christmas Day and Boxing Day and it was so hard to exercise in her parents cramped and overheated flat.

But what was the alternative? Dana was going back to Oxford for the hols and she couldn't bear to be here alone for a fortnight. And if she stayed with Aunt Gretchen, rather than just visited her, her parents would be deeply hurt.

As she pulled her suitcase out from under the bed, Amy thought over exactly what she could tell them about Jeff. She'd be honest about his age and his scientific background, but would just let them assume that she'd met him at university. They'd get the impression that he was a mature student. Perhaps they'd even be impressed.

Maybe this year would be different. For one thing, she'd promised to buy and cook the Christmas Day lunch. For another, she'd invited Aunt Gretchen over. Third, she wouldn't be the child of the house any more - she'd be returning as a woman who lived in a different town.

Amy tried to hang on to the feeling of grownupness as she queued to get on the train then stood nose to armpit with undeodorised strangers in the crowded carriage. *You'll be home soon. They'll have missed you this time. You'll have lots to talk about.* The train jolted and she was almost thrown into a man's lap. He glared and growled at her. At least Jeff was spared days like this.

When she at last reached Aberdeen, she had to queue again for a taxi. By now the cold was biting into her very bones and her shoulders ached from lifting and lugging the heavy suitcase. Still, it would be nice to have a break from Dundee.

It was lunchtime when she arrived at her parent's tenement, walked slowly up the stairs to their oh-so-familiar door then rang the bell. There was no answer. After a few minutes she put her ear to the letterbox and could hear the television's drone.

'Mum, it's me!' After another long wait she heard the thump, thump, thump of overstressed footsteps. At last the door creaked slowly open. Amy smiled brightly. 'Hi, did you not hear me ring?'

'I thought it was those Jehovah's Witnesses back.'

'Oh right.' She held out her suitcase. 'I come bearing gifts.'

Her Mum's face clouded further. 'I haven't been out much - don't know if your Dad's got you anything.'

As if she cared about that. Amy searched her mother's features for signs of illness. 'Are you okay?'

'Just a bit tired. All them envelopes...'

All that weight more like. But she didn't want to go down that road again.

'Well, I don't restart uni till the 4th of January. I can address the envelopes.'

'Oh, you'll have your studies to keep you busy. Your dad can help.'

Amy followed her into the living room which smelt unpleasantly stale. She felt frozen as a fish so didn't want to open the window.

'No, I'm up to date with my essays. I'm all yours. How about I make us lunch and we have a chat?' She went into her suitcase and found the family-sized sachet of fresh minestrone soup that she'd bought for this purpose.

Her mother glanced at the food. 'I'll have two of them pan rustique rolls with mine. Well-buttered, mind. They're lovely rolls, Amy. I get the baker to put them aside special every Wednesday.'

Alongside a huge slab of fruit cake and six buns, no doubt. Drinks might be a safer subject. 'D'you want a tea?'

Her mother nodded. 'Cream and three sugars.'

Amy went to the kitchen and added a teaspoon of sugar and a gnat-sized portion of cream to the older woman's mug, making her own tea black and unsweetened. She buttered the rolls as lightly as she could. Still, at least her mother was eating vegetables in the form of the minestrone soup.

She returned to the living room with her Mum's tray. 'Lunch is served.'

'Sh, *Doctors* has started and Sonia's about to tell Davie that she can't marry him. This has been coming for weeks.'

Amy fetched her own tray and ate in silence as the doctors fell out, made up and generally made very undoctorly choices. As soon as the half hour of medical malpractice ended, the voiceover introduced *Diagnosis Murder* starring Dick Van Dyke.

'That Mark Sloan's a marvel. Works all day at Community General and still finds time to help his son solve all them crimes.'

'Who?' She realised belatedly that her mother was talking about an on-screen character. 'Oh right. Is this one of your favourites?' *They were all her favourites.*

'If only I had another mug of tea and one of my fudge n' walnut brownie's to wash it down.'

Pretending not to hear, Amy stared fixedly at the screen.

'I said, if only I had...'

'I heard you.' She took a deep breath, 'Mum, I don't want to fight again but you eat so much that it scares me.'

'And you eat so little that it scares *me*. You're skin and bone.'

'I just ate some soup.'

'And so did I and I've still got a hunger.'

'But you had two huge rolls with yours.'

'So? Am I not allowed to eat what I like from my own kitchen now?'

'But Mum, you're making yourself ill. You're hardly going out and...'

'Sh, Steve's about to get attacked again,' her mother said.

Amy stared at her. The one cheek she could see was slightly flushed and her mother was breathing hard.

When the programme finished forty minutes later, the older woman turned to her. 'I'm making another tea. Do you want one?'

Amy nodded. 'Black, no sugar please.' She followed her mother into the kitchen and washed and dried the soup bowls. When she looked around three brownies had magically appeared on a plate.

'There's walnuts in them - aren't they supposed to be good for you?'

'They're great.' But not smothered in buttercream then topped with chocolate frosting.

'And your dad got things with fruit for you. Now where did he put them?' She produced a large bag of milk chocolate raisins and looked very pleased with herself.

The birds would eat well tomorrow while her parents were still asleep. Amy put the chocolate raisins in her bedroom cupboard. At least now she knew the perils in the kitchen, the hidden dangers in what Mum called her goody bag. Mum's goody bag - a carrier bag she kept by her chair and constantly dipped into - often contained a lethal mix of pork pies, cakes and family-sized packs of sweets.

She shuddered, remembering her early life. She'd eaten the same as they did for years - huge meat pasties served with masses of chips and tinned mushy peas washed down with sugary tea and followed by hot apple pie and Mars Bars. Then there would be smoky bacon crisps with *Emmerdale* and buttery popcorn with *Coronation Street*. By age nine she'd started to grow breasts. By ten she was the first girl in her class to start her periods. And still she'd kept growing so that the school had to get her a larger chair, a larger desk. She'd been excused from the circuit training part of gym after she got stuck in the climbing bars. She'd only felt safe at home - out of doors she was a freak.

Then a very nice lady from the surgery along the road had come to give a talk to the class called *You And Your Body*. It was mainly about periods, and, though Amy already had hers, it explained lots of things she didn't understand. 'And it's especially important that you eat healthily now that you're becoming a woman,' the nurse had added, 'Lots of fresh fruit and vegetables, chicken, fish and at most two portions of lean red meat a week.'

Afterwards the nurse had said that any girl who wanted to could come and talk to her privately in the TV Room. Amy's teacher had beckoned to Amy. 'You go, dear. Take your time.'

She'd hated being singled out, but she understood - she sometimes had to use the sanitary towels machine in the teacher's room so they knew about her grown-upness. The other girls had stared extra hard at her as she left the room.

And suddenly she was talking to the nurse and admitting that they hardly ever had fruit or veg though they did have deep fried chicken and battered fish with chips and pork or spam fritters. 'These are fine for occasional treats,' the woman had said gently, 'But they make you fat and ill if you eat them every day.'

Make you fat. It was as if a light had gone on in Amy's head. She'd always thought that she was just born fat, that she just resembled Mum and Dad. She hadn't known she could control it.

'Shall I write out a healthy diet plan for you?' the nurse had asked.

Amy had nodded shyly - then had carried the plan around with her until it fell to pieces in her hands.

But that first year had still been hard. Mum said she didn't have the time to cook vegetables that no one else in the house was going to eat, so Amy had had to spend her pocket money on carrots (which the nurse explained you could peel and eat raw) and apples and celery. Luckily the head teacher owned one of the plots next to the school playground and they were all allowed to grow peapods and broad beans and take them home, and in class they grew beansprouts and baby tomatoes and cress.

Then when she was twelve Aunt Gretchen had left London and moved to Aberdeen to be near them. After that, healthy eating had gotten a whole lot easier, as Gretchen was as slim as a pencil and was soon bringing salad packs and picnics to the house.

Her thoughts returned to the present as they went back to the living room and her mum panted 'Help yourself.' Amy looked in horror at the plate of brownies that were now located under her nose.

'No thanks, mum. I'm full.'

'A gust of wind would blow you away.'

This was why she'd spent so many years in her bedroom on her own, just exercising and reading. She took a deep breath. 'Well, Jeff likes me just as I am.'

'Jeff now, is it?' For the first time her mother turned away from the TV. 'Is he your new beau?'

'Well, we're very close.' She felt a rush of pleasure as she thought of him. 'He makes me laugh, mum - but he's bright too, has a science degree.'

'And are we going to meet him?'

Not unless you serve time in Maidstone. Taking a deep breath, she told a pre-prepared lie. 'No, he's gone home to his folks for the holidays.'

'And where do they live?'

Somewhere in Dundee. She brought out a new lie. 'In Edinburgh.' Well, it was almost true - his family had lived in Edinburgh at various times.

'Oh, they're all fur coat and no knickers through there.'

She laughed. 'No, his mum's really down to earth. You'd like her. She...' She realised it would be madness to admit that Barbara made cakes. Mum would be looking her up in the Yellow Pages within minutes. 'She's very down to earth but friendly. And...' Another lie, 'His dad's nice too.'

She knew from what Jeff had said that it was actually his *stepdad* but that sounded less of a happy families ideal.

'Maybe you can bring him through at Easter,' her mother said, reaching for a second brownie. 'I could buy simnel cake.'

'He's allergic to simnels,' Amy joked then laughed and laughed. It was so good to talk about Jeff to someone. Dana loved to talk about Ken - but when it came to Jeff she just wasn't interested. She'd tried to introduce him casually into a few conversations but Dana had either changed the subject or said that Amy was digging her own grave.

'Well, I'm glad you're fixed up at last.' Her mum wrapped a huge hand around her mug and picked it up, slurping noisily. Feeling the familiar revulsion and guilt wash through her, Amy looked away.

'I was married to your Dad by your age, you know.'

'I know.' It was her mother's mantra. Life ought to consist of an early marriage and a lifetime of cake.

'D'you think he's keen?'

'Mum!'

'You don't want to be left on the shelf - look at your poor Aunt Gretchen.'

'But she's happy as she is, Mum. She doesn't need a man.'

'Oh she pretends she's happy, alright,' her mother said, starting in on the third brownie, 'But happy people dinnae starve themselves.'

'Or gorge themselves.' Oh hell, it was starting again. She looked at her watch. 'I'll just nip round and see her. I'll be back for teatime.' She left the airless flat at a half-run.

After half an hour at Gretchen's she felt calm again.

'I got you in a few things,' her aunt said, showing her a box of seasonal fruit and vegetables in the kitchen, 'And there's a dozen eggs in there in case you can persuade them to have an omelette.'

'Well, mum ate a bowl of minestrone soup that didn't have a pie in it, so there is hope.' She smiled then felt the panic rising up for the umpteenth time. 'Aunty, I don't know if I can get through this holiday.'

Her aunt looked grim. 'Just remember that it's not personal. She wants everyone to eat. It's what she went through - it changed her for life.'

'But dad went through it too and he's not quite so bad.'

The older woman shrugged. 'Well, your dad was well built even as a child, a bit of a scrapper. He could fight for food if he had to whereas

Lenore...' She patted Amy's shoulder. 'Anyway, forget about them for the next couple of hours. How's university? And how are you getting on with your computer course?'

It's ancient history. Amy sank into a seat and dredged up yet more lies. This was turning out to be as bad as the last few Christmases, endless sixteen hours days of calorific and visual excess. The only consolation was that within the next two days she'd doubtless receive a very long letter from the sensitive and insightful Jeff.

CHAPTER TWENTY TWO

Her four year nightmare had come true - they were letting him out. Faith sat at her kitchen table and reread the letter from the authorities. They'd always been very good at keeping her up to date on the case, letting her know whenever Jeff was moved to a different prison. She'd secretly hoped that he'd commit suicide or be killed by another con. After all, he'd lost the two things he cared about most - manipulating women and having his freedom. She'd hoped that without these vital comforts he'd prefer to die. But the psycho had survived and would be free in January. Free to finish what he started? Definitely free to find another naïve and lonely girl.

Her appetite gone, Faith pushed away her breakfast toast. She'd moved house, of course, since the attack - she couldn't have relaxed in her conservatory again, the conservatory where he'd strangled her. Its glass ceiling had been the last thing she'd seen before she lost consciousness.

She tried, as she always did, to put the memories aside. He had no reason, she told herself, to return to Cardiff. He'd only stayed there out of lethargy after his BSc. Only he hadn't actually graduated, a fact that had only come out at the trial. He'd apparently attended very few lectures during his final year, had handed in scrappily written lab reports and hadn't shown up for his final exams.

She sighed as she bathed and prepared for work. He'd sounded so plausible when he told her about his degree, his career plans and the wonderful baby he wanted to make with her. But it had all been make believe, a smokescreen to allow him to go on living at her flat. He slept in her bed, ate her food, took money from her to supplement his unemployment benefit. She also cooked and cleaned for him and gave him lifts in her car. She'd given him everything she had except her virginity - and, in return, he'd almost taken her life.

Since then, she'd become convinced that she wasn't the first woman he'd attacked. He'd pointed out a former girlfriend one day when they were shopping - but when the girl saw him she'd rushed away across the road, oblivious to the motorists' blaring horns. And she'd found a photo of another girlfriend in the nude, a teenager who'd looked small and scared. They'd tracked down one of his exes before the trial but she'd just said that their relationship had been fine and that she didn't want to get involved.

But someone would have to get involved with him now that he was getting out, getting his life back. Would he go to his family and start afresh? His parents had been living in Edinburgh when he'd assaulted her in Cardiff. But she'd heard that they moved away after the trial, though she didn't know where.

As she prepared to leave the house, Faith double checked that the windows were closed and locked, that the burglar alarm was set and that her Doberman had access to the hallway. After mortising the front door, she let herself out of the six foot garden gate and locked that too. He was unlikely to track her down here - and even if he did, he'd find it hard to enter the premises. But she still feared for herself and pitied the poor female he'd prey on next.

CHAPTER TWENTY THREE

Life had just gotten better - he'd written to her yet again. Amy snatched up the letter from the hall and returned to her old bedroom to read it in privacy. Mum was still in bed but she could smell fried food coming from the kitchen so Dad must be making himself the Bartlett special - jumbo sausages, black pudding, a large tin of beans, two fried eggs and two slices of toast. Afterwards he'd waddle the fifteen minute journey to the sweet shop and start munching his way through the latest stock. Last year a neighbour had found him behind the counter gasping for breath, having choked on a piece of peanut brittle - but that night he'd still brought home several slabs.

Amy closed her door to keep the greasy aromas at bay. She usually had a slice of toast or a plate of low calorie baked beans before going to university - but since coming back here for the holidays she'd started skipping breakfast. She just didn't want to be like them in any way.

She tore open Jeff's letter and shook the three pages out onto the bed. He told her that they weren't allowed visitors on Christmas Day, that it was especially difficult for the men who had children. He told her what they'd have for their festive lunch ('Cold turkey, Amy. The catering staff have a wonderful sense of irony. Luckily I've never been a traditionalist') and how he'd spend the rest of the afternoon. A smiley face to one side of his words, he added that that he might forego the lengthy Boxing Day walk that his parents had always insisted on when he and his brother were young.

Amy lay back against her pillows and thought how brilliant it would be if her own mum and dad ever wanted to go for a walk. Dad at least walked a little bit, but Mum was in danger of becoming rooted to her armchair. And she'd probably get scurvy from eating so little fruit.

She read Jeff's next few paragraphs which mainly consisted of interested questions.

How are you spending your days in Aberdeen?

Shut in my room trying to ignore the hunger pangs.

Will you be seeing old friends?

Like who?

Did you bring books back with you? We have some new true crime books in here which are very good.

No, I've read everything and will just spend the holidays going for long walks, seeing my Aunt Gretchen and doing sit-ups in the flat.

It would make for a very dull letter, so she'd better find something to do that she could write about. Maybe she and her aunt could have a daytrip on one of the tour coaches? Or she could go to the museums and the art gallery, buy postcards of the finest paintings to send to Jeff. He was trapped in a limited environment with very few choices so it was up to her to bring the world to him.

There was a loud clatter and a yell from the kitchen as Dad presumably dropped the frying pan on his foot. Once she'd have rushed to help but now she just left both her parents to their own devices. They simply didn't connect with her - with anyone - when there was food around.

It had started when they were young, Aunt Gretchen had said, when all three of them were in the same local authority home. The day staff often took home the catering supplies so there was never enough for the children. Gretchen had coped by getting a paper round and spending the money on apples and bananas - but her sister, Amy's mum, had started scavenging through the bins behind the local bakery.

'When she was eleven the owner started to give her doughnuts and cakes,' Gretchen had said, 'We don't know what she was giving him in return.' She'd shuddered as she spoke, and Amy shuddered now, remembering. 'The man wasn't the charitable type and Lenore was big for her age...'

Gretchen had been fostered out by the time that Lenore started dating the boy that would become Amy's dad, so she didn't know if he'd also given favours to the bakery owner. 'Your dad and I were in the same home for years but he was so quiet that I hardly noticed him.'

You couldn't help but notice him now. Deciding for the umpteenth time to start a meaningful conversation, Amy left her room and slowly entered the kitchen. But her father wasn't seated at the breakfast bar so she made her way to the living room and found him in his favourite place, the settee. He had a tray on his lap which was balanced on a cushion and he was eating a slice of what looked suspiciously like fried bread.

'Great stuff,' he said, tearing into the crispy golden square.

'Mum staying in bed?' Amy asked, forcing herself not to add the word *again*. She sat down in her mother's seat and her slippers scrunched into a pile of sweets.

'Who's to say?' He frowned slightly then speared the final chunk of sausage, 'She's not herself these days, but I've taken her some of them blueberry muffins and a pot of tea.'

She wouldn't talk about food today. She just wouldn't.

'Dad, you know when you and Mum got your first flat? What was it like?' Were you ever scared and lonely? Did you find it hard to pass the time, to make friends?

'Like?' Her dad put his empty tray on the floor and reached for his tea. He looked slightly perplexed. 'Just a wee place like this only it had a toilet on the stair. Flats did in them days. Oh, and it was just a scullery rather than a kitchen - there was no place to sit.'

'And was it lonely after being with all these people in the children's home?'

'I'll need to watch my time.' Her father hauled himself forward, rocked for a few seconds then got awkwardly to his feet. 'No, your Mum worked all day in the dry cleaners and I worked in the sweetshop. By night we was just glad to put our feet up and then five years later you came along and then there were three.' He lumbered towards the door and a few minutes later she heard the power shower. She'd noticed that he always showered nowadays, suspected he could no longer fit into the bath.

He left the house and shortly afterwards she left too and walked around several of the department stores in Aberdeen city centre. 'Tis the season to be jolly,' the tannoy sang out in one shop whilst another suggested that shoppers go 'walking in a winter wonderland.' But real life was a mixture of fear and uncertainty for most people. These singers just didn't have a clue.

Every night Dad brought home more mincemeat pies, plum puddings, chocolate yule logs and packeted trifle. Every day Mum sent him out with another shopping list: 'There's four of us this year.'

'But Mum, I've said I'll buy the lunch and do the cooking and Aunt Gretchen has promised to bring the dessert.'

'Aye, and if I know you two it'll be turkey on crispbread with one of them fatfree muffins for afters. Your Dad and me need a decent Christmas after working hard.'

'Talking of which, how is the envelope-addressing going?' Amy had muttered then immediately felt ashamed.

Now she made her way from the shops to the museum, walked around until she was exhausted, had a cup of black tea then bought a book for Jeff about the science behind the exhibits. When she got home it was 1pm and her Mum was seated in front of the fire in her dressing gown watching the TV.

'Mum, are you feeling better now?'

Her mother looked up at her expressionlessly. Amy noticed that the whites of her eyes were slightly cloudy.

'I'm never at my best in the winter,' she said.

'It's not that cold out. I've been round the shops, got Jeff a book.'

'Your dad's done all our Christmas shopping.'

It was another of her mother's many non sequiters. 'Oh good.'

Amy sat down and unzipped her hooded top. The silence lengthened. As usual, she felt like the parent, the one who wanted to say 'eat your greens then go out for a nice long walk.' Her stomach rumbled but she didn't want to suggest making a sandwich as that would invariably end in another fight about food.

'So, mum, what shall we do this afternoon?'

The forty year old glanced at her suspiciously. 'I've things to watch.'

'You could record them.'

'Can't, cause some of them are on opposite channels.'

'Well, couldn't you just miss one and we could go out to a teashop together for a treat?'

She waited, hoping that the bribe would work. If she skipped lunch and only had a meringue at the teashop then she wouldn't be going over her allocated number of calories.

'I've been watching them a' year.'

'But it's Christmas.'

'They put on some rare storylines at Christmas.'

'But,' she played the guilt card, 'I'll only be here for a fortnight. It would be good for us to have a couple of hours out.'

'I'm not really up to it, love.'

'If you got some fresh air you might feel better.'

'I can always hang oot the windie and feed the birds.'

Amy stood up, her throat tight. 'Okay, well I'm off to the baths for a swim.'

By Christmas Day she'd gone for so many swims that she felt like the Little Mermaid and her arms hurt so much that they were ready to fall off. But on the morning of the 25th December she got up at 7am so that she'd have time to wrestle with the turkey and have it ready to carve at midday. She peeled Brussels sprouts and carrots, chopped parsley and chives to put through the gravy and pricked the tiny sausages that both her parents insisted accompany the bird. She also cooked and mashed potato, seasoning it well but adding only a tiny amount of skimmed milk to turn it into duchesse potatoes that would be delicious but low fat.

Half way through the morning her parents got up, exchanged

bumper-sized selection boxes, and took turns under the shower. By ten to twelve everyone was dressed, the table was set and Aunt Gretchen had arrived bringing sugar-free cordial, a fresh fruit salad plus their Christmas presents. Amy hoped against hope that everything would be alright.

They sat down. She served. 'Amy, this looks really nice. I'd have sent you to cookery college if I'd known,' her aunt said. She laughed and speared a petit pois. 'Talking of college, how's your computer course going?'

It's going on without me. 'Fine, Aunt Gretchen.' She'd never been any good at lying, hoped that her nose wasn't growing, 'I'm learning new modules all the time.'

'Never mind all they machines - she's got herself a man at last,' her mother said.

Amy felt herself going red.

'Couldn't he be here today?' Gretchen asked looking at her curiously.

'No, he... had to be elsewhere.' *The authorities insisted on it.*

'Oh well, maybe he can first foot us?' Gretchen continued.

God, she'd still be here in Aberdeen at the New Year. The festive holiday felt endless. *But she had to make it work this year, had to, had to.* 'He's going to be busy in January too.'

'Works, does he?' her mother asked between mouthfuls of potato. Amy noticed that she'd pushed all the vegetables to one side as if they might bite.

'Yes, in a laboratory.'

'I hope there's no rats there,' her mother said, then dug her husband in the elbow, 'Can you get me more potatoes and gravy? Oh and I'll have an advocaat to wash it down.'

Her dad got up and lumbered out of the room. Amy looked sadly at Gretchen and her aunt responded by pulling an equally sad face. Her mother finished her slices of turkey breast just as Jim Bartlett returned with four more duchesse potatoes, ones that Amy had planned to refrigerate and have as part of tomorrow's tea.

She ate the last of her own vegetable mountain before starting in on the turkey. She'd leave her one duchesse potato, the best bit, until last and would eat it slowly. She wanted to feel full so that she'd have the willpower to skip dessert.

'You seeing anyone, Gretchen?' her mother asked.

Amy's aunt pursed her mouth and pulled her shoulders back. 'I have a full enough life, Lenore, without all that to contend with.'

'I don't know where I'd be without my Jim.'

'Maybe you'd get out more.'

'He's very good when I'm ill, which I have been lately,' her mother said, ignoring her sister's taunt.

'Anyone want more sprouts?' Amy asked, standing up and beginning to collect the dirty plates.

'You eat far too many of them things,' her mother said.

'Amy, the meal was perfect. I'm so full that I think we'll leave dessert until mid afternoon,' Gretchen said warmly.

'Good idea,' Amy agreed, cheering up.

'Well, I'm still gutting. Jim, can you bring through the cake plates?' Lenore asked.

Amy followed her father into the kitchen with the trays and watched as he went into the walk-in cupboard and took out two huge platters filled with mincemeat pies and puddings he'd been bringing home for the last ten days. She walked behind him again as he thudded his way back to the living room.

'Not for me,' Gretchen said stiffly.

'Nor me,' Amy said.

'All the more for us, then. Cheers,' her mother added, reaching for a chocolate snowman. She stood up, supporting herself by holding onto the table, 'Well, I'm away to enjoy this in front of the TV.'

Eight days later, Amy boarded a train that would take her back to Dundee, back to winter salads and books for all seasons. Back to quietude without the expectation of conversation and company. Okay, she and Dana might never be close - but at least they weren't engaged in an hourly power struggle. Similarly, Shelley might not approve of Amy's life choices but she always showed she cared.

The nineteen year old forced her numerous tense muscles to relax as the train took her closer and closer to Tayside. Life in Dundee wasn't perfect, but she had to start viewing the flat as her real home, the place where she could relax and be herself.

CHAPTER TWENTY FOUR

'You have to leave,' Dana said. She'd practiced variations on this sentence for the past fortnight whilst she was in Oxford but now, finding yet another letter from Maidstone lying in the hall, she blurted out her ultimatum.

'Leave?' Amy echoed breathlessly, scooping up her letter and handing Dana her own mail. She was still in her dressing gown and looked dazed.

'Yes, Amy, I'm sorry but it... it just isn't working.' Dana wished that she hadn't started this conversation out in the hallway. She was only inches away from her flatmate and couldn't avoid her stricken gaze.

'But you didn't say anything before I went away for the hols.'

'Well, I wanted to talk it over with Mummy and Daddy.'

'And they want me to leave?'

Dana could see that Amy's lower lip was trembling. 'They do, yes.'

'Is it because of Jeff?'

Dana nodded.

'But he'll never come here!'

'I just don't want to risk it - and Ken's terrified that something'll happen to me.'

'Jeff would never hurt a stranger.'

'Mummy says that people are creatures of habit, that the best predictor of future violence is past violence. He hit a girl before, so...'

She watched warily as Amy leaned against the wall, hoped her flatmate wasn't about to faint.

'Can't you stay with Ken? I mean, you're with him almost every night.'

'But I can't actually live at his residency - and it's my name on the lease, remember? I only asked the agency to get me a flatmate cause Mummy didn't want me living on my own.'

Amy's lip-trembling increased and her voice broke. 'But where will I go?'

Dana felt increasingly awkward - but she'd talked this over with everyone she knew and her mind was made up. 'Chances are that some students will have moved out of Tayfield by now,' she suggested, naming a well known university student house.

'But that's miles away,' Amy said.

Dana forced herself to remember the woman who had been slashed to pieces by her flatmate's boyfriend, imagined how she'd feel if this Jeff stabbed her through the heart or cut her throat. 'You'll be fine there,' she said gently, 'And if they're full I'll help you look for someplace else.'

'Can't we just talk?'

Feeling guilty but determined, Dana shook her head. 'There's nothing to say.' Her mother, father and Ken all supported her, 'I'm sorry, Amy, but you have to find another place to live.'

CHAPTER TWENTY FIVE

'Can I have your white T-shirt, Jeff?'

'No problem.' Jeff nodded to his younger cellmate. Personally, he'd never want to wear another man's cast-offs but he'd soon be walking out of here so was starting to offload his older clothes.

Not that he had many clothes, or many other possessions. Few killers did, at least few of the ones he'd read about. Okay, there had been an American and an Australian millionaire who became serial killers, but they were the economic exceptions. The British murderers he'd read about had been a comparatively impoverished lot. Ian Brady and Myra Hindley, for instance, had been living in Myra's gran's council house at the time of their arrest, whilst Dennis Nilsen rented a modest flat and had hardly any belongings. Peter Sutcliffe had held a variety of unskilled jobs and Colin Ireland had occasionally been of no fixed abode.

Compared to them he was practically middle class - yet he had a smaller income than most of the working classes. That was the problem with refusing to accept the nine to five office life, it was hard to save. Still, mummy would give him some cash next week when he moved into her neat but overfurnished bungalow. At least, he assumed it was neat and ornate: all her other houses had been. Yes, she'd give him some money to get himself a nice suit to impress his future employer, but he'd use it to charm Amy into his - or rather her - bed.

CHAPTER TWENTY SIX

Her second day back in Dundee and she'd suddenly lost her home. Dana had been out when she returned from Aberdeen yesterday - and today her first words had been 'you have to go.'

Where would she live when she had so little money for rent? Amy lay on her bed and sobbed, unable to imagine the future. Dana had suggested she move into halls, but most of them provided meals for students and she simply couldn't eat breakfast, lunch and dinner that someone else had prepared.

And what if she couldn't find a suitable place in Dundee? She couldn't go back to Aberdeen now, she just couldn't. She had to find a way to live here and keep doing her course.

She must have cried herself to sleep for she awoke half an hour later as a door slammed shut. Amy peered out cautiously. Oh good, Dana had gone.

She needed Shelley like she'd never needed her before. Amy quickly showered and dressed, grabbed an apple from the fruit bowl and ate it in nervous gulps as she half ran along the road. She reached the Youth Crisis Clinic at 10.30 and hurried in, hearing the door make its usual warning ring. Within a moment the youngest counsellor, Zoe, joined her in the hall.

'Hi, can I please see Shelley as soon as possible?'

'She is not here. She has flu,' Zoe said.

But I'm homeless. Amy felt a lurch of fear followed by the familiar dragging sensation of disappointment. 'Do you know when she'll be back?'

'Not for some days,' Zoe said in a strongly accented voice. She smiled brightly 'But I am free.'

'Right, thanks.' Despondently Amy followed her into the nearest counselling room.

'So, what problems do you have?' Zoe asked after they'd both sat down.

'I've just heard that I have to leave my flat so I need somewhere to live.' She looked tearfully at the counsellor but the woman just looked steadily back. 'I don't want to go into student halls unless they're self-catering,' Amy continued, 'I might be allergic to dairy products and I hardly ever eat red meat and...' *And I'm terrified of getting fat like my mum and dad.*

'What about a flat share? I do this myself, share a flat with three other women.'

She'd hated sharing with her parents for all these years and hadn't exactly managed to become soul mates with Dana. She must be an unsociable creature. 'I think I'd be better in a bed-sit but I know that some of them aren't cheap.'

'You have a job?'

Read my folder. Shelley must have written down her life story by now. 'No, my aunt is very kindly supporting me.'

'You can live with her?'

Amy shook her head. 'No, I'm a student here and she lives in Aberdeen.'

'I firmly believe that life is what you make it,' Zoe said. She leaned forward. 'What have your own experiences been?'

'Sorry?' Amy ran the question through her head a couple of times but wasn't sure that she understood. The word *homeless* kept running through her increasingly panicked brain. She'd lose her university place if she had to go back to Aberdeen - and they'd found a replacement lifeguard within a week of her leaving so this time she wouldn't have a job.

'Was your childhood good?'

Ideal if your purpose in life was to be fattened up. 'My parents did their best.' She felt her chest tighten, wondered if this was what they meant by a panic attack. 'Please, about where I might live next... Do you know of any rental agencies?'

She only had the address of the agency who'd given her the room in the current flat and they might turn her down for having an ostensibly-violent penpal and for asking for alternative accommodation within four months.

'Try the Yellow Pages,' Zoe said. She tented her fingers under her chin and stared at Amy. 'I can see that you are worried more about this than most would be so I am wondering, were you breast or bottle fed?'

CHAPTER TWENTY SEVEN

Five more days till his release. Five more days of being good as gold - or of faking it. Five days until fifty two percent of the population would have to start watching out for their pretty little necks. Not that he planned to kill again, at least not immediately. Why would he when he had a brand new girlfriend on tap?

He'd start her, Amy, off gently - big bunches of flowers, cheap costume jewellery in expensive jeweller's boxes and long walks in the park and along the River Tay. His mother had already sent him descriptions of the more attractive parts of Dundee and he planned to study a map when he got out, explore other seductive places. He'd be equally romantic in the sexual department, kissing Amy's eyelids and her neck, caressing her hair and spending as long as he had to stroking or licking her clitoris. Only when she saw him as her soul mate and as the source of her best ever orgasms would he start to regularly encircle her neck.

'It's a power trip,' he'd say, keeping his voice light, his features even, 'Just imagine that I have the power to let you live or die.'

Some of them liked it at first - but they stopped liking it when the pressure intensified, when their airways became constricted. Thereafter, even the lonely and grateful ones fought like hell. But this one was especially isolated - isolated enough to stay home night after night writing to him instead of going clubbing and beer swilling at the student's union.

Alienated enough to still write to him daily when she was home with her family at Christmas and New Year.

Would she accept the trade off - a boyfriend to parade before her parents at the cost of a twice-weekly sex session? An end to loneliness in return for the occasional bruised neck? Some women stayed with men who broke their ribs, blackened their eyes and kicked their foetuses out of them. In comparison a little erotic asphyxiation wasn't so bad.

Other girls accepted the man's violence as long as it wasn't directed at them. He'd heard of several rapists in here who'd been falsely alibied by their wives and girlfriends. The girl knew that hubby was going out at night dressed in black and carrying a sheath knife, but somehow convinced herself that he was only communing with the stars. The arrangement suited them both, for during the day she had a man to play house with, and at night she watched her soaps and he did whatever he had to do.

'Dad, I didn't mean it,' Dermott said.

'Shut the fuck up,' Jeff snarled. He stared across at the nutter on the hard, musty prison bunk then turned his thoughts to Amy's bed. He was willing to bet that she was still a virgin. There was something enticing about being a teenager's first lover and about knowing that he might also be her last.

He remembered one killer he'd read about who had broken in his girl and then persuaded her to help him catch and rape a young female stranger. They'd had regular sexed-up threesomes until they tired of their victim, killed her and dumped the corpse. A few months later they'd become bored with their sex life and abducted another girl to rape and eventually kill.

He felt personally overwhelmed at the thought of a threesome but at the same time he knew that little Amy wouldn't always be enough for him, just as Faith and her predecessors hadn't been enough for him. No, in time he'd have to go further with another call girl in some out of town flat. But that would have to wait for a few months - after all, if a whore was strangled the police would look at all recently-released stranglers, and next thing he knew they'd be battering down his door. Instead, he'd make do with this friendless nineteen year old student for as long as possible and train her to accept his sexual needs.

CHAPTER TWENTY EIGHT

Her dry cough had started up again. Determinedly Shelley made her way to the kitchen and prepared herself a glass of hot water flavoured with honey and lemon juice. It was a whole lot better for you than those chemical concoctions the chemists sold.

She glanced at the kitchen clock. It was only 9pm but she was beginning to yawn like an alligator. She'd just watch this documentary on anorexia then go back to bed. She'd been sleeping for twelve to fourteen hours a day since going down with this flu that was sweeping Tayside. But at least she was over the worst of it - several men and women, one her own age, had died.

Her own age of forty. Her birthday, as usual, had coincided with Christmas so was a bit of a non-event. Usually she was too busy to really notice, but this year, with no reports to write, she'd felt comparatively friendless. Jean and Zoe had given her birthday cards before they broke up for the holidays and Netta had popped one through the door on December 25th.

Forget about getting old. Forget about having flu. Live for the moment. Sliding back into her sleeping bag on the settee, she aimed the remote control at the set.

A moment later the documentary started. 'More and more young British girls are succumbing to the ravishing disease of anorexia,' boomed the doom-laden voiceover, 'Tonight we show you the horrors endured by them and their families.' Oh great, it was going to be yet another voyeuristic and over-dramatised hour.

'Trudy is only eleven but already she refuses to eat breakfast, pretends to her mother that she's had a school dinner and will only eat salad and fish for tea.' The screen showed Trudy biting her lip as the cameras zoomed in on her. Why expose such a young child to public scrutiny? Shelley mentally shook her head. 'Giselle,' the voice over continued, 'Became anorexic when she was fourteen but still had the slimming disease when we started filming her at age twenty three.'

Shelley stilled in shock as Giselle appeared on her screen. She'd lived at the unit, been one of its success stories. The then nineteen year old must have put on four stone whilst under Shelley's care. Now her cheekbones were accentuated, her hair limp and her breasts non-existent in a loose fitting top as she stared hauntedly into space.

She'd better keep a copy of this so that she could contact Giselle after the programme. Shelley pressed *record* on the remote control.

Anna is the third desperately thin girl who we filmed over fifteen months. Anne is seventeen but only weighs six stone and can still buy children's clothes.

The documentary continued on its patchy way. It didn't mention that boys became anorexic too or admit that anorexia sometimes shaded into bulimia. It gave the impression that its three subjects only cared about cosmetic slenderness. But Shelley knew that for some anorexics what they ate, and how and when they ate it, had nothing to do with wanting male approval or looking good in fashionable clothes. Instead, it was their only means of control.

Giselle had initially been in the eating-for-control category, She was the only child of an army man and his clinically depressed stay-at-home wife, living in a household where everything was regimented. In the end, she'd asserted her teenage individuality in the only way she could: *I ate earlier, I'll just have an apple, I'm not hungry*. It was the only way to reduce her dictator-father to impotence.

The documentary switched back to eleven year old Trudi who'd clearly picked up her obsession with remaining thin from her constantly-dieting mum. Anna's situation was at first more complicated but as the hour went on Shelley could see that the teenager's parents treated her as if she was a ten year old. So she'd starved herself back to the body of a ten year old to avoid the endless parents-controlling-their-teenager fights.

Giselle didn't appear much during the first third of the programme as all three of the girls had been asked to keep video diaries and Giselle's entries were the shortest. Shelley could see from the girl's drooping shoulders and reddened nose that she was seriously ill. 'It hurts to lie down because my bones stick out so much,' she said weakly, 'And I want to eat more but somehow I can't.'

Shelley shuddered as she stared at the screen. Sometimes a girl couldn't eat because her stomach had shrunk and even a sandwich made her nauseous. But, more sinisterly, the brain started to shut down as an anorexic approached death so that she no longer got hunger pangs.

The documentary began to concentrate on Trudi's mother who proudly showed them her fridge full of low-calorie everything whilst Trudi hovered anxiously in the background. 'Her dad thinks her dieting is my fault but I tell her she's got to eat,' the woman added forcefully.

Anna's parents were shown next, taking her to the fairground and trying to persuade her to eat icecream, candy floss and toffee apples. It would have been funny if it wasn't so serious. Anna trailed behind them, a near-voiceless waif, politely refusing everything.

Then it was Giselle's turn. Shelley waited to see her narcissistic father and emotionally-crushed mother appear but instead the cameras focused on an elderly grey-haired woman. 'Giselle lives with her grandmother in Birmingham.' The grandmother started to speak and her name, Veronique, appeared in the caption box underneath. Shelley froze, immediately recognising it. A few weeks ago she'd had several hang-ups on her answering machine and when she'd used last number redial she'd gotten an answering which said that Veronique wasn't at home. Shelley hadn't recognised the name or the tired-sounding foreign voice and hadn't rung the number again.

Now Veronique spoke sadly of the various ways she'd tried to help Giselle. 'Her parents took her to a private clinic for many months and for a while she was much better. But then they took her abroad to Saudi and she got sick again. I don't have the money for the clinic and she doesn't want to go into hospital so the GP says the only option is to section her. But I'm hoping she'll eat more by herself and it won't come to that.'

The film then showed Giselle and her grandmother walking around the supermarket together, the younger woman walking much more slowly than the older. *'Giselle fainted as she left the store and would have crashed to the ground if it hadn't been for our film crew,'* the voiceover said. Oh, they were a regular bunch of philanthropists, Shelley thought sourly. Giselle wouldn't have been out burning calories in the first place if it wasn't for them.

There were some more photos of the girls in their bras and pants, showing their ribs, their skeletal arms, their slightly bluish skin tone. 'How many more children and teenagers have to go through this,' the voiceover asked, 'Before we have the courage to dismantle our dieting industry?'

The theme music and end credits started up then the voiceover added 'Since this documentary was made Giselle Liebenstein has died. She was twenty four.'

Jesus. Shelley sat there for a moment staring at the screen - then she replayed the last two minutes of the DVD. 'Giselle Liebenstein has died' the voice repeated. Shelley switched off the machine, feeling close to tears. She'd spent untold hours writing about psychology for the past few months and all the time Giselle or her grandmother had been crying out for practical help.

Slowly Shelley took the stairs up to bed and lay beneath the duvet wishing that she could live the last year differently. In the end, it was people who mattered, not article-writing for vocational magazines.

CHAPTER TWENTY NINE

'Do you have a single end?' Amy asked.

'A what?' The man looked as if she'd made an obscene suggestion.

'You know, a little house for one person at the end of a terrace? My aunt said to ask for one, that a lot of councils offer them.'

The clerk stared at her in obvious bewilderment. 'If you could give me your name and your reference number, Miss?'

What reference number would that be? Amy swallowed, feeling increasingly out of her depth. It was difficult to speak through the glass window and already a small queue had started to form behind her. 'I'm afraid I don't have a number. I've never been here before.'

'So you're not actually on our housing list?'

'Not yet. I just found out on Monday that I have to leave my current address.'

The man grimaced. 'All that we've got at the moment is the hard to let.'

'The hard to...?'

'Housing that no one wants to rent.'

Her parents had grown up in a flat with a toilet on the stair so surely she could cope with just basic amenities. 'Is it really bad?'

The clerk nodded. 'Off the record, I wouldn't put my dog in one of them.'

'Are they damp?' She could put a waterproof sheet over her bed, buy lots of cosy second hand jumpers.

'No they're structurally sound but usually the neighbours are drug addicts or alcoholics who fight all night. Others are flats which are repeatedly burgled even when the tenant is at home.'

She couldn't have herself and her fruit bowl carried off in the middle of the night. 'Shall I put my name on the housing list to get a better house then?'

The man looked unconvinced. 'It depends how long you're planning to be here. I mean, it can take seven years to get a house in one of the best areas.'

Amy felt her spirits sink even lower. Ideally, Dana wanted her out in a few days.

'Have you tried the private sector?' the council worker continued.

Amy nodded and named the three agencies she'd so far visited without success.

'There are others,' the man said helpfully and found her a list.

Revitalised, Amy set off on her housing mission again. But the letting agencies on the list turned out to be too expensive or unavailable or allergic to students. Some wanted an eight hundred pound deposit and others wanted a reference from your current landlord and from a professional who'd known you for at least two years.

Eventually, her legs moving stiffly like stilts, Amy found a telephone kiosk and called the clinic. The phone rang for ages then a breathless Jean picked up.

'Hi, it's Amy Bartlett.' They must see her as an accident waiting to happen. 'I was just wondering, is Shelley back?'

'No dear. I think she'll be off for a few more days. Can I help?'

'I hope so.' She watched a tramp shuffle past with his lifetime's possessions in two carrier bags, fought back a growing sense of panic. 'I need to find a new place to live.'

'We have a list of private landlords.'

Amy delved into her shoulder bag. 'Is it the one that the council gives out? Does it start with...' She named the first two rental agencies on the list.

'That's the one,' Jean said glumly, 'Drat.'

'I've looked at the university notice boards but there's nothing there. I wondered if you knew of a newsagent who puts accommodation cards in the window?' She'd known such a newsagent when she lived in Aberdeen.

'I don't dear, not offhand. Let me think about it,' the counsellor said gently and Amy's coin ran out and the phone went dead.

CHAPTER THIRTY

Oh good, Amy was back - at last she could get her sorted. Dana popped her head around the kitchen door as she heard her flatmate walking down the hall.

'I've found you someplace - a friend's moving out of Ensley House.'

Amy joined her in the kitchen and sat down heavily at the table then smiled tiredly. 'Really? Thanks Dana.' She blinked hard and seemed to have difficulty in ordering her thoughts, 'What's Ensley House?'

'Student accommodation that's self catering. It's only a few minutes walk away from the city centre and some of the rooms are really big.'

'Honest? I haven't tried Student Accom yet as I was so scared they'd put me into halls,' Amy said. She accepted the black tea that Dana poured, sipped it, said ouch and sipped some more, 'But I've been everywhere else.'

'I believe you.' Dana again felt guilty at how windswept and starved the other teenager looked. She found a bottle of mineral water and used some to cool down her flatmate's black tea. 'As I said, I've nothing against you. It's this prisoner...'

'Jeff.'

'Whatever.'

'He really isn't the monster you think he is, Dana. He even found time to write to me during the holidays - and it's a busy time in prison. I mean, the staff and inmates put special concerts and musicals on and give the money that they raise from ticket sales to local charities.'

Ken had told her that one of America's worst serial killers had done lots of charitable work for children. Dana changed the subject, determined not to talk psychopaths.

'Ensley House is really sought after. I expect it'll be snapped up by tomorrow. But my friend's just handing back her key this afternoon cause she's moving in with her boyfriend instead.'

'It sounds brilliant, being so central. I'll go and see the Student Accommodation Services as soon as I've finished this tea,' Amy said.

'I've got caramel shortcake,' Dana offered, moving towards the refrigerator. She felt pleased when Amy ate two bars and washed them down with another mug of tea.

CHAPTER THIRTY ONE

None of these bastards appreciated their freedom or how quickly they could lose it. Jeff stood with the other commuters at the train station and watched them yawn and pace and look repeatedly at their watches. They only noticed that the train was five minutes late, didn't seem to see the blue sky above them or the arousing female bodies all around.

He was glad to be alive, glad also that they'd let him out in January. Everyone looked peaky at this time of year so his prison pallor didn't stand out. It was vital that he blend in with his surroundings, especially once he went in search of prey.

But for now he was keeping the prison service happy by going straight home to mother. She was expecting him and would doubtless have baked and iced a special cake. He'd never liked sweet foods but they had so little to talk about that it created an easy, if banal, conversation piece.

Life in the suburbs was banal, he thought as he boarded the first train that he'd been on for almost five years. Oh, he'd never seen his mother's Dundee house but he knew from past experience that it would be like the Edinburgh house, the Horsham house and every other house his family had lived in. Saturdays were spent in a district-wide mowing of the grass and cutting of the hedges, Sundays were dedicated to pouring soapy water over the house windows, garage floors and family cars. Weekdays involved the nine to five (or more often nowadays the nine to seven) followed by a traditional British meal and a documentary before bath and bedtime. Even the thought of it made him want to scream. But he wouldn't have to live like them - he'd have his foolish little virgin to indulge his sexual fantasies, Amy the teenage misfit who believed all the lies that she'd been fed.

Talking of feeding... he stopped the railway worker pushing the trolley and bought himself a bag of salted peanuts and a polystyrene cup of coffee. Both tasted wonderful. It was an incredible feeling being in a moving carriage after years mainly spent in a tiny cell. He smiled at a young girl as she swayed her way down the train and she smiled back at him. He still had it, then, the power to attract. For a second he was tempted to follow her, attempt to strike up a conversation, but there were too many potentially observant people around. He much preferred quiet daytime bars with shadowy corners or expensive busy night time venues where, providing you wore the right clothes and spoke with the right accent, you didn't stand out.

He people-watched as the train took him further and further away from HMP Maidstone and closer to the English-Scottish border. He could tell the regular commuters as they'd brought books and newspapers with them to pass the time. In contrast, the infrequent travellers stared out of the window and bought cola, crisps and Mars Bars from the trolley service when they eventually got bored. He looked at the women's necks and knew that he could rescue them from boredom. They didn't fully appreciate being able to breathe.

At last, after two changes of train and lots of eye candy, they reached Dundee and he hailed a taxi. Reaching into his jacket pocket for her latest letter, he gave the driver his mother's address. He wasn't surprised when it drew up outside a whitewashed villa with an immaculate square front garden and an over-trimmed hedge which all but shuddered when he looked at it.

His mother walked down the path to greet him as he exited the cab.

'Welcome home, son.'

Another bag of flour had been sacrificed: he could already smell her home baking. 'Thanks, mum.' He let her hug him before he told his first lie of the day. 'It's good to see you again.' *Well, good to escape the mad and sad bastards he'd shared with in prison.* He followed her into the house.

'Your dad's at work,' she said as they entered the lounge.

Martin wasn't really his dad but she insisted on calling him that. She'd been widowed early, only meeting and marrying widower Martin (and taking on his six year old son Damien) when Jeff was three. Martin was head of sales for a large insurance firm, work which kept him away from the marital home for days at a time.

'Insurance business still good?' He knew that it wasn't. There had been too many storms, too much flooding and too little stock market growth for the sector to do well.

'Oh you know your dad - he doesn't give much away.'

But you could watch the news, mum. There again, she'd always been someone who metaphorically stuck her head in a bucket of sand. It had allowed her to ignore the family's problems, to remain oblivious to Jeff's distress during his childhood years.

He sat down on the soft beige settee and put his bag on the little coffee table in front. His mother immediately whisked it off. 'I'll put it in your room, keep everything tidy. Be right back - I've made a triple-decker cake.'

Lucky me. Still, eating a slice of coffee cream gateau was a small price to pay for being out in the big wide world, his world. And it was good to be living in a new place where no one knew his name - or his past.

'Are you warm enough?' his mother hurried back into the lounge.

'Perfect.'

He smiled at her and she flushed with pleasure and began to pour the tea.

'Nice place you have here,' he added, getting up and wandering over to the window. He stared out at the rows of houses. Such houses, and a few shops, were all he'd seen so far as the taxi ferried him through

Dundee. But his mother had told him it was named the City of Discovery - and he already knew just what he wanted to discover. The only question was *when?*

CHAPTER THIRTY TWO

Faith stared through her schoolroom window. He was out now, prowling through the English, Welsh or Scottish streets, his eyes feasting on a woman's wealth the way that other men's eyes feasted on legs or buttocks. Most men saw soft female parts that they wanted to caress and kiss - but Jeff only saw property that he could gain access to, minds that he could mould. He'd wanted her to be there whenever it suited him, but she had to keep out of the way when he wanted her house to himself.

Yet he'd hidden it so well at the start, had touched her in a way that no one else had ever touched her. He'd made her previously unexplored body reach a level of ecstasy that she'd only read about in the other teachers' lifestyle magazines. He'd stroked her and held her and told her again and again that he loved her. She'd have done anything to keep him and yet...

Remember that there's a janitor here to offer protection. Remember that you've got a good guard dog at home. But even as she silently reassured herself, Faith scanned the school playground looking for a predator. Oblivious, the children bullied or were bullied, swapped toys and traded cards. Most had no idea that violent death could suddenly threaten in a school playground or a suburban home.

The danger had built slowly with Jeff, just harsh words at first when she failed to please, then he'd started to grab her arms during arguments, his fingers digging deep. Next, the fights had involved a little pushing. She'd backed off each time, wanting to keep him, wanting him to love her as she so yearned to be loved. And for a time all would be well again and he'd hold her close at night and wave her cheerfully off in the morning. She'd still been looking to the future, even offering to teach him to drive. He'd never taken her up on the offer, though she'd once heard him boasting to her teaching assistant about giving Faith lifts everywhere. By then, she'd been ignoring his many lies and prevarications, afraid of making him angry again.

She shuddered, remembering the suddenness of his final assault, the pliers-like strength in his fingers. If her parents hadn't arrived when they did then she'd have been strangled to death. As it was, she couldn't see properly for days because her eyes were so badly haemorrhaged and her skin had looked like an alcoholic old woman's, all bluish blotches and red broken veins. The bruising around her throat hadn't faded for weeks, and the multi-faceted memory still remained.

Yet it had been such a trivial argument. She'd always stayed on at work for an hour each night to help run the after-school club, organising games to keep the children amused until their parents arrived. Jeff had made it clear that he resented her volunteering, but she hadn't capitulated because the children needed her and it was easier to befriend them properly outwith class. Many of them weren't thriving on an hours so-called quality time with their parents and clearly relied on her for adult conversation and company.

That night - the night she almost died - she'd come home and Jeff had asked her to wake him up tomorrow because it was his signing on day.

'Okay,' she'd said, walking into the conservatory with a geranium that one of the children's mums had given her that lunchtime, 'But I'll have to get you up at seven rather than eight as I've said I'll help run the school's new Breakfast Club.'

He'd let out a roar as he charged at her, but she had no idea if there were words inside the yell. All she knew was that suddenly he was throwing himself at her and that she was falling heavily. She landed, with him on top of her, on her back on the conservatory floor. Suddenly his hands were encircling her throat, squeezing, crushing. She clawed for what felt like two or three minutes at his fingers but couldn't pull them away.

He was looking down at her but his eyes were strangely unfocused. She thumped with her heels on the ground and tried to shout through her compressed vocal cords. The pain was intensifying now, every cell in her neck and her brain screaming for mercy, a pain which turned increasingly to panic as she realised that she could no longer breathe. *Please, please, please.* He kept crushing, crushing, crushing. *Please...* Her brain could no longer form the desperate plea. She could see the greenery and glass beyond him, familiar surroundings encircling an unfamiliar agony.

His face started to fade, though she could still feel his hands and was aware that his weight was still pressing down on her. Seconds later the sensation left her and her vista went dark. But then, as if from very far away, she'd heard a crashing sound, a crash that she now knew was her father breaking the glass and rushing in.

She'd been unconscious when her father hit Jeff and briefly knocked him out, semi-conscious when the ambulance arrived, heavily sedated for days afterwards. She'd still been on tranquillisers months later when the case eventually went to trial. Her mother and father had testified as to what they'd seen and how her father had stopped it and the police photographs taken at the hospital had been shown in court. Nevertheless, the defence had somehow presented their client as a high-spirited young man who had been kept on a short leash by a repressed older woman, a woman who wanted him to perpetually stay at home.

The defence had talked about how difficult it was for him to be unemployed - but she, Faith, suspected that he hadn't ever looked seriously for employment. Her neighbour had spoken honestly of how devoted he was to their dog. Jeff looked good, spoke well and came from a family that was financially and emotionally supportive, albeit not to the extent that they attended the trial. Unsurprisingly, he'd received a lesser sentence than he really deserved.

So now he was free and how long would it be before he found himself a new girlfriend? How long until she angered him with an unassuming act or unwitting remark? She, Faith, had had her life saved by the timely intervention of her father, but what if Jeff's next girlfriend didn't have a dad?

CHAPTER THIRTY THREE

'There are jobs in the *Dundee Courier*,' his mother said.

'Fancy that.' It was only his third day at home and already she was trying to find him gainful employment.

'Are you thinking of another laboratory position or...?'

'Probably *or*,' he said, aiming for levity.

'I'm making a Silver Wedding cake so if you wanted to mix the royal icing?'

Christ, she was treating him as if he were six years old.

'Can't - I apparently have to find a job within the hour or bring eternal damnation on the family.'

'I didn't mean... It's just, well none of us have ever signed on before.'

Yesterday he'd registered at the social to her intense disapproval. She had no idea that he'd signed on in Wales after dropping out of university. He'd invented a top job for her benefit and sent a few letters home giving her the details, information he'd found in the library's science magazines.

'My parole officer said it takes some time for ex-cons to find work,' he said now. He'd reported to the man the day after he got out of jail and was going to make damn sure that he kept all of his subsequent appointments. If he didn't he could be recalled to prison for being in breach of parole.

'Did he say how long?'

'Several months. He said that the main thing was to keep trying and also to try and relax when I was at home.'

He'd better get her used to the idea that he'd sometimes be here doing some serious relaxation. He'd normally read or listen to the radio in his bedroom but was in the lounge this morning because he wanted to watch the television news. He was going to surprise Amy later today and might want to discuss local happenings and current events.

'Will your last employer give you a reference?' his mother asked now.

Christ, that was all she cared about, turning him into a fucking workhorse. He'd never had a job in his life - and even the thought of one made him feel trapped and scared. He liked to awaken without the shriek of an alarm clock, have a leisurely breakfast followed by an equally unhurried and lengthy walk. When he lived in Wales, he'd taken next door's retriever out for most of the morning, had a snack lunch at home then sometimes hit the bars looking for cheap white trash to play with in the afternoons, before taking the dog for a second shorter walk. By night Faith was home to cook him a meal and they'd watch a TV film or DVD together, after which he'd sometimes put his tongue and his imagination to work, keen to keep her sweet. She needed more rest than he did so a couple of nights a week he'd go out on his own, ice-skating, swimming or just walking. All three gave him a chance to admire the female form.

'Can you get a reference?' his mother asked in an insistent voice.

'Mm? Doubt it.' He realised belatedly that he'd been daydreaming. It was the thing he'd gotten into trouble for at school on a daily basis, but he still couldn't stop doing it.

He simply had to find himself another Faith, someone who'd provide him with a house and a few quid to supplement his unemployment benefit. He'd have to check out the better lounge bars in town and target someone plain.

But for now he'd be content with Amy. He took her photo - a snapshot he'd had to beg for as she was so modest - from his wallet and stared at it again. She looked so compact that he knew he'd be able to pick her up and carry her around like a living doll. She was seriously cute but her posture wasn't that of a slim, confident young woman. No, the slope of her shoulders and the awkward way she clasped her hands spoke of an innate uncertainty.

The same emotion showed in her pretty face which held a watchfulness, a sadness. *Been there, got the T-shirt* - but unlike her, he'd gotten over it.

He thought about her all through lunch, and after the meal he re-read each of her letters. He was going to turn up on her door as the answer to her prayers, a walking Amy encyclopaedia.

'Mum, which bus do I take into town?' He was really going out the Perth Road but could see from his map that the road was accessible from the city centre. If he told mummy dearest where he was really going she'd want lots more details and might even want to come with him to see Amy again. Instead he'd hinted that his penpal friendship with her former computer course friend had virtually faded. This was doubly useful as she might find him someone else, someone rich.

He caught the bus to the city centre and bought himself a *reshape your life* book in one shop, a comb in a second and was given a free sample of male cologne in a third. They were all his insurance policies. If anything happened to Amy he'd have an alibi that he was shopping in town. And his purchases were ones which would impress any jury who could see that the cleancut young man before them was trying to turn his life around.

Not that he planned to hurt Amy, at least not in a way that would land him back in court. No, he'd always moved slowly with potential new girlfriends. But the rage he'd felt when Faith had disrespected him had made him aware that he could suddenly lose control. One moment he'd been planning his day, the next she'd showed a complete disregard for everything he'd been telling her. He'd snapped, lunged at her - and the rest was judicial history.

It was time to look to the future, start again. He walked on to the Perth Road, went into one of the shops and bought a small bottle of mineral water, reeling inwardly at the price. Christ, at that money he expected shares in the shop. Everything was so much more expensive than it had been when he went inside.

'It's thirsty weather,' he joked, referring to the unusual January sunshine.

'You're telling me! We've sold lots of that today,' the assistant said.

With her large dark eyes and shoulder length brown hair she was alluringly pretty but he forced himself to leave the shop. He just wanted to give himself a casual alibi, not an obvious one.

Now that he'd shopped in the area, given himself a genuine reason for being there, it was time for action. He walked the final short distance to Amy's flat and rang the bell.

CHAPTER THIRTY FOUR

This should be her ninth weekday off work but she'd woken up feeling fine. Shelley made a medium strength prawn curry and froze it in single-sized portions then had a generous helping with broccoli florets for an early lunch. Like most people who lived alone she kept a well stocked freezer but Netta her next door neighbour had been very good at bringing her everything from crusty bread to fruit. Now that she was craving curry, she knew that she'd returned to her pre-flu health.

At 1pm she dialled the clinic and was relieved when Jean rather than Zoe picked up the phone.

'It's me. I'm back in the land of the living, wondered if I should come in this afternoon?'

After a slight pause Jean said 'No, no. You take it easy. As I said earlier, we've got this work placement student till the end of the week.'

'Tomorrow then?'

'Well, we've given her your office, Shell. Just put your feet up for today and Friday and come back on Monday. My niece went back too soon and now she's off ill again.'

'Fair enough.' On the one hand, she welcomed a few more days of freedom, but on the other she was more than a little bored.

Jean lowered her voice. 'It's all been happening here. I was going to phone you yesterday but was scared I'd wake you up.' She broke off and spoke to someone then Shelley heard a door closing and Jean came back on. 'Dougal and Zoe have got engaged - matching rings imported from

Russia, no less. He was here again twice this week. Oh, and remember that nice boy who was phobic about college? He committed suicide.'

'Alan? How did he...?' She reminded herself that the method wasn't what mattered. 'I really liked him.'

'It was in the *Courier*. His mother must be desolate - he was all she had.'

'And Dougal and Zoe are really getting hitched?'

'Moving in together this weekend, apparently. I asked about the wedding, of course, but they haven't set a date.'

'Oh, Zoe'll probably want to get married on top of a mountain during the Equinox,' Shelley said.

She could hear the smile in Jean's voice. 'The three musketeers, remember?

'Anything else this particular musketeer should know?'

There was a pause then Jean said. 'I'm just flicking through the book. Oh yes, Sheila Crane has started a catering course and wanted to thank you for all your help - and Amy Bartlett phoned asking to speak to you. She was almost crying. Seemingly she has to get out of her current place and can't find an affordable house.'

'Are the student halls still full?'

'I suspect they must be. Shelley, she sounded really scared.'

'I'll bet she is.'

Not knowing where you'd live next was frightening for anyone - she'd been through it herself after her marriage broke up. But for someone as isolated as Amy it must be terrifying.

It was unfortunate the girl wasn't on the phone or she could call her now. Shelley drew larger and larger dark whorls on her notepad. 'Jean, if she phones back tell her to come in and see me first thing on Monday. And if she turns up before that in person, phone me at home and I'll speak to her there and then.'

They talked for another few minutes then Jean explained that another client had just walked in. Shelley said a hurried goodbye, made herself a cup of tea then checked her watch. It was 1.30pm. There was a very good chance that Amy would be at her flat now having a spartan lunch.

Don't get involved just because you're at a loose end. Go out for a walk. She popped her head out of the back door to confirm that it was an exceptionally mild afternoon and that there was even a little warmth in the sunshine. *Or do a little shopping in Albert Street or go to the Central Library and exchange your books.*

Shelley put on her favourite scoop-necked scarlet top and added scarlet star-shaped earrings, adding a brightness to her otherwise muted denim jacket, denim shoulder bag and lightweight jeans. She was aware that she was paying slightly too much attention to her appearance for someone who was just going for a solitary walk.

What the hell - she'd just take a bus out Amy's way, have a casual stroll past her flat. If she was out, Shelley could do some shopping in the west end and if the teenager was home, she could offer her housing suggestions. For example, she'd known students who rented caravans as a temporary measure and many families offered a room in their house at a reasonable weekly rate.

The counsellor jotted down a list of suggestions and put it in her bag. It was time for Operation Amy. She'd failed a girl last year - Giselle - and wasn't going to make the same mistake again. And there was nothing in the Youth Crisis Clinic's rules which said that a counsellor couldn't counsel a client in the client's own home.

The sky looked especially blue and the air smelt especially fresh after so many days convalescing indoors. Shelley took her time strolling to the bus stop and didn't mind the bus's numerous stops and starts as it slowly took her closer to Amy's house. She looked at the sandstone tenements and brightly painted shops with new appreciation. It was good to be alive.

At last she alighted and walked the rest of the way to the teenager's place. It was fortunate that the address was so close to the Youth Crisis Clinic that she'd easily remembered it. She'd also remembered that the girl lived in house number one. She realised belatedly that the front of the building was located in a dark and dingy basement. No wonder the girl was edgy and depressed. Still, the backs of the houses where the doors were located had a pleasant sunny aspect and the little path which led up to them was even and clean.

She'd only taken a few steps along the communal path when she saw an attractive, dark haired man sitting on the wall. He had a neat little bag strapped to his back and held a carrier bag emblazoned with the name of a bookshop. He half-smiled at her as she passed him and she smiled back.

There were three doors to choose from now - and none of them had any names on them, but she saw that the green door had a large metal numeral *one* above the letterbox. She rang the bell, waited for a few minutes, then rang again but the house remained eerily silent and it was clear that there was no one home.

Feeling absurdly disappointed, Shelley turned to go. Only now did she realise how much she'd wanted company. For the past two weeks, apart from the daily visits from Netta and phone calls from various acquaintances, she'd had no one to talk to. It was a culture shock for someone used to conversing with clients every day. And she'd genuinely wanted to help someone, to show that she wasn't just a nine-to-five counsellor. She'd wanted a chance to care.

She walked along the little pathway trying to decide where to go next.

'Have you been stood up too?' asked a casual but friendly voice.

Shelley looked to her right and saw the man on the wall. She'd forgotten all about him.

'Oh, well not really. It was just a surprise visit.'

'Lucky you. My friend's clearly had a better offer elsewhere.'

Shelley stood on the path and studied him more closely. With his glossy thick brown hair and hazel eyes he resembled a young Pierce Brosnan and was well worth looking at - not that she was in the marketplace. It seemed rude to ignore his comment so she asked 'Are you just going to wait for him?'

The man shrugged lightly. 'I don't have much choice. I'm supposed to be staying with him. He'll presumably return some time today.'

Shelley finger combed her fringe. 'I suppose I should wait for a few minutes too. My...' she realised that it would be breaking a confidence to use the word *client*, 'My friend's a university student so she's always popping home.'

The man smiled, showing even white teeth. 'Wish I'd lived this close to uni when I was a student.'

Shelley brushed a little dust from the wall then sat down next to him. 'Did you study here?'

'No,' She could smell peppermint on his breath when he spoke, 'At Cardiff. And I could have had university accommodation only you're not allowed animals in halls and I was looking after a dog for a friend.'

There was something incredibly sweet about men who loved animals, Shelley thought. She realised that she was staring at him and added hastily 'Seemingly you have the same problem when you're old - I was reading that pensioners often refuse to go into care because they're not allowed to take their pet.'

'Typical institutional approach. No wonder some people opt for euthanasia,' the man said, looking sad.

'Looks like we'll soon be able to offer it legally in this country so terminal patients no longer have to travel abroad.'

'Especially as many can't afford it,' the man agreed, 'But politicians don't even consider that.'

'Too true.' It was good to be having a conversation that didn't involve first love or period pains. She thought of how politics affected the Youth Crisis Clinic. 'There's a political emphasis on the family but all the attention's focused on the parents and none on the teens.'

'I wouldn't be a kid again for anything,' the man said with feeling.

'Nor me - my parents idea of conversation was saying "pass the salt"!'

'Do they live in Dundee?'

They'd never really lived in the full sense of the word. 'No, they died of lung cancer years ago.' It hadn't come as a surprise to her as they both smoked like chimney stacks.

'My dad died too. I was only a year old and can't remember him.'

Shelley felt a momentary pity. 'Memory's so variable, isn't it? Some of the people I talk to say that their first memory is of starting school age five.'

Her new friend smiled. 'Oh, I definitely remember my first day. I was so small for my age that I couldn't reach my cloakroom peg and had to leave my blazer on the floor!'

'It's enough to start you on a life of sartorial indifference,' Shelley joked then looked at his cobalt denim jacket and realised that it was much better cut than hers.

'Start me on a course of growth hormones, more like. Luckily I caught up.' He stretched languidly, revealing what must be a six foot frame.

A slightly chill breeze had started up and Shelley sneezed. 'Sorry, I recently recovered from the flu.'

'Oh, you too? Everyone on my... everyone I know has had it.' He was clearly very popular. He glanced at his watch. 'I don't think Kenny's coming, so I'm going to head off to that café along the road for a late lunch.' He stood up, hesitated for a moment then murmured 'Want to tag along?'

To her surprise, Shelley felt her heart start to beat a little faster but she aimed for the casualness she heard in his voice. 'Why not? I don't want anything to eat but a big mug of tea would be great.' Realising that her hands were cold, she pushed them into her jeans pocket and found the housing list. 'Hang on, I'll just leave a note for my friend.' Fishing out a pen she wrote *Amy - hope this list helps. I'll be back at the clinic on Monday if you want to call in or phone.* She signed it *Shelley*, folded it several times in the hope that the flatmate from hell wouldn't read it and wrote Amy's name on the outside.

'Is she an old friend?' the man asked after she returned from pushing it through Amy's door.

Shelley kept her tone light, determined not to break a confidence. 'No, young.'

'If you'd rather go to a pub than a café?'

She grinned. 'Uh uh, I'm a tea junkie. Lead the way.'

The café was filled with students, lecturers and the occasional shopper who'd succumbed to hunger pangs, but a young couple hurriedly finished their post-meal drinks and surrendered their cosy corner table. Her new friend ordered a baked potato with grated Edam and a side salad. Amy, Shelley thought, would probably like this man, providing he ditched the cheese. But he was talking about staying with someone called Kenny, so he might well be gay.

'So did you come all the way from Cardiff to see your friend or...?'

'No, I live in... in Edinburgh now.'

'That's not so bad, then. I mean, you can be home in two or three hours if your friend doesn't show.'

'Oh, I'd rather book into a bed and breakfast here.' He looked at her with a very earnest expression. 'I've been cooped up at work for months so this is my chance to see a different city.' He patted his bag, 'And I've everything I need.'

'Well, it's not nearly as majestic as Edinburgh,' Shelley admitted.

'But you must like it?'

She nodded slowly. 'My work's here and I have a nice house so it suits me fine.'

'What line of work are you in?'

It was Shelley's turn to hesitate. Some people felt exposed when you admitted that you were a counsellor. They assumed that you were hypercritical, could see all of their secrets and virtually read their minds.

'I work with teenagers.'

'Teaching them? I have a friend whose a primary school teacher back in Cardiff.'

'No, dealing with their problems. I work in an advice centre for the under twenty ones.'

'That must be challenging.'

'It is - but rarely dull. We get all kinds of problems.'

'I can imagine,' the man said, finishing his pot of tea. They spoke about his scientific research, about her magazine reports, about their childhoods and about the failings of modern parenting and the education system.

After an hour Shelley realised that she still didn't know his name.

'I'm Shelley by the way,' she said with a self conscious laugh.

He smiled. 'And does Shelley have a surname?'

'Don't laugh - it's Shelley Smart.'

'That's not so bad. My surname's Metcalfe so the other kids had a field day at school - Metal Mickey, Baby Calf, Caffeine. The irony is, my surname was Johnston, which is hard to make fun of, but my mother remarried when I was three.'

'Is Mickey your first name, then?' It was a clumsy attempt to find out his Christian name.

'No.' He looked at her full on. 'Didn't I say? It's Jeff.'

Jeff Metcalfe. It was a nice name. She thought that he was even nicer when he ordered them both another pot of tea. The waitress clearly had similar taste in men and brought complimentary sweet granary biscuits which she placed beside Jeff.

'How long will you stay here then?' she asked eating the biscuit with self conscious care to avoid spraying crumbs.

'Here in this café or in Dundee?'

'In Dundee of course!' She was aware that if they stayed in the café much longer they'd sprout roots.

'Oh, a couple of days then I'll go to Perth, Aberdeen, maybe as far as Inverness. I deserve a change of scene.'

'Go for it!' She knew from her work that many people led fairly joyless existences. But this man was obviously not in that particular camp. She smiled at the word. He probably liked men.

'Maybe you can show me the local highlights?'

Shelley nodded, grateful to have a new friend. 'I can, but won't Kenny want to do that?'

She watched Jeff frown - then he smiled again. 'He's hardly the most reliable tourist guide.'

'Okay.' She could take him to the docks to see the famous ship *Discovery* but it would be cold down there so she should really go home for her winter coat and ankle boots. Shelley turned to him. 'I can show you around now but I really need some warmer clothes. Do you want to wait here for me or try your friend again?'

She watched him look around the busy café. 'No, we should leave before they throw us out. I'll have a look around the shops again then just take up my place on Kenny's wall.'

He'd be miserable in the increasingly cold January wind. Shelley turned to face him as she slung her shoulder bag on. 'Look, why don't you come back with me and I'll grab my coat? We can take a taxi to my place then walk around my district and gradually work our way back into town and on to the docks.'

'Sounds like a plan,' Jeff said, picking up the bill and taking out his wallet. She noticed that he left the waitress a generous tip.

Outside they stood stamping their feet on the pavement until hailing a cab. They tumbled gratefully into the back and she gave the driver her address.

'They said it would snow but I didn't believe them as it was so sunny earlier on,' he said a moment later. Shelley looked out of the window and saw a few fine snowflakes swirling around.

By the time that they reached her bungalow the snow was falling much more quickly and the pavements had started to turn white. 'Shall I make us a cup of hot chocolate till we see if this goes off?' She didn't want to go walking in a winter wonderland so soon after having flu.

'I'd love one.' Jeff rubbed his hands together as Shelley fished out her keys. 'Nice house,' he added, looking up at the whitewashed walls and red-painted door. 'Very nice,' he amended as they stepped inside.

'I bought it a few years ago,' she admitted proudly, 'It's a good quiet neighbourhood and the rooms are sufficiently small that they're easy to heat.' She showed him into the lounge and they both sat down on the settee.

'I had a similar bungalow in Wales,' Jeff said, sounding somewhere between wistful and slightly angry.

Shelley looked at him in surprise. 'So why did you leave?'

'Mm? Oh I got promoted to the company's Scottish lab. Didn't mind at the time as I'd always loved what I'd seen of Edinburgh but the housing market there is out of control now so I'm renting until prices go down.'

'Or you could live on the outskirts and commute,' Shelley said. Talking of housing belatedly reminded her of Amy. She hoped the nineteen year old would pop in and see her at work on Monday so that they could get her accommodation problem straightened out.

'It may come to that,' Jeff said and it was clear that he'd given some thought to his options, 'I mean, I love the freedom of the country - I used to take my neighbour's retriever out for hours at a time - but I also appreciate the shops and night classes that the city has.'

'Have you taken any night classes recently?' Shelley herself did a different type of dance class most years and had also taken courses in everything from home plumbing to vegetarian cookery.

She watched Jeff hesitate. 'Uh huh - a pursuit of happiness course.'

'It must have worked - you seem happy enough to me!'

'Oh, I was happy enough before but a... a friend suggested it.'

'And did he - or she - do it too?' She wondered again if he had a girlfriend or a boyfriend to stake their claim.

'Mm? Yes, he did.' Jeff looked more closely at the books on the little in-built bookshelf, 'Oh I've read most of them.'

'There's more in the dining room,' Shelley said, 'Well, the last owner called it his dining room but I eat here on a tray.'

'Can I have a look?' Jeff was already on his feet before she could agree.

Shelley followed him out of the room, 'I'll make that hot chocolate.' She hurried into the kitchen to put the kettle on. By now the snow was swirling around the back garden and coating the window sill and her winter plants were thickened white versions of their former selves.

What an odd - but good - day this was turning out to be. She wondered idly where she would take Jeff if the snow continued. Would he want to go to the cinema or would that be too passive for a man who'd planned to see the sights?

He was still studying her dining room bookshelves so she walked past him and deposited their mugs and a plate of chocolate ginger sweets in the lounge. A moment later he came in and joined her on the settee.

'Sorry. I just love books.'

'Same here.'

'Have you been... I mean, you have a lot on anorexia.'

'Oh, I used to work with anorexics. The correct term is actually anorectics but no one uses that nowadays.'

'I saw a documentary on it recently.'

Shelley stilled, remembering the final pictures of a once-beautiful young woman. 'I knew the girl dancer, the one that died.'

'That must have been terrible.' He put his hand on her arm and she flinched with surprise, the movement making his hand brush her breast. The feeling was electric. He must have seen from her expression that she was excited for he stroked her breast again. She turned to face him and their lips met, moving from a gentle exploration to a long and increasingly arousing kiss. He definitely wasn't gay, Shelley thought as he pushed her onto her back and she felt his erection digging into her lower belly. He started to stroke her softly and breathe increasingly hard.

They continued to kiss and she sat up slightly so that he could pull her denim jacket off. Moments later he lifted her scarlet top over her head and dropped it on the floor. Shelley was glad that she was wearing her black bra rather than one of her white-that-has-faded-to-grey ones. She helped him shrug off his own denim jacket and began to unbutton his shirt. His chest, she was pleased to see, was darkly hirsute. She licked his nipples and ran her hands down his smooth warm back.

'Is this why they call it the city of discovery?' he murmured as he unhooked her bra.

Shelley smiled, unable to think of a clever answer. A few hours ago she'd been wondering how to get through the rest of the day - and suddenly she had the answer in the form of this incredibly attractive and intelligent man.

She moaned softly as he turned his attention to her now-naked breasts, stroking and cupping them before gently sucking on her nipples.

For a moment she felt almost maternal as she caressed his head. He must be ten years younger than her and she'd never been attracted to toy boys but for now she didn't care. And anyway a decade didn't matter so much when the younger party was so thoughtful and well read.

'What else can I discover?'

She watched as he kissed his way slowly down her stomach, and for the first time she was glad she'd had the flu. She must have lost half a stone in the past fortnight as she just hadn't felt like eating and now her stomach looked relatively flat.

When his lips reached her panties he pulled them and her jeans down, taking off her socks at the same time. She was now completely naked whilst he was only undressed to the waist.

'Come back up here so that I can make us equal,' Shelley laughed, feeling slightly self conscious. Then his tongue found her clitoris and she forgot about everything else.

For the first two minutes she kept waiting for him to surface spitting hairs as her ex-husband had done on the few occasions he'd gone down on her. But after a while she realised that he was enjoying the tonguing as much as she was and she gave herself up to the rhythm. His tongue circled her clit again and again, sending out long-forgotten sensations. Shelley could hear herself whimpering and she began to press her sex harder against his mouth. She'd been so busy with work these past few years that she hardly ever felt the need to pleasure herself, but now this man was lapping at her core and every cell in her body felt alive.

'Ah, uh.' Her voice sounded hollow as she made little unplanned cries. 'Mm, uh.' She pushed down against his tongue and he obligingly licked harder and she cried out, gutturally signifying a climax which went on and on.

He continued to lick until the very last frisson of pleasure had been forced from her flesh and his licks became painful. Gently she pulled at his head and he moved up to lie next to her on the settee. She could feel liquid on her inner thighs and lower belly and knew that she was soaking. She slid her hand down and stroked his hardness through his jeans. 'Want to discover some more?'

He nodded, smiling down at her, and she marvelled again at how good looking he was. 'But if we wait a few minutes I can make you come again.'

Shelley shook her slightly damp head. 'After that I doubt if I'll need to come for a month.'

He kissed her nose. 'Trust me.'

She trusted him.

Soon he took off his jeans and his underpants, staring at her all the while. Shelley again felt self conscious and covered her breasts but he took her hands away and put them by her sides. 'You look beautiful.' He kissed her nipples then sat back on his heels 'Roll over onto your tummy.'

If he wanted anal, he had no chance. Shelley heard the uncertainty in her own voice. 'What are you going to do?'

'Trust me. I'll make you come again.'

She could always throw him off if he tried anything that she objected to. Shelley turned over and felt his fingers playing lightly with her labial lips, separating them then caressing her vaginal rim. Seconds later she felt his cock probing at her entrance then he moved slowly forwards so that he entered her vulva a centimetre at a time. It felt so good that Shelley gasped again and heard his triumphant laugh.

She gasped some more as she felt his fingers sliding under her to locate her clitoris. So that's why he wanted her on her stomach - this way she could press against his fingers as his cock slid in and partially out. It meant that she could enjoy the sensation of him inside her whilst still benefiting from the clitoral stimulus that she needed if she were to come.

In, out, in, out. Soon Shelley knew that she was going to climax again. The wetness of her insides and the warm lust of her outsides increased to a level that was almost unbearable and she shoved her body down harder against his fingers and groaned long and loudly as she came and came and came. She heard Jeff mutter something then his thrusting speeded up and he strained into her, his only other sound a restrained grunt.

'You were brilliant,' she murmured, as she lay, like a beached whale, on her belly.

'You too. We make a very good team.'

She cried out as he withdrew and added 'I hate that bit.'

'Next time I'll stay inside you until after you've gone to sleep.'

So there was to be a next time, she thought as she turned around to face him - this wasn't just a one afternoon stand.

She realised that he was shivering and pointed to the blankets which lay folded at the foot of the settee. 'Do you want to pull them over us?' She'd used them when recovering from the flu.

'Your wish is my command,' Jeff murmured, turning away and leaning over to reach the blankets. Shelley took a moment to admire his small but muscular ass.

'You must work out a lot.'

'I do. There's nothing else to do in... in my district.'

'You said that you weren't happy where you were?' Shelley said. She wondered vaguely if he had a flatmate or if he lived alone, wondered what his Edinburgh apartment was like. But the excitement of the day was catching up with her and she began to yawn.

'Let's keep you warm,' Jeff murmured and she felt the soft cotton bedspread being tucked gently around her. *I've found the perfect lover*, Shelley thought to herself as she drifted towards sleep.

CHAPTER THIRTY FIVE

She must trust him already to fall asleep so soon. Jeff shifted his weight slightly on the settee so that he could stare down at Shelley. Her head was tilted back, showing the silky vulnerability of her oh-so-compressible neck. She'd probably be a screamer, leastways she'd climaxed noisily. He'd been worried that the sound would alert her neighbours but no one had come to investigate.

He looked around the room, admiring the large ornate fire surround and heavy mahogany table, the overstuffed armchairs. He'd landed on his feet here: a psychologist was much better than a primary school teacher and it was clear that she hadn't sussed that he was a recent ex-con. Not that her lack of insight made her unusual: in his experience psychologists weren't particularly bright.

It was something that he'd clocked in prison over the years - the shrinks gave good reports to the guys who attended the rehabilitation courses and made all the right remorseful noises. In contrast, the honest ones who continued to think for themselves were denied parole and seen as entrenched personalities. So they let the actors out and stamped *rehabilitated* on their files and they soon offended again.

He'd soon offend again: oh, the urge was dormant now when he'd just had a good fuck and had a whole new female project to work on. But history told him that within days or weeks the compulsion would return.

The woman stirred in her sleep then settled down again. He stared at her clear skin and felt renewed surprise that she was forty. At her age she wouldn't want children, which suited him nicely. She might not want a dog either but if he brought a puppy home and pretended that it was a stray...

Thinking of strays reminded him of his poor little Amy. Shelley had knocked on Amy's door so it was a safe bet that she was counselling the lonely little soldier. He'd been incredibly lucky to meet the rich bitch rather than the impoverished waif today. Shelley had property and money yet was clearly hard up enough to fuck a total stranger. She was his.

Not that he planned to give up on Amy. Hell, no. She was younger and more isolated, which meant she was more likely to be up for a regular semi-strangling. If Shelley ever refused him he'd simply go to Amy's for the day. He could walk his new dog in the mornings, see Amy for some of the afternoons and have Shelley to take care of him at night. It meant he'd no longer have to live with The Stepfather and Mommy Dearest. More importantly, it meant he wouldn't have to find a job.

'A euro for your thoughts.'

A vaguely familiar female voice broke into his reverie and he felt a momentary irritation. 'Oh, you're awake,' he said, then, realising that sounded brusque, added 'I missed you.'

'How long have I been out for?' Shelley looked at her watch. 'God, no wonder I'm hungry - it's after seven.' She stretched then pulled the blankets more firmly around her breasts, 'Could you throw a pizza in the oven while I take a bath?'

What did your last slave die of? 'Pizzas are my speciality.' He kissed her nose, 'Shall I also do us a side salad?'

'Yeah, Netta couldn't get any winter lettuce but she handed in tomatoes, cucumber and grapes with the pizza yesterday,' Shelley said.

He'd try to find more than that, make her a *Jeffrey Surprise* and burrow further into her good books. Jeff hurried to the kitchen and put the oven on then systematically worked his way through the fridge and cupboards. He grated an apple, chopped small pieces of cabbage and carrot, combining them with mayonnaise to make a sweet-tasting coleslaw. He chopped a raw onion finely and squeezed fresh orange juice over it as a marinade.

He cut tomato, lettuce and black olives into small pieces and dressed them with a mixture he made from olive oil, lemon juice, mustard and a chopped garlic clove.

Half an hour later, Shelley came back into the lounge looking pink and healthy from her bath. He noticed that she'd changed into a mid-calf cotton shift dress, clearly a house dress. That suited him - he really didn't want to go out on the town tonight.

'Dinner is served.' He garnished her pizza-and-salad plate with the red grapes and brought her the meal on a tray.

'Wow, at this rate you can move in!' Shelley said.

I already have. He smiled apologetically: 'I couldn't find any wine so I just made us tea.'

'Tea's great.' She scooped up some of the homemade coleslaw with her fork, 'So is this.'

He'd learnt that particular recipe in prison cookery classes. He smiled. 'Maybe it's genetic - my mother makes cakes.'

'Just remembered - I've got a DVD we can watch with our meal.' She knelt before the machine and he turned his attention to the screen which was already showing the opening credits of a recently televised thriller. He'd seen it already but it clearly hadn't occurred to her to ask. That was the problem with people who'd lived on their own - they became selfish. They thought that the world revolved around them.

Still, the food was good and the bungalow was warm and there were no parents or step parents to ask about his career plans or tell him to tidy his room or clip the hedge into submission. And Shelley was starting to look tired so would hopefully nod off soon, allowing him to explore the house. He'd spent days exploring Faith's house when he first moved in there, going through everything from her lingerie drawer (big white cotton knickers, sand-coloured tights and maxi-flow sanitary towels) to the boxes of Faith-as-an-ugly-baby photographs that were gathering dust under the bed.

A repetitive noise broke into his thoughts and he realised that Shelley was laughing at the movie. He smiled at her with pretend indulgence and put down his fork to ruffle her hair.

'More tea?'

She nodded, intent on wolfing down the pizza. He poured carefully, determined to make everything right.

'This is brilliant.'

You've said that before. He wanted the place to himself now, needed his freedom. If it was a normal working day he'd have had the house exclusively from around eight until after five. By then he was always in need of company, at least for a couple of hours.

They finished the meal and watched the rest of the film, just making occasional comments about the actors and the storylines. Then Shelley switched off the set and kissed him on the cheek: 'I really must let you go to Kenny's now. He'll be thinking you've fallen in the Tay.'

'Mm?' He stiffened. There wasn't a Kenny and he was fucked if he was going home to mother tonight. At least, not if he could help it. 'Oh, Kenny'll have given up on me by now, gone out to the pub again.'

'Still, you could take a taxi there and leave him a note with my phone number so that he can call you when he gets back.'

'That might be really late.' He had to take her mind off sending him away. 'Give me one more kiss and I'll go,' he murmured, kneeling on the settee so that he faced her, sliding his hands down her back and to the sides of her breasts. She whimpered as he continued his ministrations, cupping her arse through the soft cotton dress and squeezing both buttocks. Only when she was breathing fast and hard did he push her down onto her back, slowly edge up her dress and slide her panties down.

This time she tasted of bubble bath, a taste that was soon replaced by a saltier and slightly metallic tang. He wondered if her period was imminent. He'd always kept out of Faith and his mother's way when they were on the rag. They got very tired, always asking for bacon sandwiches or strong black coffee and cake.

He licked long and hard, knowing that it would buy him a bed for the night, a break from his mother. Christ, he hated being at his stepfather's home, subsisting like a little kid. He was twenty eight years old and had to live by his own rules, needed a house to call his own.

The thighs at either side of his head moved restlessly and he realised that he hadn't been concentrating fully on her clit. A clit needed a rhythm it could rely on. He resumed his cadenced licking and was rewarded by another moan. He gently lapped around the enlarged dark pink bud for long, luxurious moments and eventually her legs began to tighten and he knew that she was about to peak.

Going, going... She went over the top with a broken-up yell, as if the pleasure robbed her of every other second of vocal energy. He kept licking, forcing out every last iota of desire with his determined tongue.

At last she pulled his head away and he crawled up the settee to join her. Oh good, her eyelids were drifting down.

'Let's get you to bed where you can sleep properly,' he murmured, picking her up.

'I'm no lightweight. I sleep upstairs. You'll drop me,' she said drowsily.

'Trust me.' They always relaxed when you said that, the fools.

His leg muscles trembling with the effort, he carried her through the bungalow and up the stairs. Luckily the bedroom door was open so he didn't have to search for it. He walked in and lowered her gently to the divan, sat down next to her and helped her pull off her dress. Her thighs and pubis were streaked with wet lust and for a moment he felt cheated of his own orgasm - but the main thing now was to lull her off to sleep so that she couldn't thrown him out of the house for the night. Quickly stripping off his own clothes, he covered them both with the duvet and curled close.

She slept. He held her for a while, enjoying the warmth and smoothness of a woman after all these lonely years surrounded by men in HMP Maidstone. Oh, some of the men had jammed their cell doors shut and fucked each other, but it had never been his way. No, until he'd strangled that little punk in the showers he'd never laid hands on another man, not even when...

Forget about that. You've got a new house now, a new girl and a second girl who's going to be rapt to see you. Forget the past. Concentrate on the now.

He realised he had an erection, something he often got when he was afraid. Gently he rubbed it between her buttocks but she was sleeping so soundly it was clear that she wouldn't awake.

Slowly he took his hands from her waist and edged them upwards until they gently encircled her throat. He'd just keep them there as he bucked against her flesh, wouldn't let them tighten. He'd fantasize that he was strangling her but wouldn't carry out the act.

As he took himself closer to the edge, he was reminded of the American cop, Gerald Schaefer, who'd initially written short stories about hanging women for his own sexual gratification. *I know that I'm going to do this,* Schaefer had written, *but I don't know why.* Later, when the written fantasies were no longer enough, he'd taken girl after girl into the woods, told them they were about to be hanged - and then hanged them. Watching them dance on a noose had been the biggest thrill of his life.

His own thrill was fast approaching. Jeff groaned softly as he climaxed between the sleeping woman's arse cheeks and his hands tightened around her throat.

CHAPTER THIRTY SIX

Everything was going to be fine - Shelley would be so proud of her. Amy hugged herself as she looked around her large new study bedroom in the student house.

'The students share two bathrooms and a kitchen. Here, I'll show you,' the janitor said and proceeded to do just that.

The kitchen had two cookers, a fridge and a little ante room with a coin-operated washing machine. It also contained a large sink and a spin drier so she could wash her clothes by hand if she wanted to and save cash. Granted, sharing a kitchen with several other students would be daunting but she could make salad sandwiches in her room, eat apples and just heat up her low sugar baked beans and toast during quiet times.

'It's perfect.' Her parents would love this house if they could be persuaded to vacate their enormous armchairs.

The elderly janitor looked pleased. 'Soon as you give your deposit to Student Accom, it's yours.'

It was Friday morning so if she got the deposit to them now she'd feel secure throughout the weekend. Amy speed-walked all the way to the office and gave them the cash. Then she went home and told Dana that she'd sorted everything out.

'If you want to move in on Sunday, Mummy can take you in the car,' Dana said.

'I could pay for her petrol costs and give her a cup of tea and...' She realised that, as usual, she was talking too much and added 'That would be brilliant.' She'd bought quite a few books plus an exercise bike since moving here so the offer of transport would really help.

She spent Friday afternoon at various seminars and lectures but by Friday night was at a loose end and went to see her new house again. Some of the other tenants were on their way out and greeted her warmly. Amy was still smiling when she unlocked her new bedroom door and studied every cupboard and shelf determining where her possessions would go. She'd put the bike in front of the window so that she could look out at the tree-lined gardens as she pedalled her way to a thinner her.

This was a nice spacious house, nicer than any caravan. Not that she wasn't grateful for the counsellor's written suggestions - Shelley must really care to have left her sick bed to visit her. It was such a pity that she'd been out.

It was with some regret that she left Ensley House and returned to Dana's for what would be her penultimate night. Then, on the Saturday, she awoke at seven and couldn't get back to sleep. She wanted to tell someone else about her new room and the beauty of the surrounding house and grounds. She'd already phoned her aunt, of course, and had written a long letter to her parents describing every facet of the building - and she was almost finished writing an even longer letter to Jeff. Usually she got a letter from him every other day but the last one hadn't arrived yet. Luckily he'd explained that Maidstone was undergoing administrative changes which meant that the mail might be late going out.

Now, after her usual baked beans on toast - Dana had once joked that it was closer to baked *bean* on toast - Amy picked up her pen and finished Jeff's letter. *So please use my new address from now on. I'll probably be here till I graduate. I love it already! It's a picturesque old house which has everything a student could need.* She signed it *love Amy* and added a smiley face. She still didn't think of him as a boyfriend, for all that she'd told her mother, more as an incredibly dear best friend.

An hour later she was dressed and walking towards the local post box with his five-page letter. Where could she go next? The day stretched before her. Tomorrow was going to be exciting but today was all about playing the waiting game. She could fill up some time at the swimming baths or walk to The Howf again and look at the Victorian gravestones or... *Or go to Shelley's house and thank her for the housing list.*

Re-energised by the prospect of tea and a chat, Amy upped her pace, knowing it was a long walk to Shelley's. Should she take the woman a few flowers or some other kind of gift?

Suddenly the teenager stopped, remembering that she wasn't supposed to know where Shelley's bungalow was, had only discovered it when she followed the counsellor. She'd think that Amy was stalking her, would never want to see her again.

Unless... Stopping by the Central Library, she took four leaflets on intensive animal farming from a leaflet-heavy shelf. Now she could knock on Shelley's door and just look like she was canvassing the entire area. After all, people did it all the time. Just this week she'd opened the door to reps from two pressure groups who wanted her opinions and her time.

Now she was ready for anything. Smiling inside, Amy set off with renewed vigour towards the counsellor's pretty red-doored house.

CHAPTER THIRTY SEVEN

This man certainly got intimate very quickly. Shelley woke up to find Jeff pressed against her, one of his hands resting lightly on her throat. She tried to move away and for a second his grasp tightened then it totally relaxed. There was a small snore as he turned on his other side followed by a few longer snores as he drifted into a deeper sleep.

She squinted at the clock. It was 5am, which explained why she felt like a limp dishcloth. She and Jeff had had sex - their third session of the day - at around 3am. After years of hardly ever thinking about men, she was amazed at her sexual responsiveness, at how often she wanted to orgasm and at how intense these orgasms were.

He was an exceptional lover, she thought, turning on her side and gazing at his glossy black hair and smooth shoulders and back. And he was equally good in the kitchen. He'd produced an impressive variety of meals and snacks over the last couple of days.

And therein lay the problem - he'd now been in residence for far too long. She'd brought him here on Thursday afternoon and he was still in situ on Saturday morning. Her hints that he should now go to Kenny's had fallen on very deaf ears. Oh, she wanted to go on seeing him and getting to know him, but at the usual dating pace.

In a week he'd have to go back to Edinburgh, back to work - but he couldn't stay here for a full week, he just couldn't. She wanted to do the sorts of things she could only do by herself. She longed to put on her virtually-antique leisure suit and watch the *Coronation Street* omnibus, wanted to make up a big batch of barbecue spare ribs and eat them with her hands.

Today she was definitely going to throw him out then she'd do a mammoth grocery shopping and have a lazy day. They could arrange a date for Sunday but she wouldn't let him stay over as she was going back to work on the Monday. Shelley smiled, wondering what Jean would make of this week - first Zoe getting engaged to The Digit and now Shelley picking up a toyboy outside a client's house. On second thoughts, she wouldn't mention her new boyfriend to her colleagues, would wait and see how it worked out.

Tired as she felt, she just couldn't get back to sleep. She got up at 5.30am and made herself a pot of tea and some muesli. Afterwards she bathed and dressed in her best chambray shirt and matching bootcut trousers, wanting Jeff's last view of her today to be an attractive one.

At 8am she made him tea and toast and carried a tray upstairs.

'Breakfast!'

She had to say it twice before he sat up against the pillows and smiled at her before reaching for a buttered slice.

'Hey, you're dressed.'

'I've been up for hours, even cleaned the house.'

'I would have done it.'

She felt a momentary disquiet at the thought of him sharing the chores so soon.

'No, your mission for today is to go and stay with Kenny.'

She noticed that he'd suddenly stopped crunching his toast. He made a grab for her: 'You look good enough to eat.'

Laughing lightly, Shelley dodged out of his way. She'd noticed that he made a pass at her every time she talked of his leaving. Not that she could really blame him - it was obviously more fun staying in an attractive bungalow with a willing woman than bunking down in a decrepit flat with a drunken mate.

'Jeff. I have to go out to the shops before they get busy.'

'Want me to prepare something for lunch?'

'No,' She realised that she was saying no a lot, tried to soften her words, 'Listen, I love being with you but I need at least a day to myself. Go to Kenny's now and maybe we can meet up in town tomorrow and I'll show you around the city.'

'Sounds like a plan.'

She was glad that he'd capitulated at last.

At 9am, after many more kisses in the porch, they both left the bungalow and Shelley set off in the direction of the nearest supermarket whilst Jeff walked away in the opposite direction. Feeling an uplifting sense of freedom, she all but skipped through the cool winter streets. Jeff had taken her phone number and promised to call her tomorrow to fix up their next meeting so everything was going to be great.

CHAPTER THIRTY EIGHT

Fuck it, she'd only gone and thrown him out. Jeff was halfway along the road before he realised that he had no idea how to get home from here. He'd been too busy concentrating on Shelley in the taxi on Thursday to pay much attention to the locale.

On the upside, the snow had melted and it was turning into a mild January morning, the type he'd enjoyed before he was banged up in prison. Maybe he'd walk all the way back to his mother's, even if it took all day. He was in no hurry to swap anecdotes about royal icing with her or exchange grunts with step daddy dearest if he'd bothered to come back.

The odd thing was, his mother hated it when he, Jeff, stayed away. Oh, she had little enough to say to him when he was there - but if he stopped out overnight he was greeted with tight-lipped glares and an awkward silence. She'd also treat him like a school kid, complaining 'you should have phoned to let me know.'

He'd phone her now and get the lecture over with. Maybe he could soften her up by offering to bring in something for their evening meal. She'd given him fifty quid when he arrived in Dundee and he still had most of it left.

He was standing in the phone kiosk before he remembered that he needed coins: the prison phones used cards called green-and-friendlies. Digging into his pocket, he was relieved to find a fifty pence piece.

As usual, his mother took an age to pick up. He could imagine her part-way through some crucial flour-folding process. She'd always made it clear that Lots Could Go Wrong if a small boy interrupted a cake-making mum. Now that he could cook for himself, he'd formed the impression that most recipes were recoverable and that nothing terrible happened if a cake mixture was left unstirred for a minute or three.

'Hi Mum,' he said lightly as soon as she answered, 'I'm just on the way home from a friend's and wondered if you wanted anything from the shops?'

'Guess who's here?' she murmured sounding slightly breathless.

'Martin?' he asked, giving his stepfather's name. He had a horrible feeling that wasn't the right answer.

'No - Damien. He only arrived ten minutes ago. You should see his suit!'

I should see his hands. I should smell his breath. I should get as far away from him as possible.

'Right,' he said in a voice that didn't sound like his own.

'He's really looking forward to seeing you.'

No he's not. Mum said things like that all the time, pure wish fulfilment. Damien only looked forward to causing pain.

'So when can I expect you? I'm making bacon rolls for Damien now because he hasn't eaten but I could put one aside for you if you don't mind it cold.'

'Oh, I'll be ages, mum.' *Like next century.* 'Just go ahead without me. I've got things to do.'

It was only after he set down the receiver that he realised he was shaking - and he jumped slightly when the kiosk clankingly returned his unused coins.

Christ, that was a turn up for the books, the return of the prodigal. Damien must have fucked his business or lost his home. He simply wasn't the type to play happy families. No, he'd be wanting cash or accommodation or his pound of flesh.

His stepbrother had taken numerous pounds of flesh over the years. At six, he'd bloodied the noses of half the boys in his class, pulled out chunks of the girls hair, spat on their parents. Jeff had only been three then, had been at the school's adjacent nursery and was enjoying it. Yet his parents had callously uprooted him and moved to a much smaller town which didn't have facilities for pre-school kids. Looking back, they'd moved to avoid having Damien expelled, to avoid the humiliation. They hadn't given much thought to what the upheaval might do to Jeff.

Now, as he leaned heavily against the back wall of the kiosk, he felt sick and abandoned. Damien was at home - so Jeff wouldn't go home. Damien had fucked up at school after school so Jeff had had to leave schools that he loved. They'd moved house approximately every eighteen months, ostensibly for his father's business but really so that Damien could have a new start.

He'd have to start sweet-talking Shelley all over again when she came back from the shops. He'd have to... His spirits lifted slightly as he remembered Amy. Oh course, he could spend the day - if not the night - with her.

But first he had to get rid of any Shelley-signs, had to look as if he'd arrived at Amy's door straight from prison. She'd see that as a romantic gesture, the man being freed early and making straight for his beloved's home.

Was he even walking in the right direction? Remembering his map, Jeff fished it out and found the name of Shelley's road and the name of Amy's street. Oh good, if he kept walking in this direction he'd eventually hit a sloping road that would take him into town. From there it was a straightforward if lengthy walk to Amy's - but that suited him as he didn't want to arrive too soon. He wanted her to be up and dressed and breakfasted, ready to devote the day and night to him.

Jeff walked until he found a large waste paper bin and deposited his two pairs of dirty underpants and dirty socks. He hesitated, then kept both his sweat-stained shirts, his favourites. Luckily he'd had a long bath at Shelley's this morning so was free of the scent of sex.

Stopping for a half hour coffee-and-cooked-breakfast break in town, he made his way to the student's flat. Was it only Thursday afternoon that he'd last been here? It seemed another life away.

He rang the bell. After a brief pause it was answered by a girl with long, honey coloured hair. Christ, she looked ten times better than her photo.

'Amy?' he said, smiling widely.

'No. Amy's out.'

Fuck that was stupid of him. Now this girl was aware that he didn't know what Amy looked like. He kept his smile constant. 'She'll be back in a minute. I'll just wait in her room.'

'No you won't.'

He opened his eyes wide, held his palms out in an open, trusting gesture. 'But she's expecting me.' He stared at her uppity little neck. *And you could do with a bit of strangulation to be going on with.*

'Sorry.' She shut the door.

Little bitch. He rang the bell again. Knowing the British penchant for politeness, she'd answer, and this time he'd simply walk in. Amy had told him that she had the bed nearest the window so he could stretch out on it and rest until she came back.

He waited and waited but the flatmate didn't return to the door. As he prepared to ring the bell for the third time he saw the curtain move and realised that she was standing there with her mobile phone. Fuck it, if she called the police and made a harassment charge his parole could be revoked.

He'd have to go back to Shelley's. She'd have finished her shopping by now and he could make love to her until she virtually passed out then cook her a very special lunch.

Jeff walked to the nearest supermarket and bought a large bunch of scarlet carnations intertwined with equally vibrant ferns before hailing a taxi to take him back to his new girlfriend's. She'd have had some time to herself by now, would be surprised and hopefully pleased to see him. Everything was going to be just fine.

CHAPTER THIRTY NINE

Oh good - this was Shelley's street. Now she just had to look for the red door. As she approached the right house, Amy realised that the figure approaching from the opposite direction was Shelley herself. The counsellor had her head dipped slightly so hadn't yet seen her. She was weighed down with four supermarket carrier bags.

'Shelley, fancy seeing you!' Amy said, hoping that she didn't sound over the top. Surprise, she realised, was a hard emotion to fake.

The older woman took a moment to focus. 'Amy? What brings you out this way?'

What indeed? For a panicky second Amy forgot her story then she remembered and pulled the four leaflets from her pocket, waving them in front of the counsellor. 'I'm helping put an end to intensive farming. There's a student club I joined and they needed canvassers and as I love animals and like to walk I thought that...' She ran out of breath and stood there, clutching the leaflets and blushing hard.

'I'll take one in a minute. I just live in there.' Shelley nodded towards the red door. 'If you let me dump my shopping I'll have a free hand.'

'Can I?' Amazed at her own daring, Amy reached for two of the carrier bags. She was pleased when Shelley surrendered them without a fight.

'Thanks, I'm out of it.'

'You do look pale.' She blushed again as she realised that she was staring.

'I've not had much sleep.'

'Jean said that you had the flu.' This was great, they were chatting like old friends.

'Hasn't everyone?' Shelley said, 'But I'm over it now, going back to work on Monday.'

'I'll have moved house by then,' Amy admitted, unable to keep the news to herself.

'Well done you!' Shelley smiled weakly at her as they walked up the path towards the red door. She set down her bags, put her key in the lock. 'Do you want to come in for a quick cup of tea?'

'That'd be great. I've been walking for ages and...' As usual she was talking too much and too quickly. 'That'd be great,' she said again.

'Right, you have a seat in there and help yourself to a bottle of mineral water. I'll be through in a few minutes when I've put this lot away.'

'Do you want me to help?' Amy hovered outside the lounge door as Shelley started to disappear into the depths of the bungalow. She could see a large dining room with a door leading off, presumably to the kitchen or breakfast bar.

'No, just put your feet up and watch some TV,' Shelley called back, 'I'm fine.'

Feeling slightly self conscious at being left alone in the counsellor's lounge, Amy sat on the part of the settee which was nearest the bookshelf and scanned the titles, realising that she was familiar with most of them, but then they were the classics. She wondered where Shelley kept all her counselling books. The mantelpiece had two wooden carved statues that must be from history or mythology and there were equally Oriental-looking paintings on the far wall.

It must be brilliant having a beautiful house like this to yourself, though her new room in the Georgian house was the next best thing to having her own place. She'd give Shelley the address today in case she wanted to take a walk in her direction, see for herself.

Suddenly her thoughts were interrupted by the doorbell's ring. Amy waited, expecting the woman to answer. After a minute or so it rang again. Looking out between the slats of the blind, she could see an attractive man holding an enormous bunch of carnations. Someone was presumably hoping that Shelley would get well soon.

'Shelley - door,' Amy called, going out into the hall.

There was no answer and just then the doorbell rang for a third time, even more insistently. Hoping that the counsellor would appear at any moment, Amy walked towards the porch. She opened the door and the man looked surprised.

'Hi there, I'm here to see Shelley.'

'Hi, I think she's in the kitchen.'

'Putting away the groceries, no doubt,' said the man, walking into the house and heading for the lounge.

'That's right. Er, do you want a glass of water? She said that I could help myself.' She followed him into the room and indicated the little bottles and glasses on the gate leg table.

'I'd love one,' the man said and he looked at her so intently that Amy could feel herself blushing yet again.

Remember that you've got a new room. Remember that you're doing well at uni. Remember that Shelley cared enough to visit you. She poured two mineral waters, put one on the table for herself and handed the other to Shelley's friend. There was a brief silence after he said thanks.

'I was just admiring her books,' Amy said, resuming her seat on the settee next to the man.

'Oh, I've read most of them,' he said.

'Me too.'

'So have you known Shelley long or...?'

'Since last year.' She hoped that he wouldn't ask in which capacity. She didn't want anyone knowing that she visited the Youth Crisis Clinic almost every week. She wondered how long the man had known Shelley. He was probably a long term boyfriend, given that he'd read most of her books.

'Tea at last.' They both looked up as Shelley entered the room. She stopped just inside the door and stared, 'Oh, you're back.'

'Kenny was out. I brought you these.' The man stood up, walked over to Shelley and handed her the carnations, kissing her on the forehead as he handed them over.

'Right. Thanks.'

Watching, Amy was surprised at how offhand Shelley was. If she, Amy, had been given such a bouquet - hell, even a couple of daffodils - she'd have been truly honoured. She'd have held them close and pressed her nose into the blooms to enjoy their scent.

'I'll get another cup,' Shelley added, putting down the tray. A moment later she returned. 'Amy, this is Jeff - he's touring Scotland. Jeff, this is Amy. She's studying English Literature at the university.'

CHAPTER FORTY

Christ, this little girl was Amy - his Amy. The girl who he'd just been to visit, the girl who was out. He'd realised on Thursday that she knew Shelley in a client-and-counsellor capacity but had never expected her to end up together with him in Shelley's house. Somehow he had to keep Amy from realising that he was her pet prisoner because if she told Shelley he'd be thrown out.

Maybe he could make Amy feel so uncomfortable that she'd leave? He got up from the settee, put his cup on the little table then walked over to Shelley's chair and perched on the arm of it.

'I missed you,' he said, kissing the top of her head and stroking the back of her hair.

'I didn't have time to miss you.' Shelley's voice was clipped as she pulled away. He looked over at Amy but the teenager was staring at the floor. *Leave, leave, leave.*

'Amy, you were going to tell me about your new house,' Shelley said.

The girl looked up and smiled at them both. 'It's brilliant - I've got a really huge room and it's within walking distance of the city centre.' She named the street. 'I have to share a kitchen of course but there's lots of cupboard space and you can keep fruit in your room.'

Shelley smiled. 'Fruit, eh? And is this a bedsit or...?'

'Oh no, it's student accommodation. You pay termly in advance for your accommodation and fuel bills - but they take a deposit which they can keep if the fuel bills are especially high.'

'And your aunt's okay with that?'

Amy nodded. 'She's really pleased that I'm sorted. She's going to come through next month for the day.'

'And your parents?'

Listening, Jeff wondered what the teenager would say for she so rarely mentioned her parents.

'I've told them too.'

Shelley picked up her cup and sipped from it for a moment. 'Well, the main thing is you're happy. I was worried when Jean said you were facing homelessness.' She turned to Jeff, 'Amy's been living next door to your friend Kenny for the past few months.'

Shit, shit, shit. Now Amy would say that her neighbour wasn't called Kenny and he'd be fucked. This was all going pear shaped. A bright man just didn't expect to find his girlfriend and potential mistress in the same room.

'Oh, is he the tall man with the cats?' Amy asked, looking at Jeff.

He nodded, smiled. 'That's the one.' *Jesus, that had been a close call.* He was starting to feel caged-in, suffocated. But he couldn't run home to mother, not with Damien there. And as long as he stayed here he could possibly control the situation whereas if they started talking about him when he'd gone...

He gave Amy his best smile, glad that the small photo he'd send her had been taken years ago. 'So you're studying English, Shelley said?'

'Uh huh. We're doing poetry, drama and prose this year - but later I get to specialise in Victorian Literature.' She droned on, telling him all the things that he already knew from her letters to the jail.

'And have you always lived in Dundee or...?'

'No, I'm from Aberdeen originally,' Amy said. There was a silence during which she reached for her tea and finished it in three noisy gulps. Jeff again kissed Shelley's head and ran his hands over her shoulders, hoping that the teenager would realise that she was playing gooseberry. His spirits lifted when she took the bait: 'I should go.'

'No, stay. I want to hear more about this new place.' To his amazement Shelley then turned to him, 'Jeff, can you make yourself scarce? I want to talk to Amy. Maybe you can call me next time you're in Dundee?'

Jesus, she was only throwing him out again - and she no longer wanted a date for tomorrow. That vague next time was polite speak for go to hell.

'Sounds like a plan.' Trying to keep it casual, he stood up and walked towards the door. His throat felt tight just as it had during all those years when Damien moved in for another torture session. Was he really going to enter the demon's lair again? Oh his stepbrother wouldn't attack him now that he was a man - but he'd look at Jeff and remember. And Jeff would know that he was remembering and would feel powerless and increasingly ill.

'I'll see you out,' Shelley said in a neutral tone, standing up and following him as he walked slowly towards the door.

You mean you'll throw me off the premises, make sure I don't pocket the key.

In the porch he turned to her, the condemned man pleading for a final meal. 'Kenny really was out.'

'You could have gone to a guest house.'

He tried to pull his tense mouth into a boyish grin. 'But I missed you.'

'Jeff, you're suffocating me.'

'Can't I just sit upstairs and read a book for the afternoon? You wouldn't know I was there.'

'I would.' She shook her head forcefully.

'But I've got nowhere to go. I'm virtually homeless.'

He waited for her to relent, to realise that she was being too hard on him. Instead, she said 'That's your problem, not mine.'

White rage rushed through him and he pulled back his arm and punched her hard in the face. For a second she stood there and he rebunched his fist, ready to hit her even harder. Then she started to fall, her eyes rolling back in her head. Grabbing her, he lowered her to the porch's linoleum floor, propped her up against the side wall. Working quickly, he took the mortice key from the hook, locked the door and pocketed the key.

She might not be out for long so had to be neutralised. He took off his shirt and tore off a strip, wound it around her wrists so that he tied her arms in front. He used two larger strips to firmly bind her ankles, making sure that she couldn't kick out at him or at the door. He'd have to leave her here alone for a few minutes until he sorted Amy out.

He walked back into the lounge and the student turned round, already smiling - but her smile faltered when she saw that it was him rather than Shelley and her eyes focused on his newly bared chest.

'I should go,' she mumbled, standing up and reaching for her bag.

You sure about that? I thought we were soul mates. He wondered if he should tell her who he was but decided against it - he had no idea how this would pan out, so why admit his true identity? He'd given Shelley his real name, of course, but he could always decide to silence Shelley, whereas Amy still thought that *her* Jeff was in an English jail.

'You're not going anywhere for a while.' He saw the fear in her eyes and it pleased and aroused him. 'Thing is, I need to stay here for a few days and I really want company.'

'But my parents will worry.'

'No they won't.'

'My dad likes to know where I am.'

'I don't think so.'

She stared at him, her face an almost-comical mask of confusion. 'Where's Shelley?'

'She isn't feeling very well. She's having a lie down in the porch.'

To his surprise, the girl suddenly made a dash for the opposite door which led into the hall, rushed through it and into the dining room, heading towards the kitchen. Damn, there was a kitchen door which led out to the back garden. She could presumably alert a neighbour from there.

He raced after her and caught her around the waist as she scrabbled at the kitchen door, trying to bust the lock in her panic.

'Bad girl.'

She went limp and he scooped her up like a bride and carried her back to the lounge.

Now he had to tie her up - or, more importantly, tie her down to stop her racing off again. He settled her in a standing position, his right arm around her neck so that his forearm pressed against her throat. Holding her in front of him, they walked four-leggedly across the lounge floor.

'Open it,' he said when they reached the door that led to the porch. She did so, but let out a little cry when she saw Shelley. Looking down, he saw that the older woman's eyes were open and that a large reddish mark now stained her brow. She was still lying exactly as he'd left her and looked reassuringly dazed.

'Pick up my shirt,' he said to Amy, moving his hand to her hair and holding onto a clump of it. She squatted down slowly and came back up equally gingerly, the torn garment trailing from her right hand. Taking it, he manhandled her back into the lounge and tore further sections from the thick cotton, using it to bind her arms above her head then securing them to the table legs. He also tied her feet firmly together and warned her not to move.

Now he had to get Shelley out of the porch in case she became fully compos mentis and started kicking. He hurried out of the lounge door and knelt down to reach under her arms. As he did so, he heard a piercing scream. Fuck it, that Amy was calling for help. Ripping a sleeve from Shelley's blouse, he raced back towards the well tied teenager. She stopped screaming when she saw him though she tried to say something as he forced the gag into her mouth and tied it behind her head.

Breathing fast, he went back to Shelley again and pulled her into the lounge, leaving her just inside the door. Now he had to get the bedroom prepared for one of his prisoners. He might be holed up here for days and was going to have some serious fun.

Jeff took a last look around the lounge before he exited it. Everything was in order, Shelley lying silently on her back, her limbs bound tightly, Amy tethered to the table and soundly gagged. He could safely go upstairs and find the ropes and belts that he needed to remind them both that he was their new master, their nemesis, their king.

CHAPTER FORTY ONE

Shelley watched as the psychopath - Jeff or whatever his real name was - left the room. He was probably going to use the bathroom. Her voice trembled so badly that she hardly recognised it as her own.

'Amy?' A muffled *uh* came from somewhere beyond the settee. Either he'd punched her too or he'd gagged her. 'Amy, there's a little door in my bedroom leads to a toilet cubicle with a window. Try to get out of it. Go to my neighbour for help.'

She listened intently, heard another *uh*. Shelley wanted to go on talking but forced herself to keep quiet, knowing that he could come back at any second. She tried to pull at her bonds but the blow to her head had left her feeling weak. Deciding to conserve her little remaining energy until she really needed it, she lay motionless, her heart beating fast.

A few minutes later he reappeared in the doorway and smiled coldly at each of them in turn.

'Mm, who should I enjoy first? The shy young virgin or the middle aged whore?'

He was going to rape her now. She knew it. She just knew it. After all, she was the one who'd told him to leave. He didn't even know poor little Amy, but was sufficiently deranged that he'd hurt her or tied her up.

She kept her eyes downcast as the man approached her again, not wanting him to read the terror in her eyes. Some psychopaths fed on that terror. Her only hope was in reminding him of the many good hours that they'd had.

'Get up.' He pulled her roughly to her feet but she couldn't walk because he'd tied her ankles too tightly together. Muttering, he loosened the bindings so that she could take small, hesitant steps. 'Go to the bedroom.' She pigeon-walked obediently in front of him, her body demure, her thoughts pleading *escape, escape, escape.*

But there was nowhere to run. The hall and dining room that they walked through were windowless and she knew that there was no point in making a run - or rather a hop - for the kitchen door as she always kept it locked and he'd catch up with her in seconds. He'd also locked the front door and presumably pocketed the key.

'Get up the stairs.'

'I'm going.' She kept her voice light, a trembling mixture of pretend-teasing and appeasing. Something - presumably her rejection - had set him off and he was viewing her as the enemy. Somehow she had to convince him that she was still his friend.

They were coming to the top of the stairs now and she knew that he wanted her to go into her bedroom - but she wanted Amy to end up there as she might just be slim enough to squeeze through the concealed toilet window. That meant that, she, Shelley, must aim for the other upstairs room. Pretending to trip, she crashed into the door of the spare bedroom, stumbled through it and fell heavily on the bed.

'What the...?' Within seconds he thundered into the room after her.

'Sorry, I tripped.' She rolled over onto her side and looked up at him expectantly.

'Who sleeps here then?' He looked around the small room suspiciously.

'No one - it's for guests.' Realising that she could use the information to her advantage, she added 'I always put my friends in here. You're the first friend in years that's shared my bed.'

'So why the fuck did you throw me out?'

He sat down on the chair next to the pillow and glared at her as if she was the source of all his hatred. *Christ, this guy really was livid.* Shelley felt her heart race even faster than before.

'I didn't throw you out. I just wanted a few hours to myself - and I felt sorry for your friend Kenny.'

'There isn't a Kenny.'

'I... I didn't know that,' Shelley said. So he was a compulsive liar as well as being a possessive control freak. 'Can't we start over? We had such a good time,' she added forcing her bruised mouth into a smile.

'We have started over. Hell, I'm back, aren't I? Only this time I'm here for good.'

Here for good. In other words, she was facing a siege situation. As she smiled at him and tried to look accepting of the situation, Shelley desperately tried to remember what she'd read about such things. She knew that sometimes the captors bonded with the captives and no one was harmed but in other instances the situation turned dangerous when the police arrived.

At what stage would the police arrive? The clinic would definitely phone her neighbour when they couldn't get hold or her on Monday and Netta would let herself in with her key. Would Jeff attack Netta and possibly her husband or would he race out of the kitchen door and return home?

'What are you thinking about?'

He sounded angry again and her mind went blank. 'Can't remember so it couldn't have been important.' She smiled some more but he scowled and scowled.

'Shrink school not prepare you for this?'

Not in a thousand years. She tugged surreptitiously at her wrists but they were bound so tightly that she'd never free herself. She shook her head.

'Didn't take a seminar on dealing with violence?'

She nodded. 'They just said to sit down so that you didn't appear threatening to an angry client.' She held out her bound arms, 'Hey, I'm no threat to anyone.' But the tell-tale tremble in her voice said that she found him threatening - and that trembling presumably helped him feel big and strong. The question was, would he see her as a harmless bint who now admitted to his superiority? Or would he see her as helpless prey?

'You're not much good are you, doc?'

She wasn't a doc but this wasn't the time to discuss the small print. She shook her head. 'But I don't mean any harm.'

'Don't mean any harm?' He sounded like a school bully now, 'Picking nice guys up then throwing them out? Inviting your stupid wee clients around to the house to keep you company? Where's the fucking ethics in that?'

'Jeff, I didn't throw you out. I just wanted a few hours to myself.'

'So? I said I'd stay upstairs.'

'I wanted to... to relax and rest so that I'd look nice when I saw you next.'

She noted with relief that he was leaning further back in the guest room chair, that he no longer looked ready to pounce. She must keep on appeasing him, sought for a way to answer his second complaint, something about inviting clients to her house. How did he know that Amy was her client? Unless Amy herself had told him before she was gagged...

'I didn't invite Amy here. As I said, I wanted a few hours to myself. Jeff, it wasn't personal. You know how happy you made me. Can't we start again?'

She cringed now at the thought of his licking her and entering her - but she'd pretend to enjoy it in the hope that he'd relax. The main thing was not to make him angry. She'd said one thing which enraged him so far and he'd hit her so hard that he'd knocked her out. She had to get him on her side, prevent further violence. And for most people - lust murderers excepting - having an orgasm made their aggression abate.

'What are you thinking now?'

'Just remembering how good we were.'

'So good that you needed time out?'

'Needed time to recover!' She tried to smile, willed her body to stop quivering. She could hear that he was working himself up again, getting ready to do... whatever it was he did.

'Yeah, right. You're as selfish as the rest. You know my last girlfriend wanted a baby?'

'Is that right?' She wondered if she should admit that she was on the pill, had been for years to avoid painful periods. But he might be anti-pill if he was Catholic. 'I take it you don't want a child?'

'Too right.'

'I don't want a baby from you, Jeff.'

She watched his eyes narrow. 'No, you just wanted a one night stand to cheer you up after the flu.'

'But I asked to see you again, didn't I?'

'And changed your mind as soon as your little lezzie client came round.'

'She's not...' She wondered again how he knew that Amy was a client, 'She was delivering leaflets in the area, bumped into me by chance.'

She had to keep him talking, had to, had to. As long as they were conversing he wasn't punching her in the face.

'You really don't get it, do you, doc? That lonely little cow has probably been planning this visit for days.'

How did he know that Amy was lonely? How did... *Oh Christ.* Suddenly the information all clicked together. He'd said that there wasn't a Kenny - which meant that he'd really been waiting outside Amy's flat. Amy, who had a prison penpal and though Shelley couldn't remember the prisoner's name it was obviously Jeff.

What exactly had the teenager said about Jeff? That he was serving seven years for attacking his live-in girlfriend. And she, Shelley, had explained that seven years meant he'd done far more than slap her around. Men on manslaughter charges sometimes got similar sentences so he must have come close to killing the girl.

'Jeff, aren't most of us lonely at some time? If you untie my wrists we could hold each other.'

Her heart leapt as he stood up and she held her arms out hopefully. But instead of freeing her, he straddled her with his full weight so that she could hardly move. *Oh someone help me, help me, help me.* She stared up into his face and saw that it was pitiless.

'Oh, I want to do more than hold you. Much, much more,' he said.

Shelley tensed, expecting him to rip off her already-torn chambray shirt or undo her zip. Instead, she felt his fingers encircling her neck and moving around until they found a firm handhold. Smiling down at her in a strangely unfocused way, he started to squeeze.

CHAPTER FORTY TWO

What was happening? Was he still in the house and what had he done to Shelley? Amy pulled at the twisted cotton strips which held her wrists and ankles and at the strips which bound her to the heavy table but they held fast. Her already-distended bladder twinged as she moved and she lay still again, terrified that she'd wet herself.

Shelley had told her to escape via the bedroom toilet window but she couldn't get out of this room, and the saliva-soaked gag in her mouth ensured that she couldn't call for help. And it was pointless trying to drag the table with her all the way to the porch as the door was locked. In films, heroines were always saved at the last minute by intuitive friends - but she didn't have any friends. Even Dana didn't know that she was here.

Why had Shelley's boyfriend suddenly got mad and attacked them both? Admittedly, she'd seemed annoyed when he handed her the carnations, but the way he'd called Shelley a whore made it clear that this was a million times worse than a lover's tiff. And why had he also turned on her, Amy? And what was he going to do to her when he came back?

Amy started to cry then realised that her nose was starting to clog and that she couldn't breathe fully through her gagged mouth. Desperate for any kind of comfort, she forced herself to think of nice things such as her Aunt Gretchen, her English studies and her penpal, Jeff.

CHAPTER FORTY THREE

He could do anything to her now - and she knew it. Jeff sat back on his heels and watched the forty year old gasp for breath. He'd climaxed hugely as she fought for air, as she struggled beneath him. Now he'd let her recover before he started again.

'Want to play some more?'

Her eyes were wide with panic as she shook her head, still wheezing like an asthmatic.

'But you said you wanted us to get back to normal.' He held his hands out before him and flexed his fingers. 'This is normal for me.' She continued to wheeze painfully, lips twitching and eyelids flickering in some nervous spasmodic dance. 'Cat got your tongue? Am I not good enough to speak to now?' All the things that Damien had said to him. 'You want more of what you just had?' Christ, he was even beginning to sound like his stepbrother - the boy hadn't used the English language well.

He leaned closer, just teasing her, but she started to gasp so wildly that he feared she was hyperventilating. He'd seen young prisoners in this state when they'd been cornered: you couldn't get through to them for ages after that. And he wanted to get through to this bitch, have her fully compos mentis, remind her again and again that he was in charge.

Talking of being in charge, he'd better bring young Amy upstairs. He'd meant to lead her up here as soon as he'd got this cow settled but she'd pissed him off so much that he'd been diverted. It was madness leaving Amy down there when a neighbour could knock on the door.

'I'll be back in a mo. Don't try any funny business.' He took a length of washing line from the various ropes and belts that he'd brought upstairs with him, closed the guest bedroom door and tied a rope to its handle and to the balcony railing. Hoping that Amy hadn't managed to extricate herself, he raced downstairs.

At first he looked at the settee and the chairs and his heart sank. God, there was no sign of her. Then his gaze swept over the thin, wet-faced figure lying in bondage on the floor.

'Missed me, have you?' He stepped over her carefully, and undid the cotton bindings which secured her to the table legs. He helped her up but she immediately swayed heavily against him and he realised that she couldn't stand. He knelt - ready to tackle her to the ground if she tried to kick - and loosened her bonds but she was still unsteady. At least she was a lightweight, he thought, as he picked her up and carried her towards the stairs. He'd put her in Shelley's bedroom until he was tired of the older woman. Thereafter it would be Amy's turn to plead for breath. If only she'd been sensible and stayed home today rather than complicating matters. She'd have ultimately become his mistress whilst he lived here in the bungalow with Shelley and had a very nice life.

Now he'd have to settle for a nice few days then go on the run. It was such a pity that Faith didn't have a sister. Her parents had warned her about the lowlife found in bars and clubs, but had been oblivious to the danger that lurked within her own four walls.

This little scrap of nothingness knew where danger lay. He stared down at Amy as he kicked open Shelley's bedroom door. She'd probably spent her entire sad little life being a victim. At the moment he felt no malice towards her, but that could change.

He looked around Shelley's bedroom. Yes, the teenager would be fine here. The windows, set high in the wall, were tiny and he'd locked them both so she couldn't call for help.

He carried her over to the bed and set her down on her back. 'Stay there and you won't come to any harm.' That was probably the three hundredth lie he'd told her. He'd lied about his employment, his prison record and his previous relationships.

She didn't answer - and it was only when he glanced at her that he realised she was still gagged. He'd play safe and leave the gag in place, as well as her wrist and ankle bindings. And he'd tie the door shut so that she couldn't escape that way.

He took a last look at her before he left the room: she was lying there, motionless, the perfect victim. He could forget about her until he tired of strangling the forty year old whore. Jeff closed the door, knotted an end of rope around the handle and secured the other end to the balcony. Now he could concentrate on his uppity shrink, his rejecter, his prey.

CHAPTER FORTY FOUR

She had to act fast before he returned. Amy rocked back and forward several times to gain momentum then catapulted up into a sitting position. A heightened energy flowed through her, allowing her to jump to her feet. Luckily he'd loosened the binding between her ankles so she could walk, albeit with small, careful steps.

She scanned the room, desperately looking for a door, shuffled towards the nearest wall and began to feel quickly along its centre. If she heard footsteps she'd have to throw herself back onto the bed. *Smooth wallpaper and more smooth wallpaper and...* suddenly she felt a long crack in the smoothness and, focusing more closely, could see the outline of a small door. Moving even more swiftly, she felt along till she came to the inlet which served as a handle, curved her fingers into it and pulled. *Oh god, it was stuck.* As nothing happened, she fought back new waves of panic. *Think, think, think, think, think.* She tried again, this time pushing rather than pulling. Immediately the door flew inwards and she could see into a sunlit cubicle which contained a toilet, a wash hand basin and a small window, her only chance.

Realising that she'd run out of air, Amy took a few deep breaths as she stretched out her bound wrists and pushed at the window, expecting to meet further resistance. It opened easily and she looked out at a garden that was neatly fenced in. Immediately below the window was a ten foot drop onto a concrete path and her senses balked at the thought of jumping onto cold stone - but if she could land on the big plastic patio table it would break her fall.

Do it, do it. He could be battering Shelley now and might return for her, Amy, at any moment. What if he raped her and she became pregnant? She couldn't bear to watch her breasts and belly swell. *Do it, do it.* She clambered awkwardly onto the inner cill, her bound hands and ankles restricting every movement. Manoeuvring herself so that her feet left the window first took ages and she was sure that at any second he'd return.

Following gravity now, her feet and calves slid out, then her thighs. There was a terrifying moment when she became stuck at the waist and hung there, half in and half out, like Alice In Wonderland. Then she sucked in her stomach and pushed harder and suddenly her body was free. But the suddenness of the move meant that too much weight was held in place by her hands as they clutched the cill and they lost their grip and she felt herself falling with sickening speed, landing on her feet with a violent jar.

Immediately she hit the concrete she fell to the ground. She tried to move towards the garden gate but as soon as she moved, a terrible pain shot through her right ankle. It was accompanied by a wave of sickness that was stronger than anything she'd ever experienced before.

Move, move. She tried again but the sickness - now accompanied by a convulsive, all-over trembling - overwhelmed her. *Try to shuffle.* The hellish pain emanating from her ankle held her in place like a giant pin. She couldn't afford to be sick, not with the gag still in situ. She'd choke on her own vomit and die a horrible death. But if he found her lying here he'd surely rape or kill her and he might be assaulting Shelley right now...

Drag yourself. Crawl. Her mind urged her to move but her body just couldn't do it. As wave after wave of nausea rippled through her, Amy lay down and closed her eyes, waiting for unconsciousness.

CHAPTER FORTY FIVE

He was back again and this time he'd changed out of his torn shirt and into a pristine one. What had he done with the torn garment, done to Amy? And - more importantly, if she was brutally honest - what was he about to do to her? Already her throat felt so bruised that it was difficult to swallow and her wrists were scraped and swollen from struggling against her bonds.

'How's Amy?' If she could only keep him talking, take his mind from thoughts of further strangulation.

'She's lying on your bed feeling very sorry for herself. Your little lesbian playmate, is she doc?'

'I'm not a doctor.' She had to stop him from seeing her as someone elevated, someone he wanted to denigrate. From what he'd said earlier, she suspected his family was similar to hers. They'd both had parents - albeit in his case a mother and stepfather - who didn't have much to say to each other but who weren't deliberately unkind.

'Whatever you say, doc.'

Jesus, he really seemed to hate her now. When he'd been staying here he couldn't do enough for her - snacks and meals and as many orgasms at her body could handle. But now this pretend-love had turned to hate and she didn't know how to make things right.

'Amy isn't a friend, exactly.' He knew who Amy was - but he didn't know that Shelley knew. She could act as if she were sharing a confidence.

'Off the record, she's a client from the Youth Crisis Clinic. She's had a little trouble adjusting to student life. She's new to Dundee, her home town is Aberdeen.'

'And you've been kissing it all better?'

She watched him warily as he sat by the side of the bed. Meeting her gaze, he smiled and clambered onto her so that he had one knee at either side of her thighs. Shelley fought back a cry, terrified of what he was going to do next. Still smiling, he slid his right hand over her, toying with her breasts then brushing her belly. He'd made no attempt to remove her clothes so - apart from the sleeve he'd ripped off earlier - she was still fully dressed.

'I've been trying to help her settle here.' Damn that trembling in her voice. 'I can understand her predicament. I remember how strange it felt when I first went to university.' He said nothing, so she forced her bruised throat to talk on. 'My mum and dad had nothing to say to each other so our house was very quiet but suddenly I was in halls and there was constant noise.'

'Poor little rich girl.'

'I wish!' She tried to force her mouth into a smile, tried to ignore the fact that his fingers were now unbuttoning her blouse, 'No, I got a full grant. They still had grants in those days.' She was feeling increasingly remote from the situation and her voice seemed to be emanating from high above her head.

'So you've always had it tough? How come you managed to buy this place?'

Sheer hard work. 'Well, I had a live-in job for years so that allowed me to save up the deposit - and I walk home from work, hardly ever socialise, write articles for a magazine in the evenings.' She realised with a sense of panic that she might never write another article or ever walk home from work again.

'And here I am giving you the whole weekend off!'

When she'd thought of her death, she'd always imagined it taking place when she was an old woman. She'd either die peacefully of natural causes or take her own life to avoid an undignified end.

Maybe he was starting to see her as a human being again. She tried out a simple request. 'Jeff, could I possibly have a glass of water?'

'Possibly you could. I mean technically it's very possible. But do I want to fetch you one?' He cocked his head to the side. 'Mm, let's see. No, I don't think I do.'

Shelley felt her trembling intensify. She wasn't really very thirsty but what was going to happen when she *did* need food or water? Could a healthy woman die of dehydration in a weekend?

'What shall I do with you next?'

Please no, no, no. She'd never felt so helpless.

'What do you think, doc? Time for a little more strangulation? I mean, I know how quickly you got tired of ordinary sex.'

'I didn't get tired. Honest. I'd like us to...' She smiled invitingly, held up her bound arms, hoping desperately that he would untie her.

'No you wouldn't.' He was putting on a pretend-child voice now, 'You're just saying that.'

'I want to, Jeff, really. Please.' She relaxed slightly as he trailed his fingers down her belly and started to unbutton her jeans. Oh thank God, he wasn't going to restrict her breathing.

'Nah,' he said suddenly, taking his hand away, 'I'd rather play a little more of the gasping game.'

No, no, no. She looked up at him, searching for the words that would make him see her as a fellow human being. 'Please, I...'

But she felt his fingers wrap themselves around her neck and all too soon they were robbing her of air.

CHAPTER FORTY SIX

Unconsciousness clearly wasn't going to claim her - but at least the nausea had abated whilst she lay motionless. If only she could lie still forever, Amy thought to herself. But the day was growing colder and she was now shivering as well as trembling. Somehow she had to get help.

Slowly she raised her head and shoulders, supporting her weight on her elbows. From there she pushed herself into a sitting position and stared at her ankle which still felt incredibly odd. Jesus, it looked as if someone had pushed an orange down her sock: she'd had no idea that flesh could swell so much.

Don't look, don't think - just move, move, move. She lifted her injured leg and pushed it out in front of her then shuffled forward on her rear. Again the nausea claimed her. Amy rested for a moment then shuffled a little closer to the garden gate, which was at the end of a very long path.

How was it possible for so little movement to make her feel this sick? She remembered the heroic feats she'd read about in Aunt Gretchen's *Readers Digest*. One man had fallen into a machine which had cut off both of his legs below the knee but he'd dragged himself out of the machine and pulled himself to an occupied part of the building to summon help. There had been another man - a hunter - who'd had his arm torn off by a bear and who'd given himself first aid in the wilderness and driven one-handedly to the nearest hospital. Shuffling along a path was nothing compared to that. *You can do it*, she repeated to herself over and over as she moved slowly forward. If she didn't, both she and Shelley might die.

At last she reached the gate. *Please don't let it be locked, please don't let it be...* She took hold of the bottom and pulled inwards and it opened creakily. Amy froze, terrified that Jeff might hear and drag her back into the house. But the bungalow remained reassuringly - or should that be ominously? - silent, and after a few seconds she resumed opening the gate by careful stages until she'd created a gap that she could shuffle through.

Now she had to drag herself down Shelley's drive. She kept her injured leg held high, but every so often her thigh muscles gave out and she had to lower the leg to the ground and rest for a moment. Her ankle and foot felt so strange that she suspected she'd broken them. Amy gazed down the driveway, willing someone to pass by on the pavement so that she could call for help, but no one came.

At last she reached the pavement, saw that the street was deserted and begun to pull herself up Shelley's neighbour's path. *Almost, almost*. She concentrated on the door, but her vision started to blur. She was sweating heavily by the time she reached the step and her body shook violently as she reached for the letterbox set low in the door. Amy rattled it again and again, a metallic *help me*. She repeated the *help me* inside her head again and again but no one came. The teenager leaned back against the wall, her strength fading then tried to find the energy to speak as the door opened and a woman said 'Oh my God.'

CHAPTER FORTY SEVEN

She was sounding asthmatic again. Jeff lay beside the forty year old and watched her gasp for breath. At some point in the proceedings she'd obviously pissed herself as there was a growing stain on her chambray jeans. Fuck her, she could live with it. He'd had to do so himself often enough as a kid when his mum was out at her patisserie classes or at the boutiques and beauty shops. He'd come home from school only to find himself alone with Damien. His stepbrother would grab him by the throat and Jeff's bladder would go...

He flexed his fingers, aware for the first time that they were beginning to hurt. He'd taken longer to orgasm this time, must be tiring. He should really overcome his inertia and find himself a bottle of wine then go and liven shy little Amy up.

At last the counsellor's gasping was replaced by stenosed breathing. He propped himself up on his elbow and stared down at her. 'Feeling better?'

Her movements betraying her panic, she half nodded then shook her head.

'Want me to get you a nappy?' he asked, aware that he wasn't humiliating her as much as he wanted to.

To his surprise she croaked out 'Is that what your stepfather did?'

Put him in a nappy? His stepfather hadn't even come on the scene until he was three so... His head cleared as he realised she thought he'd been shamed and abused by the man. 'Hell no, he was always out at work.'

'But someone mistreated you?'

He didn't reply but his mind replayed, yet again, the memory of being strangled by his stepbrother, of the older boy pinning him against the tennis court grounds, the bedroom wall.

The bitch, Shelley, seemed determined to go on talking, though her voice sounded so hoarse that it was almost masculine. 'And you never told anyone before?'

Of course he'd told someone. He'd told his mum numerous times that Damien kept choking him. Sometimes he even had the red marks or fingerprint bruises to prove it, but she'd just said that boys would be boys. And anyway, Damien's mummy had died at birth so he'd spent his first three years with various babysitters whilst his daddy was working. Wasn't that a good enough reason to be extra nice to him now?

He stared at the heavily-bound woman on the bed. 'Don't try to psycho-analyse me, doc.'

Maybe if Damien had had a shrink at the time it would have made a difference. Christ knows, a couple of his teachers had suggested it. But his mother and stepfather were so convinced that they were a normal family, a Stepford-like cake baking family, that they refused to bring the professionals in.

He must have started every other childhood sentence with 'Mum, Damien has...' but she'd just smiled and fed him walnut gateau, murmuring 'You must get on with your brother.'

'But he hates me.'

'Oh Jeff, of course he doesn't hate you. He's just got a lot of energy.'

'He held my neck so I couldn't breathe.'

'How about an eccles cake? There's lots of fruit in it.'

'Look, mum,' He'd pointed to his neck, 'It's all red.'

'Well, you know he can be a bit boisterous so just keep out of his way.' So many kids had kept out of Damien's way that the school were ready to expel him when - surprise, surprise - they'd moved house and area again.

But moving house and area didn't do him, Jeff, any good. After all, he was living with the enemy.

'If he kills me you'll be sorry.'

'Jeff, you're exaggerating as usual.'

'Am I bruised or am I bruised?' Damien would get him after school on days when he couldn't get any of the younger kids.

'Well, Mrs Mansfield's son used to be bullied but now he's taking ju-jitsu lessons so that he can defend himself.'

He'd gone along to a few of the classes but he had no particular aptitude for ju-jitsu. And he was so scared of being bruised further that he found it hard to practice the moves in a realistic way.

He glared at the bondaged woman lying on the bed. Why did so many adults refuse to listen to children? Kids begged to stay off school because they were being terrorised in the playground but the parents delivered them to their torturers regardless. Others cried when the babysitter arrived and the parents said 'Oh you'll be fine' and swanned off to the theatre, leaving the poor little bastards to be sexually abused. Adults thought that children's tears didn't matter so children toughened up and became mad as hell.

He was mad again now. He repositioned himself so that he was hovering over the bitch who had rejected him.

'Please, why are you doing this?' she asked in a trembling, hoarse and strangely alien voice.

So even in her last hours of life she was searching for meaning. 'Because,' he said simply, fetching a scarf from the pile and using it to gag her, 'I can.' It was a nice move, silencing her with the gag. It added to her feelings of helplessness and made her look the part of the victim. And there wasn't a downside as he'd tired of her groans and cries.

He squeezed some more, starting and stopping as if he was milking a cow. Not that he'd ever milk a cow. It was an obscene fucking practice, taking newborn calves from their mothers so that the farmers could steal their milk. Man was the only creature who drank the maternal milk of another beast. For many years now he'd preferred beasts to humans - and nothing in Shelley's simplistic personality had made him change his mind.

He sat back as the counsellor wheezed ever closer to unconsciousness. It was time to check on his little penpal Amy though he didn't want to strangle the teenager yet. In fact, maybe he'd sweet talk her for a while. His spirits lifted as he left the room. If she took his side then there wouldn't be a witness to what he'd done to Shelley - at least, not if Shelley died.

Oh good, the rope which he'd tied to Amy's door handle and the banister was still in situ. Jeff untied it and quietly opened the door. He'd offer her a drink and a snack, would maybe build up to asking for a hug. She'd be very grateful. The situation could still be salvageable if he played his cards exactly right.

He looked at the bed. *Shit, she wasn't there.* She must have rolled under the divan to hide from him. Taking no chances, he got down on the floor a good few inches away from the edge of the bed so that she couldn't grab hold of his hair or kick him in the face.

But there was no one hiding in the dark, dusty gap: only a few box files and photo albums. He stood up and hurried to the little high-set windows but they were still locked shut. How the fuck had she managed it? He looked at the ceiling but there was no loft hatch. She must have escaped by the door then tied up the rope again so that he wouldn't suspect anything. She deserved to die.

Taking the stairs two at a time, he searched the downstairs lounge, bathroom, dining room and kitchen but the bitch had gotten clean away.

CHAPTER FORTY EIGHT

For a second, Netta simply stared at the girl slumped in her doorway. The teenager's wrists were bound tightly together in front of her and there was a rope between her ankles. Her mouth was bound with a heavy cloth strip and her face was a greyish white and wet with perspiration, a perspiration which also soaked her hair.

'I'll fetch an ambulance,' she said and raced for the phone. For the first time she wished she had a mobile. She wanted to stay by the girl, to reassure her, but it was vital that she summon help.

She dialled 999 and the operator asked her which service she required. 'Ambulance please. Oh, and police.' Someone had tied up this poor stranger and goodness knows what they'd put her through. She gave a few more details plus her name and address then hung up and raced back to the teenager, only to find that she'd slipped into unconsciousness.

Maybe it would count as interfering with the evidence, but she couldn't leave her like this. Netta knelt down and removed the saliva-soaked gag then unpicked the simple knots that held the girl's wrists and ankles. Trying not to touch any more of the ropes, she dropped them into her apron pocket then hurried back into the house and grabbed the cotton throw from the nearest armchair, using it to cover the teenager and keep her warm. There wasn't much more that she could do, so Netta simply sat down next to her and spoke quietly, ready to be a reassuring presence when the teen regained consciousness.

After ten minutes or so she heard a vehicle approaching, stood up and waved to the ambulance. Within minutes two paramedics had the girl strapped onto a stretcher. She opened her eyes as they carried her down the path.

'Can I go with her?' Netta asked.

One of the paramedics nodded and moments later the vehicle started up, presumably headed for Ninewells Hospital.

'Can you tell me your name?' the medic asked.

The girl's eyes flickered and her lips moved. It was clear that she was desperately trying to speak.

'She was gagged when I found her. She may be thirsty,' Netta offered, aware of an increasing sense of unreality. Girls simply weren't found gagged and bound in residential areas like this. She watched as the man fetched a thin cloth and used it to wet the girl's corner-cracked lips.

'Shelley,' the teenager gasped, 'Jeff.'

'Shelley, can you tell me if you have any pain?'

Netta's brain switched into gear. 'Oh God - Shelley's my neighbour. Please, stop the ambulance!'

The paramedic looked at her blankly.

'She may be in danger. I've got her spare key.'

'You shouldn't go into the house if you think that...' he started.

'Just tell the driver to stop the ambulance,' Netta yelled, and the ambulance stopped. The paramedic opened the doors and she jumped out, relieved to see that they'd only travelled two streets from her home. 'Call the police,' she shouted back, forgetting that she'd already asked for them during her original 999 call. Then she was running, her slippers slapping against the pavements, intent on saving her friend.

As she neared her house she was relieved to see two police cars drawing up outside. She shouted and waved as she ran, could see that the four constables who emerged were regarding her warily. By the time she reached them she was gasping for breath.

'In there,' She pointed to Shelley's house. 'That's where the injured girl came from. I think my friend Shelley may still be inside.'

The most senior looking policeman consulted his notes. 'And this other injured girl was tied up?'

Netta nodded, sucked in lungfuls of breath. 'She must have escaped, crawled to my door. She said something about a man called Jeff. Please, I think Shelley is still in there. I have her key.'

'We should really knock first,' one of the policemen said.

Panicking further, Netta shook her head. 'No, he tied this other girl up and gagged her. If he's tied Shelley up and hears us, he may kill her. Please, I have her key. I'll be responsible if it's all a mistake.'

The WPC of the quartet nodded sympathetically and they all began to move towards Shelley's red door.

'You two stay here,' the senior PC said indicating Netta and the WPC. As he unlocked the door, they stared at him mutinously. Netta felt helpless as she watched the three men disappear inside.

CHAPTER FORTY NINE

Hell, he needed a drink. Anger tightening his forearms, Jeff found a bottle of white wine in one of the kitchen cupboards, opened it, and took a long swig. He stared out of the window facing the garden for a moment, wondering what to do next, then took another lengthy drink.

What was...? He listened, sure that he'd heard noises at the other end of the house. Fuck it, now he heard voices. As several pairs of footsteps thundered into the lounge, Jeff took the kitchen door key from his pocket and swiftly let himself out.

Her visitors might have manned her garden gate as well as the front door. Taking no chances, he scaled the four foot fence which divided Shelley's garden from her neighbours. He did the same thing for three consecutive fences, glad that most people weren't at home on a Saturday afternoon. When he reached the garden of the fourth house, he let himself out of the garden gate, strolled casually down the driveway and into the street. As he'd feared, there were two police cars outside Shelley's house.

Forcing himself to go at a pace which wouldn't attract unwanted attention, he walked to the end of the street, only starting to run when he was out of sight.

Where would he go now? He couldn't go home to mother, not if Amy knew who he was. And she'd figure it out for sure when the prison sent back her latest letter. It would give a whole new meaning to *Dundee, City Of Discovery.*

No, he had to get out of town, away from identifying eyes, telltale throats and pointing fingers. He'd head for one of the unemployment black spots such as Newcastle where the natives were friendly, find himself a cheap rented flat and sign on for a while. When the heat died down, he'd start to travel further afield in the evenings, checking out the classier bars and hotels for an older woman who wanted a live-in man.

He half ran and fast-walked for the next hour, looking out for a taxi but not finding one, until he reached the station. Only when he slowed down did the sweat on his body begin to cool, making him sneeze. He rubbed both his arms and realised for the first time that he wasn't wearing his jacket. Oh Christ, he'd left it at Shelley's and it contained his wallet with his cash and credit cards. There was no way that he could afford a train ticket now with only a few coins in his jeans.

He'd have to take the bus back to Mum's after all, borrow some money from her and take a later train to his new location. He'd have to see Damien.

CHAPTER FIFTY

He was approaching the guest room door again - and this time he'd surely kill her. Shelley screamed through her gag but her vocal chords only produced a reedy cry. Belatedly she realised that two policemen - *two policemen!* - had entered the room. The oldest constable rushed to ungag and untie her and kept promising that everything was going to be okay whilst the youngest spoke into his walkie talkie, requesting an ambulance.

'Have you got him?' Shelley asked, her voice so hoarse that she couldn't recognise it.

'We will do. You just relax and save your strength,' the younger policeman said.

'Amy's penpal did it.' She had to let them know this before they tranquillised her or whatever it was that the hospital was going to do. She feared unconsciousness.

The older man got out his notepad and pen. 'Who's Amy?' he asked.

Oh Christ. They didn't know. Had Jeff killed Amy?

'She was visiting me. I think he tied her up.'

'Could be the young girl who jumped,' the other constable said slowly.

Shelley nodded, forced more air into her damaged throat. 'Is she okay?'

'She's gone ahead of you in an ambulance. She's going to be fine.'

Moments later a WPC came up the stairs. 'We found his parole papers in his jacket - he only got out last week. They've despatched a car to his mother's house.'

'So he's got previous for...?'

The woman nodded. 'For doing this.'

'His mum bakes cakes,' Shelley said. It hurt like hell to talk but she had an overwhelming urge to tell them everything she knew, 'He's read the classics.' She began to cry as she added 'He likes dogs.'

She stiffened as she heard heavy footsteps on the stairs. The older policeman stepped out onto the landing, came back in and said 'The paramedics are here.' Two men entered the room. Shelley scanned their faces but they looked nothing like Jeff and she relaxed back against the pillow though she still listened hard for other telltale sounds. *They hadn't got him which meant that he could be anywhere. He could come back and finish what he started while she lay helpless in a hospital bed.*

'You won't knock me out?' she pleaded through her scalded airways, 'He's still out there.'

The WPC stepped forward. 'You're going to have police protection at the hospital until he's caught.'

'And Amy?'

'And Amy,' the WPC said.

'Have you any pain, Miss?' one of the paramedics asked. Shelley nodded and indicated her neck. The man checked carefully that she still had full movement in the area. 'And can you move your arms for me?' She lifted them a centimetre from the duvet, aware that they felt like lead. Her throat felt dry as well as incredibly bruised and a low dull pain was spreading across her forehead. When the man offered her a pain killing injection she nodded gratefully.

She was vaguely aware of an acrid smell as they lifted her onto the stretcher, watched with increasing detachment as they carefully angled their bodies in order to carry her smoothly down the stairs. They carried her out of the kitchen door and down the driveway where Netta was hovering by the ambulance.

'Shelley, everything's going to be fine. I'll lock up the house and bring your nightwear up to the hospital.'

But why would she be staying overnight at the hospital? All that she had wrong with her was a very sore throat. Shelley opened her mouth to explain to Netta that nightwear wouldn't be required but suddenly the effort was too great and she shut her eyes. She heard various clanging noises as they presumably lifted her into the ambulance and she tried to look at her new surroundings but her lids remained obstinately shut. Then she heard a radio or walkie talkie crackle into life and a male voice said 'possible fracture and risk of a stroke.'

CHAPTER FIFTY ONE

He could sneak in the back door of his mother's house and steal her purse - assuming that she'd left her bag in the kitchen. That way he wouldn't have to see Damien or explain to Mummy Dearest where he'd been for the past three days, or, more importantly, where he was going next. He could take a train to Newcastle tonight, book into a cheap bed and breakfast. Shortly after that he'd start looking for ladies in search of love.

Jeff walked quickly into Dundee's city centre and caught a bus to his mother's house. Christ, he hated using buses. The proles all had coughs and the fat ones took up three quarters of the seat.

He walked to the back of the bus so that he could sit by the window. It was a nice bright January afternoon and he'd have loved to keep walking but it was best to get out of Tayside as quickly as possible - after all, the police would eventually figure out his identity and make straight for his mother's house.

Christ, his fingers hurt. He flexed them but only succeeded in extending the throbbing to his palms. Just how many times had he strangled the counsellor into submission? He smiled at the irony: she'd spent years analysing the human condition, only to pick up an ex-con and invite him home for tea.

He peered across the bus to see if he recognised the view from the far away window and a girl glanced at him and then looked quickly away.

Stupid cow, dissing him because he wasn't wearing a jacket. Faith had bought him two brilliant jackets, one black with a pure silk lining, the other a tailored beige cotton for spring. Admittedly her main motivation was to make him look nice for her mummy and daddy, but still...

Strangling wasn't good for the hands. He'd steal a bottle of his mum's headache pills and a couple of her prescription tranquillisers, otherwise he'd never sleep tonight. And he had to be bright-eyed and bushy-tailed tomorrow to start his new life. He'd have to invent a name and a last address, phone a couple of other ex-cons who'd make him some fake ID to fool the social. He'd have to give his hair a home tint then get it cut in a radically different way.

Damn, he'd been so busy planning tomorrow that he was about to overshoot his mother's street. He hurried down the bus and leapt off as soon as it stopped, keeping the momentum going. He wanted to be in and out before she, and Damien, even knew he was there.

The lack of a car in the driveway cheered him up somewhat. His stepbrother must be seriously down on his luck if he hadn't driven here. Keeping close to the hedge, he hurried up the path which led to the back door. As he let himself in, he mentally went over what he would need - cash, of course, and a jacket to replace the one he'd left at Shelley's. He could get that, and some other clothes, if he tiptoed up to his room. Shutting the back door quietly behind him, he stood in the kitchen and scanned the table and work surfaces for his mother's purse or bag but neither of them were there.

Walking with exaggerated stealth he made his way up the stairs and into his bedroom. What had he left in his jacket that he needed to replace? A comb, of course, and a handkerchief and money. And... he froze as he realised that his parole papers were in the inside pocket of his jacket, had been since his appointment a few days before. It would take the police about a minute to find them, after which they'd know exactly who he was and where he lived.

He turned to flee but found the door blocked by a burly policeman who must have been hiding in Damien's old room. Jeff got ready to tackle him but the man shouted and was answered by other men who must have been waiting in the lounge.

'So what am I supposed to have done?' he asked, heart beating overtime but trying to keep it casual. The policeman - now joined by two of his colleagues - told him as they read him his rights.

The first thing he saw as they reached the ground floor was Damien. The vicious bastard was grinning. Mummy dearest, in contrast, had a downturned mouth and was heavily flushed.

'I'll need a lawyer, mum,' he said.

'I'll phone your daddy.'

He'd need her on his side again for the next few years so managed a smile. 'And send one of your cakes.' *Preferably containing a file.*

'You're just picking on him because he's had difficulties in the past,' his mother was saying to a fourth police officer (who had what looked suspiciously like cake crumbs around his mouth) as they frogmarched him out of the door.

Seconds later they put him in an unmarked sedan that was parked in next door's driveway. That explained why he hadn't been alerted by the usual panda car with flashing blue lights and sirens. They must have been on the enhanced thinking course he thought drolly as they drove him to the local nick.

CHAPTER FIFTY TWO

'Everyone's been so nice here,' Amy said. She pushed her wheelchair back from Shelley's bed so that the counsellor could see the various gifts on her lap. 'The girls from my new house brought me these chocolates and this huge tin of sweets - I thought you might like them.' She watched Shelley closely and was relieved when she smiled and nodded. 'Gosh, Shelley, you've got even more flowers than me.'

Shelley nodded a little more. Amy glanced at her more closely then quickly looked away. Poor Shelley's eyes were completely bloodshot and her skin was a mass of broken veins. The collar around her neck hid the worst of the damage but the nurse had told her that the counsellor's throat was very badly bruised.

'I'm so glad they've caught him,' she continued, 'The police came here to tell me when I was still being X-rayed and both of the technicians cheered and...'

'I'm glad too.' Shelley's voice sounded like the boy next door's had when it was in the process of breaking.

Amy realised that she was staring. Hastily she reached for the boxes and tins of surplus calories and deposited them at the end of the woman's bed. 'Oh and Aunt Gretchen came straight through when they phoned her and the university are letting her stay in my room for a few days for free.'

The counsellor nodded and gave the thumbs up. Amy felt her heart start to beat faster. She'd been so looking forward to seeing Shelley but now she'd run out of things to say.

'Time we were taking you back now. Miss Smart needs her rest.'

Amy looked up gratefully at the nurse then back at the patient. 'I'm getting out tomorrow so...' She wanted Shelley to say that she'd see her at the Youth Crisis Clinic or that she could visit her here again.

Shelley made another thumbs up sign and closed her eyes. She must really hate her. Amy felt bereft as the nurse wheeled her back to the ward. If only she hadn't befriended Jeff, this wouldn't have happened. If only she'd listened when the counsellor said that violent men rarely changed their ways. But his mother had been so convincing as she sung his praises and his own letters had seemed equally heartfelt and sweet.

'She's really amazing, your friend,' the nurse said as they reached Amy's bed.

'I know.'

'She'd gone into shock when they brought her in - yet here she is sitting up and she's already written a statement for the police.'

'Oh, they just took mine verbally,' Amy said. They'd written it down in policeman-speak and when they read it back she'd hardly recognised her own account of what had happened. But they'd been so nice to her that she didn't mind. 'Has... has Jean from the clinic been round? And Netta?' Amy asked, keen to keep the conversation going. Visits from nurses and offers of drugs were all that livened up the hours spent in a hospital bed.

'They have but we just let them wave to her from the doorway. She's not really up to seeing visitors,' the SRN explained.

'But she saw me.' Amy winced as she pulled herself onto the bed and her injured ankle twinged. The heavy support that the technician had put on meant that her torn ligaments felt secure as long as she didn't attempt any movement.

'Oh, you're the chosen one. When we said that you'd asked about her, she insisted on seeing you. The consultant relented but advised her not to talk.'

'I... they just told me not to tire her out,' Amy said. She realised for the first time that she'd been incredibly selfish. She'd been so busy worrying about being boring that she hadn't seen things from the counsellor's point of view. The woman had been in agony whilst she prattled on about chocolate Hob Nobs and maiden aunts. She smiled tremulously, hating herself and wanting to make amends. 'Can I see her again tomorrow before I leave if I tell her not to talk?'

'I wouldn't advise it.' The nurse shook her head. 'She needs to rest, do a lot of healing. You're being discharged after breakfast by which time she'll probably have gone back to sleep.' She looked doubtfully at the flowers and plants that were taking over Amy's locker. 'Can I get you a magazine?'

'That would be brilliant, thanks.' She'd rather have had a book but apparently the library trolley was only for long-stay patients. She'd been brought in on Saturday and was leaving tomorrow, which was Tuesday. A magazine would have to suffice.

The kindly nurse brought her a teenage weekly with a cover which promised an end to boy trouble and spots. Aware that this would have to keep her occupied until bedtime, Amy scanned the pages of fashion, make up and ring tones, looking for something with which she could identify. Did no one else need articles on shyness, fear and feeling different? Did no one else run out of things to say after they'd said hello?

There was a Thin Tips column and she turned to it avidly: *fill up on salads and fruit, climb the stairs at work, get off the bus a couple of stops early.* She already walked for miles and pedalled for Scotland and it wasn't nearly enough.

Hearing footsteps approach the bed, she looked up to see a middle aged man in a white coat followed by several young men and women in equally white coats. She half expected them to produce a box of Persil.

'I'm...' She missed his name but smiled and smiled, 'So how are we?'

'Fine, my ankle feels a lot better since they strapped it up and I've visited my friend in a wheelchair and I'm getting to go home tomorrow morning in an ambulance.'

The man - presumably a consultant - looked at his notes. 'And we're arranged for you to have a physiotherapist?'

Amy nodded. 'She's already shown me how to use my crutches but next week she's going to show me specific ankle and foot exercises. Apparently there's too much swelling to start now.'

'That sounds about right.' The consultant turned a page, 'Do you have any questions?'

Any chance of a diet pill? Amy forced back the thought. 'I just wondered when I could go back on my exercise bike?'

To her surprise, the man looked shocked. 'Exercise bike? Oh, preferably never. You'll always be left with a weakness in that area. You don't ever want to twist it again.'

Never exercise again. Amy felt an internal pressure, as if someone had pushed a thick tube from her lungs to her abdomen. She had to persuade him to let her use her bike - and that need overcame her usual shyness. 'But it's not as if I broke a bone or anything.'

The man grimaced. 'Sometimes a clean break is much better, because the bone just knits smoothly together. What you've got is altogether more complicated, as some of the ligaments are badly stretched whilst others are stretched and torn. That's why we've got you on such strong anti-inflammatories and regular icepacks, to try to bring the swelling down.'

'So, if I can't use my bike, can I work up to a fast walk?'

Again the medic looked doubtful. 'It'll be several weeks till you're off the crutches and then you'll have to walk slowly for a few more weeks to avoid losing your balance. After that, you'll still have pain if you try to speed up or put weight on that limb for very long.'

God, she couldn't even walk aerobically any more. For the first time, the full realisation of her injury hit her. The X-ray department had told her to keep her leg elevated as much as possible when she got home and to use icepacks every three hours but she hadn't realised that her mobility would remain so limited. The physiotherapist had said 'Let's get you back to normal as soon as possible' so she'd just assumed...

'You need to learn patience with an injury like this,' the man concluded. He talked to the medical students about the importance of early treatment in such injuries, and everyone went away.

Amy lay back against the pillow as new levels of dread washed over her. If she couldn't exercise she'd put on weight and she already felt far too heavy from lying around in here for the past three days. She was sure that they were buttering the toast rather than using low fat margarine and yesterday they'd tried to give her chocolate sponge for dessert. She'd always assumed that hospital were healthy places but now she knew that they made you lethargic and fat.

Wearily she returned to the teenage magazine. Typical - the page after *Thin Tips* was followed by a *Chill Out* column which suggested inviting your mates round for pizza, deep fried chicken wings and garlic bread.

Hastily she turned the page again and found a Pick-Up-A-Penpal piece. *Been there, got the blood-spattered T-shirt.* Unsure whether to laugh or cry, she pushed the magazine towards the bottom of the bed. The movement spread a strange new pain up her ankle and down her foot whilst a different, sharper pain ricocheted up her calf.

She had to keep fit, had to, had to. Maybe she could do some arm exercises to burn off a few calories? Amy extended her arms and began to windmill them back and forth.

The woman in the next bed sat up and stared at her quizzically. How she wished she was alone in her room. 'I'm trying to keep fit,' she admitted.

'Kit? I think she's at the nurses station,' the patient said.

'Oh right.' Amy smiled politely and tried to keep windmilling. But she soon had to admit defeat, her arms aching from pulling herself along to Netta's house to summon aid.

'You're lucky to be alive,' Aunt Gretchen had said, but at this moment Amy didn't feel lucky. The careful dietary routine - occasional binges excepting - that she'd followed since she was eleven was starting to break down and she felt vulnerable and scared. What if she ballooned up like mum and dad and all the girls at her new house laughed at her? What if she was so fat by the time she graduated that no one ever wanted to share a house with her again? Would she have to live alone, her thighs rubbing together and bleeding as she addressed envelopes for a living until she died?

'Hot chocolate or tea?' the orderly asked as they brought the trolley round.

'Black tea with no sugar, thanks,' Amy said, smiling gratefully. She continued to smile after refusing the digestive biscuit (eighty calories) and the coffee cake (don't even think about it.) When she'd been given the room in Ensley House she'd felt hopeful and happy but now the future was dark with uncertainty again.

'There's a huge box of crystallised fruits making the rounds,' the orderly said, 'Come all the way from Australia from a grateful patient. Apparently he took ill whilst he was here and wanted to thank the nurses with some Aussie fare.'

'Not for me. I'm full thanks,' Amy said when the enormous basket of glistening syrupy peaches, pineapple rings and sugar-speckled pears reached her bed. She exhaled with relief as the woman took the basket away. This time her willpower had held out but what about the next time and the next? How would she distance her mind from food now that she no longer had Jeff to write to? How could she burn off the calories when she could hardly move?

Amy looked around the ward, a ward where almost everyone was eating and drinking. Suddenly she understood why people overate and then pushed their fingers down their throats.

CHAPTER FIFTY THREE

The lounge was cold and dimly lit when they entered.

'I'll put the kettle on,' Netta said, 'And bring through that sponge I made.'

'You're an angel.' Shelley put down the carrier bag containing the two dozen cards she'd received at the hospital. She switched on the gas fire, opened the curtains and moved the gateleg table back to its usual position. By the time that Netta brought the refreshments, the place was beginning to look and feel like home.

'I put today's mail on top of the TV,' her neighbour said as she cut and served the buttercream sponge. Shelley investigated and found a subscription magazine and yet another get well card. She opened it and saw that it was from Dougal: he'd always been spectacularly slow.

'I'd have had so much to do if you hadn't helped me,' she said now and watched her neighbour flush with pleasure.

'I'm just glad to have you back.'

They ate the cake and drank the tea then Shelley went to the bathroom to wash the buttercream from her fingers. On the way back she noticed that the ansaphone was indicating that the tape was full.

'I'm just going to listen to my messages,' she called - and it was only when her voice cracked mid-sentence that she remembered it wasn't yet back to normal. She'd gone down with a bad cold after being admitted to hospital, something which had further complicated her recovery.

Hoping that it wasn't bad news, she sat down, pressed play and listened as various counsellors who she'd previously worked with wished her well. There was also a lengthier message from the owner of the anorexia clinic where she'd lived and worked for several years.

Suddenly there was an ominous silence then an unfamiliar male voice said *'He hasn't forgotten you and he never will.'* The tone wasn't that of a well-wisher. Shelley trembled as the rest of the messages were played, kind words from former clients and the editors of two psychology journals. *He hasn't forgotten you, hasn't forgotten you, hasn't forgotten you...* At the end of the tape she talked to Netta and they listened to the male stranger again.

'Take the tape from the machine and I'll drive over to the police with it now,' Netta offered.

Shelley hesitated then shook her head. 'No, we can't even prove that the message was meant for me, far less that *he* had anything to do with it. I'll keep the tape but won't take it any further unless I get a similar call.' Knowing that she had to get back to normal, she added 'Can you come for coffee tomorrow morning? Say about ten?'

Netta looked slightly surprised. 'Are you going to be okay on your own till then?'

'Hey, I'm forty now - practically middle aged! I've lived alone for years. I'll be just fine.'

'If you're middle aged, just what does that make me?' asked Netta, who was pushing fifty.

They both laughed then Shelley touched the older woman's arm: 'Really, thanks for everything.'

She looked at the clock when Netta left. It was 11am. She might as well put a baking potato in the oven for lunch at 12.30. She walked into the kitchen, noting its unused, slightly musty smell. Shelley opened the wall cupboard and saw that her neighbour had bought her a few extra tins, but that the bottle of wine that she kept for visitors had gone. She felt puzzled for a moment, then realised that Jeff Metcalfe must have taken it. At the thought of his hands all over her cupboards - and, she fought back the thought, *all over her* - she felt sick and dirty. She showered and dressed again then remembered that she'd initially gone into the kitchen to switch the oven on.

Concentrate on the good things. Remember how many people phoned and sent cards. She double checked that all of the doors and windows were locked then phoned the clinic.

'We've had three unwanted pregnancies today,' Jean said.

They passed the unwanted pregnancies on to a young people's contraceptive agency, passed the over and under eaters on to their family doctors, passed... As she sat there clutching the phone, Shelley realised that at work she was little more than a human signpost. Go here for employment information, go there for housing benefit.

'Are you okay?' Jean asked.

I had sex with a psychopath then was almost strangled to death. I feel just brilliant.

'I'm just... I'm re-evaluating a lot of things.'

'I could come round after work.'

No, she had to get back to normal, couldn't let her friends babysit her.

'Jean, I'll be out of it by then. Don't laugh, but I'm going to spend the afternoon digging up my carrots and harvesting my sprouts!' Several of her neighbours had sent cards and gifts to the hospital and she wanted a casual way to call by and thank them. She produced far too many vegetables for one person so had often given them baskets of fresh vegetables in the past.

'Rejected for a sprout,' Jean said in her usual droll voice. Shelley could picture her there behind her desk, could imagine her looking up and smiling as the door opened. She realised that anyone - absolutely anyone - could walk in.

'Be careful, Jean.'

'I'm always careful,' the older woman said.

'I mean, maybe we should lock the door, have a *Ring The Bell For Attention* sign.'

She heard Jean's hesitation. 'They wouldn't use it, Shelley. You know what some of them are like.'

Shy, frightened, unsure if they belonged there. She was beginning to understand how they felt.

That afternoon she did the vegetarian benefactor bit, feeling self conscious when her neighbours glanced at the silk scarf around her neck. Everyone dropped their voices and had softened expressions in their eyes as they asked her how she was feeling. 'I just want to get back to normal,' she said again and again.

When the last winter cabbage had been dispatched, she returned relievedly to the house and checked all the locks again. Then, hearing a cracking noise, she raced to the front door, only to find a free newspaper pushed through the letterbox. *Relax, relax.* She tried to watch the afternoon movie but kept dozing off then waking with a start, sure that someone was watching her. He hadn't gotten bail but was on remand in prison. What if he got out on a technicality?

As the day moved into the early evening, she wrote a few thank you letters and tried to read a health magazine but found that she simply didn't have the concentration. By 9pm she could hardly keep her eyes open and knew that it was time for bed.

As she climbed the stairs, Shelley's mouth went suddenly dry and she began to shake. She forced herself to enter her bedroom but when she looked at the bed all she could think of was waking up with his arm resting lightly around her neck, his hardness nestling between her buttocks. And she couldn't go to the guest bedroom because he'd... he'd done what he did to her in there.

He'd done it and he could do it again, even if he didn't get paroled for years. She couldn't go on living here. Shelley put on all of the lights in the downstairs part of the house then sat in an armchair waiting for morning to come.

CHAPTER FIFTY FOUR

Was she never going to answer? Amy dialled Shelley's number for the twelfth time that month and got the familiar ansaphone. At the sound of the beep she hung up. It had been three weeks since the counsellor had left Ninewells Hospital but she still wasn't back at the Youth Crisis Clinic and Jean had admitted that they didn't yet know when she'd return.

Slowly Amy turned away from the hallway payphone on her crutches and hobbled back to her room. She was just about to lie down on the bed when someone knocked on her door. For a moment her hopes rose - after all, Shelley had visited her when she lived with Dana. But when she opened it she saw that it was Marianne and Lisa who lived upstairs. The younger one had apparently become homesick last term and had gone home to her parents for a few days, a course of action which Amy could understand.

'Hi, we're all going to the Rep for seven thirty,' Marianne, the more extrovert of the pair, said casually, 'Susan's brother's going to drive us there in his people carrier so your crutches'll fit in the back.'

The Rep was Dundee's big glass-fronted theatre, a building that she'd walked past and admired. 'That would be brilliant.' Amy could tell that she was grinning too widely to look cool but she didn't care. Luckily, Aunt Gretchen had given her a hundred pounds when she got out of hospital, so she could afford this trip and many more.

'Okay, we're meeting up in the foyer at seven.' When all nine of them had visited her in hospital they'd revealed that the whole household often went to the cinema or to a musical hosted by a local amateur dramatics club.

Now that she had a purpose, Amy suddenly felt re-energised and hobbled over to her wardrobe to find her favourite scoop-necked blue top and best jeans. She also looked out the big shoulder bag from Aunt Gretchen. It allowed her to carry water - for her torn ligaments meant that she had a higher than normal temperature and was often dehydrated - yet still have both hands free. Coping for long distances on her crutches was impossible, but she took several short walks around the grounds every day. She was also keeping her weight down by living mainly off fruit.

But she'd live dangerously and have a tuna salad before she left and would take a bottle of mineral water with her to sip during the interval. She'd take another bottle for Susan who presumably wouldn't want alcohol as she was on anti-epilepsy pills.

The remainder of the afternoon was spent alternately getting ready and resting, then at the appointed time Susan's brother helped her into his car. Amy spent most of the short drive just looking out of the window and recovering her energy as the other girls chatted and laughed. Seven of them were going to see an Ira Levin play, the other two having seen it before.

At the interval she hobbled out to use the ladies whilst the other girls raced to the bar. As she made her way back across the upstairs foyer, she noticed a phone and realised that she could casually phone Shelley so that the counsellor would know that she wasn't being a burden, that she'd made new friends.

Taking the piece of paper with Shelley's number on it from her bag, Amy dialled and heard the ansaphone click into life yet again. Damn, she'd have to leave a message: the woman was permanently out.

'Hi Shelley. I'm at the Rep with some of the other girls from my house and we're having a really nice time.' She realised that she hadn't said who she was and added 'Er, it's Amy.' To her surprise Shelley immediately answered the phone.

'Amy, how are you?'

Ready to fall over. She tried to ignore the constant throbbing in her foot as she leaned heavily against the wall. 'I'm good. I've been phoning to see how you are but keep getting the ansaphone.'

There was a pause then Shelley said 'I'm screening calls.'

'Oh right.' Did most people screen calls?

'If I'd known it was you...' Shelley added. 'And you say you're at the Rep? I can hear lots of background noise.'

'Everybody's come out for a drink at the intermission.' She felt proud to be there, even if she didn't want a bottled beer or rum n' black like the other girls.

'What's on?' Shelley continued and for a few moments they discussed the play and Amy had to add more coins to the box.

'I'll have to go soon,' she admitted, 'I've just run out of change.'

'Do you have enough to get a taxi home?'

Enough for several taxis home. 'I'm sorted - one of the girl's brothers is driving us back.'

'And you can get around all right on your crutches?'

Only as far as the fruit bowl and the kettle. 'Well, I won't be back at uni for another couple of weeks cause there's too many stairs and corridors. But I can hobble out to a car or walk for a few minutes at a time.'

'So if I ordered you a taxi for 2pm tomorrow, could you come and see me? I'd pay both ways.'

This was brilliant. Amy smiled into the phone. 'Course I can.'

They finalised the arrangements then Amy hung up and made her way back to the other girls.

'We thought you'd got lost,' Lisa said.

Amy felt surprised that they'd noticed she was gone. 'Just phoning Shelley.'

'Is she any better? It was awful, what she went through.'

'She sounds fine.'

'I shuddered when I read about it in the papers,' the redhaired girl whose room was nearest the kitchen admitted, 'And we didn't have any names then. It was only when the police came round asking questions that we realised one of the girls was you.'

'Oh I got off lightly,' Amy said, forcing back the memory of Jeff carrying her up the stairs, 'Whereas poor Shelley...' She broke off, unable to imagine how the woman had survived being strangled again and again. What must the pain be like as your nerves were crushed, as your airways narrowed? And how often did you relive the terror of approaching death?

CHAPTER FIFTY FIVE

She'd been looking forward to seeing Amy but now that the teenager was due, she felt slightly nervous. She had several changes to announce - and you didn't have to be Einstein to know that the Amy's of this world resisted change. Indeed, an exercise-conscious person like Amy probably wouldn't be adapting to life on crutches. She'd seen other teenagers turn to Prozac after they'd suffered similar injuries.

Shelley was putting out the snacks-on-sticks when the taxi arrived. She watched through the blinds as the driver came out and opened the passenger door. A few minutes later Amy started hobbling up the drive on her crutches: they'd arranged that she enter through the back door rather then attempt the stairs which led to the front of the house. She stopped and stared for a moment when she saw the sign indicating that the property was for sale.

Shelley hurried around to the back but waited until she heard the teenager approach before she cautiously unlocked the gate.

'Hi, come on through!'

'Thanks.' Amy smiled widely but Shelley could see the strain on the girl's damp features. Despite the freezing February wind, Amy was only wearing a sweatshirt over her black cords. 'I see you're leaving us,' she added.

'Leaving this street - but I'll still be living locally.' She ushered Amy through to the lounge, got her settled in one of the armchairs and poured the tea.

'Will you be going back to the clinic?' Amy asked softly.

Not in Dougal's lifetime. Shelley shook her head. 'I had some issues there towards the end. This move - it's about work as well as accommodation. I'm renting a big farmhouse on the outskirts of Dundee.'

'You're going to run a farm?'

She was the tenth person to say that. The counsellor smiled. 'No, I'll run it as a residential unit for people with eating disorders. I did similar work before.'

'On the NHS?'

Shelley shook her head. 'Fraid not. Like the last place I worked it'll be private. But once we're established we can consider subsidising the occasional patient who really needs our help.'

'You're running it with other people?'

Informal bodyguards. Shelley nodded. 'There's a woman who graduated with me who's agreed to be the second counsellor. We'll live there alongside a maximum of ten patients. And I'll also employ a cleaner, driver and cook, all very much part time.'

'You seem to have thought it all out,' the nineteen year old said, looking impressed.

That was the understatement of the century. 'I've thought about... well, tried not to think about anything else.'

Amy paused then leaned forward. 'Is this due to... Are you leaving here because of what *he* did?'

She might as well be honest. Shelley nodded. 'I can't sleep here. I've been staying at my neighbours every night.'

'Couldn't you get a lodger?'

The counsellor smiled inwardly, wondering if the teenager would go on to offer her rent. 'I could but I don't want to go on living here, just in case he ever gets out.'

'You think he'll come back?' For the first time the girl looked alarmed.

Shelley mentally kicked herself for being so insensitive. 'It's a chance in a million - but moving will give me extra peace of mind.'

'He won't know where I am either,' Amy added, 'I mean, now that I'm in my new place.'

Oh good - it was an obvious subject change away from psychotic stranglers. 'So how is your new place?'

Amy's face lit up and she sat up straighter then winced and moved her ankle more carefully on the cushioned footstool 'It's great. We have all these nights out and the university got me a student to buy in my fruit whilst I'm on my crutches. And Susan who lives upstairs brings me the other students notes so that I don't get behind.'

'It sounds perfect. Is there a spare room for the oldest swinger in town?' Shelley joked. They both smiled then Shelley added 'Actually, this place that I'm setting up sounds very similar to where you're staying. I mean, every patient will have his or her own room.'

'And it's a farm, you say?'

'Well, it's a farm*house* - the neighbouring farmer has bought most of the land so it's only the house and a large fenced off yard that's for rent, and if it works out I have the option to buy.'

'And it's just outside Dundee?'

'Uh huh. It's accessible enough that girls - and the occasional anorexic boy - can come and stay there, but not so accessible that their mothers and fathers can pop through all the time.'

'Because...?'

Shelley realised that Amy was using shorter sentences than before, that she seemed to be listening rather than talking. 'Because sometimes the parents have contributed to the teenager's problems, however unwillingly.'

The nineteen year old nodded slowly. 'My parents have a problem with food. I mean, they don't think they do but they're really huge.' Her fair hair had fallen over her face but she peaked at Shelley through her fringe. 'Do you... if you decide to subsidise some patients, could my mum and dad come to you?'

So she'd been right after all - Amy's background was dysfunctional.

Shelley searched for a tactful answer. 'Amy, they don't sound like ideal candidates. I mean, if they don't recognise that there's a problem then they won't want help. I know it's hard, but they'll have to admit to themselves that their behaviour is destructive and for some people that only happens when they have a heart attack or a stroke.'

'The skin of mum's breasts tears with the weight sometimes,' the teenager added, her voice hard with tension, 'And dad gets terrible sweat rashes but they just don't seem to care.'

She'd seen such blood, sweat and tears before when she'd done a placement with a compulsive eaters group. 'Oh they probably care a great deal, and want to be different, but just can't imagine a future without excess food.'

'So it's only when they can't imagine a future at all - when they're really ill - that they'll change?' Amy asked.

Shelley grimaced, aware that some people ate their way into the grave, but she was determined not to further frighten Amy. 'Or it could happen before that. One insult too many makes some compulsive eaters go for help. Others react to the break up of a relationship. Some will be moved by reading an article written by someone who's suffered in a similar way and gone on to take control.'

The girl pushed her tea away. 'Oh, they've suffered. Mum hardly goes out and Dad's exhausted when he comes home from work and they're jealous of Aunt Gretchen so keep having goes at her.'

'They're probably jealous of you, too,' Shelley said.

Amy's head jerked up and she stared, open mouthed at her. 'Jealous of me? But they have each other and... I have no one.'

'That's not true. You have your aunt plus your new friends from your house. And I hope that you and I are going to keep in touch?'

To her amazement - she really was losing the plot when it came to reading people's minds - Amy burst into tears and it was a good five minutes before the counsellor could work out what she was saying.

'You've been so good to me and I almost got you killed.'

So that was the big lie that Amy had fed herself. Shelley leaned forward. 'Amy - you jumped from a window and saved my life.'

'But if I hadn't been in touch with Jeff...'

'All that you did was write him letters. I'm the idiot who picked him up and brought him home!'

'But...'

'There's no but about it. I had cabin fever after the flu, went out and acted on impulse. It has nothing to do with you.'

'I keep going over and over it, wishing I hadn't gone to that word processing place, wishing I hadn't met Barbara or hadn't written when she gave me his address.'

Shelley sat back in her chair, glad that Amy had at last admitted to going over and over certain events. It was healthier than repressing everything. In time - unless there was an underlying neurosis - the obsession would fade. It was advice that she repeated to herself over and over when she woke up in the night sure that his hands were about to encircle and crush her throat.

'We'll get through this, Amy,' she promised shakily.

The phone rang and she flinched, hurrying to the lounge door as the ansaphone clicked on. She relaxed as the message came through, returned to her chair.

'Oh good, that's the carpet warehouse - my floor coverings are being fitted tomorrow afternoon.'

'At the farmhouse?'

'Uh huh. The farmer's wife had a love affair with primary colours but I don't think you can subject sick people to scarlet rugs.'

She watched as Amy froze. 'And you think anorexics are sick?'

'Well, if someone is dizzy, weak, has no concentration and loss of appetite, we can hardly describe them as being fit.'

'But not sick as in mentally ill?'

Shelley shrugged. 'The yearning for thinness starts in the mind and influences the body. But a starving patient undergoes biological changes that make it hard for her to eat so by then the body is working on the mind.'

'I want to be slim,' Amy admitted tremulously.

'With your parents being large, that's all the more understandable,' Shelley said. She took a deep breath, hoping that she wouldn't scare the teenager off, 'But there's a huge difference between being healthily slim and being unnaturally thin, Amy.'

'You think I'm too thin?' the teenager looked surprised.

Shelley nodded. 'And I remember you saw something satanic in your flatmate's cheese!'

Amy stared then reluctantly broke into a smile. 'Well, it's sixty percent fat.'

'So it stays in the stomach for a long time and fills you up.'

'I didn't know that.'

'One of the things I'll be doing is helping people to stop fearing food, to think more realistically about their energy needs.'

'It sounds brilliant,' Amy said.

Shelley pursed her lips. 'You wouldn't actually say that if you were anorexic. Most of the girls who'll come to us will only do so to avoid being sectioned. They'll hate the fact that we make them eat every three hours, monitor them so that they can't over-exercise and weigh them naked so that they can't put weights in their pockets and shoes.'

'I can't imagine being made to eat that often,' Amy admitted, 'I felt bad enough when Dana used to give me her chips.'

Shelley looked thoughtfully at the girl. 'I think you're too concerned with thinness and food but I don't think you're anorexic and you definitely don't need anything as intensive as what we'll be doing on the farm.'

'Just as well if it's expensive,' Amy said.

For a moment the forty year old felt guilty. 'Well, it's hard to get public funding so I need enough to pay my wage and that of my therapist.'

'And the cook and everyone else you mentioned,' Amy said slowly, 'I can see that it all mounts up.' She paused then said casually 'Maybe I can visit some time? Susan's brother might give me a lift.'

'No need. I've employed an occasional driver - a local pensioner - so that the girls can be collected from the railway station, taken to the dentist or into town to buy new clothes. She'll be delighted to collect you and bring you home.'

'I'll be the fattest one there,' Amy said with a self conscious laugh.

Shelley smiled back. 'No, I will by at least three stone.' Then she got serious, 'Actually I thought you could come and see me in my private rooms which are at the back of the house.' She took a deep breath, not wanting the teenager to feel that she was hiding her away. 'It's just that these ten patients will be together for many weeks and will form a certain dynamic. A stranger coming in to the group will disrupt all that - and as you've recognised, they'll all be comparing their bodies to yours.'

'Okay, you can smuggle me in the back door at midnight for a private tour,' Amy said with a smile.

It would take more than a private tour to really help Amy. 'I was thinking - if you want - that we could make it a weekly thing. You know, talk about whatever's troubling you?'

'Like at the Youth Crisis Clinic?' Amy asked.

Latterly she'd spent much of her time at the clinic dispensing leaflets. 'Well, therapeutic rather than just practical. I trained as a psychotherapist so can go to the roots of a problem if I get the chance.'

Amy looked uncertain. 'Do you think I have serious problems?'

None that couldn't be cured with the right support. 'No, I think you have very few - but I suspect that you're already worrying about things like graduating, for example, instead of looking forward to the new possibilities they open up.' She leaned closer to the girl, 'All I'd be doing would be looking at where your wrong-thinking started, what's made you see the world as such a frightening place.'

'But it is frightening - we almost died,' Amy said.

Shelley paused for a second then grinned at her. 'Hey, who's counselling who?' She collected her thoughts and added, 'I know what you mean, but worrying for years about meeting someone like Jeff wouldn't have made us any less afraid when we actually met him. It would still have been years spent worrying in vain.'

Amy nodded slowly. 'I really would like to be less anxious.' She moved her foot on the cushions, winced visibly then added 'Though I'm already doing some of what you said - you know, talking less and asking the other person questions.'

'Hell, I'm already virtually redundant,' Shelley said and they both laughed. 'So, have I got myself a weekly patient?' she added casually.

Amy paused then smiled widely and nodded. 'That'd be great! I'll ask Aunt Gretchen for the money and pay her back when I start work. Just how much do you charge per hour?'

Shelley swallowed hard as she realised that the girl who'd saved her life expected to pay for therapy.

'For you,' she said softly, 'It's free.'

CHAPTER FIFTY SIX

There was hope - the old bat had come through for him again. Jeff sat on his bunk and read his mother's latest letter. Irene is a charming girl but very lonely. I'm sure that I mentioned her to you when you were home with us recently. (Dad's so sorry that he missed you.) She has her own wholemeal bakery business, supplying gingerbreads and muffins to health food stores and small local shops and cafes, but she also makes the little pottery figurines and numbers for my cakes.

That was a good sign. Artistic people tended to be fucked up. It went with the territory. Not that the teacher or the counsellor that he'd dated had exactly played with a full deck of cards. Faith had been a miserable cow yet was ready to inflict her pointless existence on a baby whereas Shelley was a workaholic who started writing articles the moment she shut the door at night.

He was willing to bet that particular door now had several more locks on it - not that they could protect her from the increasingly strange phone calls she was getting. He'd persuaded an ex-con on the outside to give her a bell - and as of next week the man was going to start leaving the occasional dead bird outside her home.

Jeff smiled to himself as he added various refinements to his plan. They had to be local birds, of course, ones which could have died of natural causes: that way she couldn't prove that it was a vendetta. And - like the phone calls - there mustn't be too many and they mustn't be too obvious a threat. In other words, nothing that the boys in blue could pin on him or on any other con. But she'd know that he was behind each subtle act of violence and would hopefully keep her evidence muted at the trial.

Even if she didn't, he'd soon get out. His lawyers were delighted that she was a divorcee, something which always made juries think *desperate woman*. And, to back this up, she'd picked him up in the street and gone to bed with him that very first afternoon. She'd had sex with him again on the Thursday night, several times on the Friday and on Saturday she'd brought him breakfast in bed and made a date for the Sunday. It was pure fucking Romeo and Juliet.

His take on it would be that she'd gotten angry when he'd left, that she'd still been enraged when he came back with his peacekeeping flowers. So they'd had a fight in the porch and she'd lunged at him and he'd struck out to defend himself. The fact that he'd tied her up was a bit more awkward, but he could say that she'd been nicest to him when they were experimenting and had told him she enjoyed bondage. He'd heard a lot less likely stories that other prisoners had told on the stand. The jury just had to accept that there had been several days worth of consensual sex which had boiled over into anger and gone too far.

Amy, of course, was harder to explain away and was probably the victim that he'd serve most time for. The daft little bat had jumped from a window to raise the alarm.

He read a little more of his mother's missive. I won't mention your earlier sentence to Irene, of course - there's no point in confusing the issue by telling her about your scrape with that religious teacher. No, I've simply explained how that jealous anorexic girl and her psychiatrist stitched you up. Jealousy is a terrible emotion and seems especially prevalent in young people. I always worked hard to make sure that you and Damien had the same toys and similar clothes.

Yeah, rubbish supermarket clothes because all of the money went on the house and the garden, on impressing the neighbours. And nice genteel toys that Damien could hit me over the head with whilst you hid yourself away in your kitchen and made currant buns.

He read on. He's back in his old room, now - apparently the second hand car market has dried up in Basingstoke and he wants to live here quietly. That said, he's been out very late most nights - Dad says the kettle is still warm when he gets up at seven for work!

Damien would be selling ketamine round the Dundee clubs or doing Christ knows what. He had a sudden vision of his stepbrother being sent here to HMP Shotts and ending up on the same wing, sharing the same showers. He, Jeff, would ask to be transferred right away.

Think positive. It was alright being here. He recognised a couple of people from his first stretch who'd been moved to Lanarkshire, and the place had a reasonable gym.

He skimmed his mother's next two paragraphs. *Here are Irene's details.* It was followed by a Broughty Ferry address which he knew to be a quiet beach-based part of Dundee. *She's thirty nine, from the Outer Hebrides, and has never been married. She came here with her parents in the seventies and stayed on in the family home when they died.*

Aha, so his new bint had property. Which was just as well, as making muffins and cake decorations presumably didn't bring in much money. There again... *She has mail order contacts all around the world who send her unusual decorations and has told me, off the record, that they fetch far more than the ones she configures herself.* Oh good, she could keep him in the style to which he'd like to become accustomed, could stay home with her baking powder whilst he enjoyed strangulation sex with desperate whores.

And he would do, only next time he'd play further away from home or choose victims that no one cared about. Just look at Fred & Rose West who'd sexually assaulted girls from orphanages - they'd gotten away with lust murders for over twenty years. Peter Sutcliffe had also chalked up a large body count through concentrating mainly on stabbing prostitutes and Dennis Nilsen had taken the same approach, strangling rent boys and homeless men. This time he, Jeff, would find similar victims and wouldn't attack whoever he lived with. After all, no one had ever linked him to the death of that junkie whore or that fellow con.

He picked up his mother's letter again. Irene prefers writing to phoning, at least in the first instance. She hopes that's okay? She also apologises for the photo which was taken yesterday in one of those little booths whilst she was recovering from the flu. (Even your daddy, who never gets ill, has now had that same flu!) I've shown her all my photo albums of you - it's such a shame that the photographer lost your graduation photos - and she was very impressed.

What photo? Christ, there it was, tucked into the corner of the envelope. He'd almost binned it. He shook out the coloured square and stared at the moderately pretty little face that smiled self consciously across at him. It was framed - or rather overwhelmed - by the heaviest mane of jet black curls that he'd ever seen. It covered her forehead, stuck up at the top and billowed out at the sides, coming to rest heavily on her shoulders. She must want to enter the Guinness Book Of Records for having the most head hair or else she was phobic about having a trim.

Her features, set in pale skin, were delicate but weren't enhanced by any make up and she was wearing a beige blouse or jumper. In other words, a reasonable looking woman who just didn't make the best of herself.

He was just the man to help. Jeff picked up his pen. Dear Irene, I'm so pleased that you found the time to write to me. It gets very lonely here and somewhat claustrophobic - I long for companionable walks by the sea. But I'm taking an arts and crafts course to extend my skills and help me usefully pass the time. I enjoy creative pursuits but my background's in science - did my mother mention that? I have a BSc.

Mother told me that you're a very caring person and that you're involved with the bakery business. I grew up watching cakes being made and have retained an interest in patisserie. Please write and tell me how you spend your days and I'll do the same. He'd miss out the part about strangulation fantasies, of course. Women like this preferred a man who was damn near asexual. By the time the trial eventually came around, she'd have convinced herself that Shelley was a promiscuous whore.

Do you have any children from a former marriage? He might as well find out if she was one of the empty-wombers. If she wanted a baby he'd come over all paternal in subsequent notes. *Or does your career come first? I know from my mother that it's a challenge to combine commissioned work with motherhood. The general public have no idea the amount of time and care which goes into home baking at a commercial level - including the stringent rules laid down by the hygiene inspectorate!* There. He and she were already part of the in-crowd, albeit on a subject as boring as fucking cakes.

He looked at her photo again, belatedly noting the small crucifix around her neck. Aha, he felt a sudden urge to sign up for a theology course, so beloved of the parole board. Even as he sat here in his dimly lit cell, he was beginning to see the light. He might even retrain as a minister or become a lay preacher, as numerous other murderers had done.

He stared at the celluloid vision of Irene and wished that her hair didn't hide her throat, a throat that he'd fantasise about crushing again and again over the next few months as he orgasmed. He'd ask her for another, larger photo in a few weeks time. And he'd eventually propose marriage to this one - freedom would beckon so much more quickly if he got religion and a wife.

Acknowledgements

Many thanks to the prisoner who answered my questions about imprisonment and parole. He's not the prisoner portrayed in this novel. The Youth Crisis Clinic and Psychology In Practice magazine are equally fictitious as are the names of the student halls.